D0170510

FRONTIERS AFLAME

FRONTIERS AFLAME

Jane Cannon Campbell

Revolutionary War Heroine
When America Had Only Heroes

by
Eugenia Campbell Lester
and
Allegra Branson

Heart of the Lakes Publishing
Interlaken, New York
1987

Cover, Frontispiece, and Wash Drawings
by Peggy Scott

Maps by Anne R. Knight

Library of Congress Cataloging-in-Publication Data

Lester, Eugenia Campbell, 1929–
   Frontiers Aflame.

   Bibliography: p.
   1. Campbell, Jane Cannon—Fiction. 2. United States—History—Revolution, 1775–1783—Fiction. I. Branson, Allegra, 1934–   . II. Title.
PS3562.E8525F7   1987   813'.54   87–8783
ISBN: 0–932334–87–3

ISBN: 0–932334–87–3
Manufactured in the United States of America

First printing—September 1987
Second printing—November 1988

A *quality* publication from
Heart of the Lakes Publishing
Interlaken, New York 14847

DEDICATION

To our families

past and present

CONTENTS

PART III
FORT NIAGARA

PART IV
MONTREAL AND CROWN POINT

PART V
THE FULL CIRCLE

ILLUSTRATIONS

SOME REMARKS BY THE AUTHORS

Captured and held hostage by warring forces, be they Iroquois Indians, Hitler's Gestapo or international terrorists, the story is as old and as new as the world itself. Although Jane Cannon Campbell's experiences among the Seneca Indians during the American Revolution were highly personal, her abysmal despair at the thought of endless imprisonment and her realization that *"one can't always die when one longs for death,"* are hauntingly universal.

In 1976, when we first decided to tell the story of Jane (Mrs. Samuel) Campbell's captivity among the Iroquois Indians, we assumed that we had nearly all the pieces. For had not the tale of her adventures two hundred years ago been passed down in the family by long-lived descendants who faithfully treasured not only the story, but also corroborating manuscripts? To our surprise, however, those manuscripts provided merely the framework and a few tantalizing pieces of what we came to call our "jigsaw puzzle."

Our search to fill in the missing pieces began at the New-York Historical Society; sent us forth by twentieth century automobile to retrace Jane Campbell's two-year journey from Cherry Valley on New York's then western frontier with the Indians; and eventually ended in Ottawa's Public Archives of Canada and London's British Museum. During our peregrinations we literally unearthed hundreds of new manuscripts and memorabilia, enabling us to fill in virtually the entire puzzle.

We have quoted extensively from letters, documents and even recorded conversations, feeling that where possible, the characters should be allowed to speak for themselves. When the exact words are used, rather than paraphrased, they are italicized. Except in rare instances, however, we have used modern-day spelling and punctuation.

Before inviting our readers to relive with us the dramatized retelling of Jane Cannon Campbell's adventures, we should like to acknowledge many debts of gratitude, first and foremost, to our families; without their patience and encouragement we should never have been able to finish this book. We also wish to thank Ann M. Lingg, Dennis D. McCrary, Eleanor Truitt Weekes and John S. Genung for their editorial advice and invaluable criticisms.

Thomas Dunnings and William Asadorian of the New-York Historical Society's Manuscript Room made available to us their innumerable Revolutionary War records—always with unfailing patience and seeming enthusiasm. David Cornelia and C. Deane Sinclair of the Cherry Valley Historical Association let us examine and photograph their memorabilia and other documents. Nina Pietrafesa of Seneca Falls' Mynderse Library was especially helpful in locating books she thought would be of value in our research.

Some other libraries and institutions in which we found valuable material are: Albany Institute of History and Art; Buffalo and Erie County Historical Society; Firestone Library (Princeton University); Geneva Historical Society; Niagara Historical Society Museum (Niagara-on-the-Lake, Ontario); Massachusetts Historical Society; Museum of the American Indian, Heye Foundation (New York); New York Public Library; New York State Historical Association (Cooperstown); New York State Library (Albany); Old Fort Niagara Association; Waterloo Library and Historical Society; Widener Library (Harvard University); William L. Clements Library (University of Michigan).

Our thanks also go to family and friends who read the text, shared with us copies of their manuscripts and memorabilia, or otherwise aided us: Jean Walker Barry; Frances Ann Kiehn Browne; Charles Lorne Butler; Christopher Campbell; Theron L. Carman; Carroll Jarvis Dickson; Tracy Campbell Dickson III; William G. Bodmer; Lora Lester Dunn; Caryl Lee Rubin Fisher; Agnes Burke Harding; Cynthia Lang; Caroline Avery Lester; Doris Van Dyk Lester; John Campbell Lester; D. Campbell McCrary; Malcolm Campbell McMaster; Eleanor Bassett Schrimsher; Stephen G. Strach; Agnes Lester Wade; A. Pennington Whitehead; Frances Thompson Wiggins.

Eugenia Campbell Lester
Allegra Branson

New York City
November 11, 1986

PART I
CHERRY VALLEY

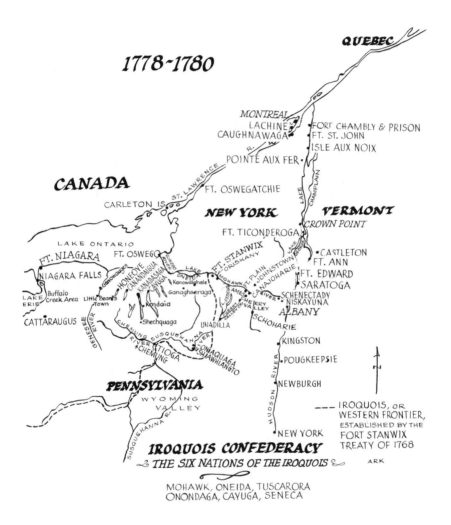

1778~1780

QUEBEC

MONTREAL
LACHINE
CAUGHNAWAGA
FORT CHAMBLY & PRISON
FT. ST. JOHN
ISLE AUX NOIX
POINTÉ AUX FER

CANADA

FT. OSWEGATCHIE
CARLETON IS.
ST. LAWRENCE R.

NEW YORK
VERMONT
CROWN POINT
FT. TICONDEROGA

LAKE ONTARIO
FT. NIAGARA
FT. OSWEGO
FT. STANWIX
ORISKANY
CASTLETON
FT. ANN
NIAGARA FALLS
HONEOYE
CANANDAIGUA
KANADASAGA
CAYUGA
Kanawalghale
Ganaghseraga
MOHAWK
FT. PLAIN
JOHNSTOWN
NAJOHARIE
FT. EDWARD
SARATOGA
SCHENECTADY
NISKAYUNA
ALBANY
LAKE ERIE
Buffalo Creek Area
Little Bean's Town
Kendaia
Shechquaga
UNADILLA
CHERRY VALLEY
SCHOHARIE
CATTARAUGUS

GENESEE RIVER
CHEMUNG RIVER
SUSQUEHANNA R.
TIOGA
CHEMUNG
ONAQUAGA
SHIAWHIANGTO
KINGSTON

POUGHKEEPSIE

PENNSYLVANIA
WYOMING VALLEY

NEWBURGH

HUDSON RIVER

SUSQUEHANNA R.

NEW YORK

IROQUOIS CONFEDERACY
~ THE SIX NATIONS OF THE IROQUOIS ~

--- IROQUOIS, OR
WESTERN FRONTIER,
ESTABLISHED BY THE
FORT STANWIX
TREATY OF 1768

ARK

MOHAWK, ONEIDA, TUSCARORA
ONONDAGA, CAYUGA, SENECA

14

1

To Be Free or Die!

Early June 1776.

The fury of the Revolution threatened New York's western frontier.

On an isolated farm along the Susquehanna River an owl hooted. Ephraim Smith looked up from his plowing, frightened. "What owl hoots at mid-day?" He scanned the newly cleared field next to his log hut. Seeing nothing, he returned to work. Suddenly his eye caught a movement among the trees: a group of war painted savages!

Ephraim raced toward the cabin, Indians in pursuit. "Martha, Martha, get the guns!" Almost within reach of the house warriors seized him. Helplessly, he watched as his frantic wife ran out the door, their small daughter following behind. An Indian took aim and fired: Martha fell dead. A tomahawk struck little Sarah. Savages whooped, pounced, then began scalping their victims. Ephraim struggled to wrench himself free; a warrior's club split his skull.

The Indians gathered up all the plunder they could carry, set fire to the cabin and with a final whoop vanished back into the forest.

July 1776.

The slaughter of Ephraim Smith and his family blackened still more the cloud of terror hanging over New York's Cherry Valley. "How can we defend ourselves?" was on the lips of everyone in the border settlement.

Armed farmers and their wives gathered in the meeting-house.

Robert Wells, one of the community's most respected leaders, rapped his cane on the floor of the church. "Today we have a vital decision to make, but first, Dominie, will you lead us in prayer?"

The Reverend Samuel Dunlop shuffled to the pulpit, hurriedly adjusting his wig. "Almighty God, give us courage as we face the threat of death and devastation from invading Indians and their Tory friends. Direct our minds and hearts to choose the right path for our freedom and for our future. Amen."

"Amen. And now, without further ado I turn the meeting over to Lt. Colonel Samuel Campbell."

"I have encouraging news," Sam called out as he strode to the front of the room. The tall, powerfully built frontiersman turned to face his audience. "General Philip Schuyler, our good friend in Albany, has pledged to do everything in his power to help Cherry Valley. He's promised us supplies, troops and ammunition to defend our exposed position. But only if, and I emphasize *if*, we provide ourselves a fortification.

"Friends," Sam continued with his usual earnestness, "you and I have a choice: stay and protect our lands and liberty or be cowards and flee. As for my wife Jane and myself, we aim to stay and fight. Cherry Valley is where my father settled thirty-five years ago, when I was three, and where our four children were born. We belong here!" Sam stopped to look around at his neighbors. "Are you with us?"

"Amen, Amen," shouted the crowd.

"Yes, Amen. Now then, what's the best farm to fortify?"

With scarcely a moment's hesitation the answer was "Yours, Colonel."

Wells spoke up. "That's right, Sam. It's the largest for miles around, even bigger than mine. Besides we can build a stockade around your two barns."

As if pondering, Campbell drew has fingers through his thick sandy hair. "I reckon we could crowd in. What do you say, Clyde?"

"Well . . . ." His cousin, Major Samuel Clyde, took a hasty puff on his pipe and lumbered to his feet. He seemed ready to launch one of his customarily long-winded speeches. "Yes, the house would make a passable fort if we strengthen it. Certainly from atop your hill we'd have a commanding view of any approaching enemy."

"All right," Sam interrupted, "I agree."

"Shall we start tomorrow morning at dawn?" Wells asked.

"So be it."

After throwing up a crude embankment of logs and earth around the Campbell house and barns, the settlers erected twin blockhouses in two angles of the enclosure. They reinforced doors and hung strong shutters at windows for defense against musket balls.

Meanwhile Cherry Valley's few Loyalists tried to slow the preparations. Those rascally Tories would have welcomed a raid; such an attack would provide cover for the men to slip away and join the King's forces while the families could remain on the farm and pretend neutrality.

Soon Loyalist leaders were warning Colonel Campbell: "Cease and desist, or else."

"Never," Sam always retorted. Even so, he knew that sooner or later the Tories would send more than just a warning; they would send a raiding party to destroy Cherry Valley.

"Perhaps we should flee after all," Sam said, putting his arms around his wife's small, slight body.

"No, darling, if we do, they'll destroy everything we've ever worked for. Of course, if we stay, they could kill us." Jane paused, reflecting: her parents had brought her and her brothers to America in order to be free of King George and his ilk. "We must stay, if only for our children's future."

Sam pulled at a reddish curl sticking out from under her cap, then drew her close and kissed her. "I hoped you'd feel that way."

By August when the fortification was nearing "ready," settlers from Cherry Valley and the surrounding communities streamed in, all burdened with their most valuable possessions. They were fleeing the Indian menace to encamp within the confines of the compound.

Among the refugees were Jane's own parents, Captain and Mrs. Matthew Cannon. Not only was Jane relieved that her family was now safely together, but also she was secretly pleased the Eleanor Cannon could help care for the children and Cap'n could assist Sam.

Once the makeshift fort was completed, Sam Campbell summoned all the refugees to a meeting on the green. "Fellow Americans, our wooden defenses alone will never protect us; we must organize ourselves." He introduced his brother, Lt. Robert Campbell, and then their cousin, Samuel Clyde.

"Friends," Major Clyde drawled, "I may be a farmer, but this much I do know. Now our safety in great part depends on all of us keeping alert against enemy attack. And so, to make a long story short, we're instituting

17

martial law."

"What's that mean for us, Major?" a voice called out.

"First of all, it means sentry duty around the clock."

Robert Campbell stepped forward; he had the same craggy face and lean body as his younger brother. "I've assigned every able-bodied man here certain hours to stand guard in the compound, in our fields and wherever else is necessary."

"Second," Clyde continued, "it means curfew from dusk to dawn. When our bell rings, everybody—men, women and children—must be in their tents, bedded down for the night."

"Only our sentries will be outside," Lt. Robert emphasized. "They'll be patrolling the compound."

"Third—and this is vitally important, it means guards will allow no one to leave or enter our stockade without permission."

"And," Robert said, pointing toward the assembled farmers, then to Sam, Clyde and himself, "that includes members of our own families. We all know secret Tories live among us, even in this very compound. It is everyone's duty to expose those concealed traitors, for they are waiting to betray us in our struggle for American liberty."

"Can we count on you all?" Sam Campbell asked.

"Hear, hear, Colonel," voices shouted. "We're with you; American liberty, all the way!"

2

Allegiances Drawn

In 1777, the flames of war began to engulf Tryon County, virtually all the territory west of Albany County to the Indian frontier. Loyalties irrevocably divided between King and country, and emotions fired to a fever pitch. Long-standing friendships broke. Even within families, fathers, sons and cousins committed themselves to opposing causes. The conflict became at once a civil war as well as a revolution, all the more bitter and devastating because the enemy was a former neighbor, friend or relative.

Before the Revolution, Tryon County had been politically dominated by one man, Sir William Johnson. This flamboyant Irishman, the King's Superintendent of Indian Affairs, scandalized the Mohawk Valley settlers by riotous drinking with his white friends and by frolicking with the Indians, painted and naked except for a breech-clout. Rumor claimed he had fathered 600 children, both white and Indian. Sir William horrified the King's authorities as well by refusing to marry the mother of his three "official" children, Catherine Weisenberg, until she was on her deathbed.

Sir William also had a long-time liaison with Mary "Molly" Brant, a member of a prominent Mohawk Indian family. Though she bore him eight children and they were married according to Iroquois custom, he always referred to her as his "housekeeper."

With the aid of "Miss Molly" and through his countless affairs with other squaws, the "Lord of Johnson Hall" came to wield a powerful influence over the Iroquois Confederacy. This Confederacy consisted of the Mohawk, Oneida, Tuscarora, Onondaga, Cayuga and Seneca Nations in New York, but sometimes included brethren in Canada, Ohio, Pennsylvania and elsewhere.

When Sir William Johnson died suddenly in July 1774, his son, John, succeeded to the title and extensive lands; his nephew and son-in-law, Colonel Guy Johnson, became Superintendent of Indian Affairs. Neither of these weak men possessed Sir William's personal magnetism or leadership, and therefore could not sway the entire population of Tryon County to the Tory cause. Essentially, they controlled only the settlers near Johnstown, the county seat; these farmers remained loyal to the King because they had been Sir William's tenants and members of his personal guard. Many Tories in other parts of the vast territory, however, pretended neutrality, hoping the war would be over before they had to commit themselves.

The inhabitants of Cherry Valley and of other similar Scotch-Irish communities were Rebels born; their forefathers had fled Scotland, and then again Northern Ireland, to escape the British yoke. In addition, the majority of Tryon County's German colonists opposed England and its Germanic King George.

On May 31, 1775, barely six weeks after the first shots were fired at Lexington, Colonel Guy Johnson left the Mohawk River Valley for Canada, taking with him a number of Loyalists and a handful of Indians. Among the group was Mary Brant's younger brother, Joseph. At thirty-three, he still owed much of his influence to his late brother-in-law, Sir William; subsequently he would gain power in his own right as a Mohawk war chief and captain in the British Army.

Also joining the Loyalist exodus north were Lt. Colonel John Butler and his son, Walter. As Johnson's Deputy Indian Superintendent, the colonel's prime duty was to persuade the Iroquois to fight for their "father" the King. His efforts succeeded except for the Oneidas, most of whom remained friendly to the Rebels. Later, when Tories began fleeing to Canada in large numbers, he recruited men for his own élite fighting group, Butler's Rangers. From headquarters in Fort Niagara, fourteen miles north of the Falls, they and their Indian allies would swoop down upon the New York frontier to lay waste to Tryon County and the fertile Mohawk River Valley. They hoped to force settlers from their lands and thus deprive George Washington's army of vital food supplies.

Colonel John Butler, however, had made a fatal personal mistake: he had left behind his wife, Catalina, and their four younger children. When the Rebels heard he was inciting the Indians against them, they seized Mrs.

Colonel John Butler, head of Butler's Rangers and father of Captain Walter Butler.
Courtesy of Public Archives of Canada, Ottawa/C-1174.

Butler and her family, took them to Albany and placed them under house arrest.

The colonel's son, Walter, swore to free his mother, sister and three brothers, but instead he found himself captured by the Rebels and condemned to death. Reprieved by General Philip Schuyler, he was sent to jail in Albany, fell ill and as a consequence was paroled to house arrest. Although confined not far from where his mother and the children were detained, Walter was never allowed to see them. Subsequently he broke parole, escaped to Fort Niagara and joined his father's Ranger Corps as a captain. From that moment on, his determination to set the family free became an obsession.

In May 1776, Sir John Johnson also fled the Mohawk, taking numerous Loyalists with him. Before departing, he buried the family silver in the basement of Johnson Hall, expecting to return home shortly, victorious. Upon his arrival in Canada, he was given beating orders to raise a regiment to be known officially as the King's Royal Regiment of New York, and unofficially as the "Royal Yorkers" or "Johnson's Greens." Their objective was the same as Butler's, the complete devastation of Tryon County.

With the flight of Sir John, future Tory soldiers began flocking to Montreal, to outposts along the St. Lawrence River and to the great Fort Niagara. Nearly all of them left behind wives and children who would work their farms until they returned.

After the departure of so many Loyalists, the Rebels' Tryon County Committee of Safety was able to seize political control. By April 1777, the State of New York had written a constitution and elected George Clinton its first Governor. This Scotch-Irishman was a leader in the rebellion and a friend of Sam Campbell.

Barely three months later, Governor Clinton's New York would be facing a massive British invasion.

3

Oriskany

Early July 1777.

Fearful news reached Cherry Valley. British General John Burgoyne, at the head of a mighty army, was pushing into New York from Canada along Lake Champlain. Everyone knew his goal was Albany. Soon even more dreadful intelligence jolted the Campbell compound. Brigadier General Barry St. Leger, commanding another British force, was poised to invade the Mohawk River Valley. First, he would seize Fort Stanwix [present-day Rome], the westernmost outpost on the frontier, then sweep east through the valley and meet Burgoyne in Albany.

August 3, 1777.

An express rider galloped into the compound at Cherry Valley. His message was urgent: "Stanwix's besieged, surrounded by an army of British, Tories 'n Indians. Colonel Gansevoort and his men are holding out. But they need help fast. All militia, get to the Mohawk. Join General Herkimer 'n his regiment. March to the relief of Stanwix."

Within the hour Sam and Robert Campbell, and Sam Clyde galloped off, Robert reporting to his company and the two Sams joining the staff of General Nicholas Herkimer's Tryon County Militia. The rest of Cherry Valley's farmer-soldiers would follow at dawn.

Jane Campbell held the new baby, Samuel, closer in her arms, tears trickling down her long, narrow face.

"Don't cry, Mama." Eleanor, Jane's only daughter, nestled against her mother. "God will take care of Papa and Uncle Robert."

"Yes, Elly dear, we must have faith."

The next morning the women, children and old men silently watched the remaining militia march away. Jane stifled a flash of panic at the full realization that she was alone, without Sam to guide her for the first time in their nine years of married life. Although her father could help manage the farm and those remaining behind could divide up the work among them, the responsibility of running the compound lay on her soulders.

As the last sounds of tramping feet died away, Jane turned to the Reverend Dunlop. "Dominie, will you please say a few words to give us comfort?"

Dunlop patted his wig and drew himself up straight. "May God protect our loved ones who have gone to do battle against the enemy, and may He return them safely to us."

"Amen, Amen."

"However," the Dominie continued, "these alarming times require much of us here assembled. Not only must we stand behind our soldiers in their belief that our cause is just, but also while we wait, we must work. For work is our saving grace."

"Yes," Jane said, "all of us can best serve by taking over the chores and guard duties our men left behind."

They worked. They prayed. And they waited for almost a week.

Finally a lone, ragged militiaman straggled back to report: Herkimer's forces were ambushed near Oriskany Creek. Out of 800 men maybe 200 remained unscathed. All the rest were killed, captured or wounded. Lt. Robert Campbell was killed, first volley. "Thank God, our militia escaped the slaughter; one day sooner and we'd all have been goners."

Jane seized his arm. "Robert dead! What about Colonel Sam?"

"And Major Clyde?" his wife Catherine choked.

"Both unharmed and leading off what's left of Herkimer's regiment."

Elly pulled at her mother's apron. "Why didn't God save Uncle Robert, too?"

Jane put an arm around the little girl and hugged her; she had no answer. She turned back to the militiaman and asked fearfully, "What about Herkimer and the other officers?"

The soldier wiped his eyes as he recounted what happened: the general was wounded in the leg and his horse shot down dead; Colonel

Ebenezer Cox took over until killed; then Colonel Campbell took charge; finally so many officers were killed or wounded that Major Clyde became a colonel and Campbell's adjutant.

"When will our husbands come home?"

"I don't know; they're off to fight Burgoyne."

Jane embraced Catherine. "Our waiting goes on." They wept.

By the time the last of the militiamen reached the compound, Jane had pieced together the dreadful story of the Battle of Oriskany: On the morning of August 6, Herkimer's forces were ambushed by 400 painted Indians and eighty Tories, their bullets raining down death and destruction. Within minutes the regiment had been cut in two. The rear forces guarding the baggage and ammunition wagons were put to flight; pursuing Indians butchered almost all of them. The forward division, surrounded and unable to retreat, fought on, refusing to surrender despite the slaughter of their comrades.

Although wounded and propped up against a tree, Herkimer remained in charge, calmly smoking his pipe while commanding his forces. He directed Colonel Campbell to form the men into pairs behind trees;

Colonel Samuel Campbell directing the troops at the Battle of Oriskany, 6 August 1777. *Courtesy of C. Deane Sinclair, Cherry Valley Historical Association, Cherry Valley, New York.*

one reloaded while the other shot. Oneida Chief Honyery accompanied him for protection.

Honyery, the leader of some sixty friendly Indians, followed with tomahawk ready and musket cocked. Three times he shot a Tory about to fire at his colonel; a fourth time he split the skull of a charging warrior.

Herkimer's new strategy caused enormous losses among the attacking Indians. But still the fighting continued, growing even more ferocious upon the arrival of Sir John Johnson's "Greens." The Tryon County Militia recognized old friends, even relatives, among the reinforcements. The struggle became so murderous that blood flowed down the hill in rivulets. A torrential thunderstorm interrupted the battle. When the rain ceased, the carnage resumed, now on ground turned slippery with bloodied mud.

A large Indian sprang at Sam Campbell with uplifted tomahawk. Sam fired, jumped back, slipped and fell; the warrior dropped dead at his feet. Campbell grabbed for his musket, but the barrel was full of mud. He searched dead comrades; not a single gun was fit for use.

Sam looked toward the enemy. At some distance lay a dead Loyalist. Desperate, he darted over, seized the man's gun and ammunition, then raced back in a hailstorm of bullets. Musket balls passed through the folds of his shirt, but he was untouched.

The battle had raged for six hours when suddenly the enemy Indians raised a mournful cry, *"Oonah! Oonah!,"* showed the white feather of retreat and vanished into the forest. The Tories fled after them, leaving Herkimer's surviving militia to claim possession of the Oriskany battlefield.

* * *

Once again Cherry Valley waited. At least for Jane, the responsibility of running the compound and the farm, in addition to her own household, dulled her fears. She never stopped working, occupied from early morn to night overseeing everything from sending grain to the gristmill, to organizing quilting bees, boiling dirty clothing, making candles and soap.

The five children were Jane's comfort and joy, but even they created anxious moments. Two-and-a-half-year-old Matthew snuffed a huckleberry up his nose, and almost five-year-old James slipped into a pot of cooling applesauce.

William, the oldest, however, gave Jane few problems. After school, he helped his Grandfather Cannon with the farm chores, paying little attention to his "baby" brothers or to his sister, Elly, who was only a girl.

Meanwhile, Fort Stanwix was still surrounded, but its commandant, Colonel Peter Gansevoort, and his men refused to surrender. Then on August 22, St. Leger's army abruptly lifted the siege and fled in confusion. They had heard that Rebel troops, "*as numerous as the leaves on the forest trees*," would fall upon them momentarily. Two days later those Rebel troops, fewer than 900 men, reached the gates of Fort Stanwix; King George's besiegers had been tricked into departing.

More encouraging news trickled back to the Cherry Valley compound. On August 16, near Bennington, American troops had defeated a detachment of Burgoyne's forces. Jane took heart, hoping this meant Sam would be coming home.

A short time later General Horatio Gates called for reinforcements against Burgoyne. Cherry Valley's militia left once again, this time flocking to Saratoga to join Colonel Samuel Campbell; but hardly had they arrived than the general commanded Sam to lead them home; Gates thought Tryon County had bled enough and the Mohawk Valley had been saved. In addition, hordes of New Englanders had by that time answered his call; thus he counted sufficient soldiers for victory.

In October, following Burgoyne's surrender at Saratoga, hopes for peace soared.

* * *

"Darling," Jane called from her spinning wheel, "do you think the war will really be over soon?"

"I have grave doubts, my dear. The British weren't defeated, only Burgoyne's army." Sam put down his book. "The King's generals probably won't invade New York again with regular troops. But the Indians and Tories will surely come back to destroy what they couldn't capture."

"And Cherry Valley?"

"We have to be one of their targets. If our compound angered them before, they'll be madder than hell now. Besides, don't forget our neighbors, especially the Moore clan. John Moore over in the Assembly, not to mention his brother James." He shrugged his shoulders. "But then most of our friends scarcely hide their revolutionary lights under a bushel."

"Nor do you, my love." Her blue eyes twinkled.

"You've got me there." He grinned, walked over and gave her a peck on the cheek. "In any case, the Indians will want to destroy Cherry Valley if only because of what happened at Oriskany."

* * *

With the first snows, the refugees in the Campbell compound returned to their farms. But as Sam had predicted, peace did not come. All that winter Mary and Joseph Brant, and Colonel John Butler fed the Iroquois' desire for revenge. "Remember your losses at Oriskany and Stanwix. Seek scalps and plunder."

Uprooted Tories, homesick for their families and farms, spent the season nursing those same wounds. At Fort Niagara they trained for the coming spring and summer campaign.

To plot that campaign of revenge Brant met with Seneca Chief Old Smoke, the foremost war chief in the Iroquois Confederacy. They divided the western frontier between them. Old Smoke, although close to seventy, chose to lead the raids against the frontiers of Pennsylvania. From Tioga [now Athens] on the Susquehanna River, he would launch a major assault against Pennsylvania's fertile Wyoming Valley. Brant decided he and his men would move north into New York along the Susquehanna to Onaquaga and Unadilla [now Windsor and Sydney]. From there they would descend upon the Mohawk region; their particular target was Cherry Valley.

Friendly Indians soon brought this information to Sam Campbell.

The colonel turned to his brother-in-law, James Willson. "Well, I guess an attack is inevitable. But damn it, all we can do is fire off a petition for help—as if any of our others ever did us much good."

The older man sighed. "This time our Legislature will have to send the troops they promised us."

They waited and waited for an answer. None came.

"Apparently no one can read," Sam fumed. "Jim, why don't we go directly to our friend, Governor Clinton?"

"Good idea. At least we know he'll read it and give us a reply."

The 23d of February, 1778

To His Excellency George Clinton Esquire . . . .

Brant and his warriors are preparing to pay us a visit, which we fear will be shortly. Send us troops to guard the western frontier. Consult with Colonel Samuel Clyde or Representative John Moore for the names of capable officers.

Experience has taught us that our safety depends much on good officers . . . .

Little did Sam and his neighbors realize the truth and tragedy of their observation.

4

General Lafayette

March 1778.

"Gentlemen, I've just received some important news from Albany," Sam Campbell announced. He and several other members of Cherry Valley's Committee of Safety were conferring beside the fire, savoring their morning glass of bitters. "George Washington has sent us a new commander for the northern department."

"What, another one?" his father-in-law, Captain Matthew Cannon, interrupted.

"A Frenchman by the name of Lafayette."

"A Frenchie?" The sea captain's normally ruddy face turned bright red. "Damn, now I've heard everything."

Sam laughed. "No, wait, Cap'n. Now he's in Johnstown on an inspection trip."

"He ought to come this way; we'd show him a thing or two."

"Any sign he might?" Jim Willson asked.

"Not that I know of."

Colonel Clyde drew a long puff on his pipe, as if deep in thought. "Then why don't we send over a delegation to meet with him, Sam; you know, 'Nothing ventured; nothing gained.' "

"You're right."

The next day Campbell, Clyde and Willson rode over to Johnstown.

When the three men met the new commander, they could hardly believe their eyes. Lafayette stood before them, a twenty-year-old Marquis dressed for King Louis' court. He might be wearing the sash of an American major general, they thought, but what does this fancy Frenchman know about fighting Indians? How can he possibly understand why we need a fort?

Campbell nevertheless unfurled his map and pointed out Cherry Valley. "As the crow flies over the rolling hills, it's some fifty miles southwest of Albany and about twelve miles south of the Mohawk River."

Lafayette studied the map, then listened attentively as the men explained.

"Cherry Valley is one of this frontier's oldest settlements—about 1741—and famous for its flowering cherry trees. Naturally it's become the most prosperous and the largest. We count upwards of 300 people, not including refugees, of course."

The Marquis was silent for a moment, seeming to ponder their words, then asked, "As a *conséquence,* it is the most *important, non?*"

"Yes. And nowadays it's wide open to Indian attack."

"*O?*"

Campbell returned to his map. "From earliest times Indians have passed through Cherry Valley; it connects their villages on the Mohawk, here, with ones along the Susquehanna and farther west." His fingers traced the Cherry Valley Creek southward to the great river. "See these two large Indian towns: Onaquaga and Tioga? Well, these, together with Unadilla, a Tory settlement, are their bases for launching raids, making our settlement, right here, New York's first line of defense. If we're destroyed, then the entire Mohawk region will become easy prey for the savages. And I do mean the entire Mohawk, all the way over to here, even including Schenectady and Albany."

"*Mon dieu!*" [My God!]

Clyde pointed to Unadilla again. "Brant's already rounded up a powerful lot of Indians to join the Tories living here; it's a bare forty mile march to Cherry Valley."

"And," said Willson, "our only defense is Colonel Campbell's fortified farm, guarded by a few old men and young boys."

"But where are your soldiers?"

"Marched off to fight with George Washington."

"*Ah, mon grand* Washington."

"General," said Campbell, looking him straight in the eye, "we're defenseless! We need a fort and soldiers."

Lafayette threw up his hands. "*Immédiatement* Cherry Valley must 'ave *assistance.* The *situation* is *grave.* I will write *mon Général* Washington, desiring him to order the *construction* of the *fort.*"

"But we also need real soldiers, Continentals from Washington's army."

"*Naturellement!* No need that I mention. Soldiers are always *nécessaire* for a *fort.*"

The three frontiersmen looked at each other; the Marquis had understood.

"You 'ave my *promesse* of *assistance.*"

"Thank you, General. We'll always remember that you came to our aid." The men prepared to leave.

"*Ah,* but wait a *moment.*" Lafayette walked to his desk, took out three silver coins and gave one to each man. "Let me *présente* to you a *souvenir* of this our *conférence.*"

Astounded, the three officers merely stammered, "Thank you," and began examining the coins.

"*Thalers* from *Autriche,* Austria. *L'empresse,* Maria Theresia, she is the mother of our *magnifique* queen, Marie Antoinette." Lafayette poured each of them a glass of sherry. "To my glorious American friends and to their *cause* of *liberté.*"

"And to our fort."

A few days later, on March 13, Lafayette wrote to his Commander-in-Chief: "*. . . The people of Cherry Valley cry for a fort in their country as they are exposed to the incursions of Indians and Tories coming up on their rear . . . .*"

He had been true to his promise.

But until George Washington received the letter, made his decision and sent proper notification, the settlers at Cherry Valley had to wait, ever fearful help would not come in time.

1760 Maria Theresia Thaler coin presented to Colonel Samuel Campbell by General Lafayette. *Private Campbell Family Collection. Photograph by Lou Gerding Photography, Tustin, California.*

5

Fate Postponed

Early April 1778.

Two friendly Indians appeared at the Campbell stockade with alarming intelligence:

> About 1500 Indians and Tories are assembled at Unadilla . . . . The inhabitants of Cherry Valley and the adjacent settlements must move from their plantations if they intend to be free from danger. The enemy will arrive in approximately four weeks from the 28th of March.

Farmers and their families once again streamed into Sam's compound. They thanked God each day that another twenty-four hours had passed without attack.

May 25.

An express rider from General Philip Schuyler, the Indian Commissioner, brought an urgent warning: "Joseph Brant and a war party of 300 to 500 Indians and Tories have arrived in the area. Attack is at hand."

"Tell the general," Campbell replied, "we lack troops, guns and ammunition."

June 2.

Joseph Brant and a small party of scouts stood atop Lady Hill. His Mohawks and Tories, their faces painted with featureless distortions of

red and black stripes and designs, peered through thick trees and foliage; the Campbell stockade lay below, about a mile away. The chief was surveying Cherry Valley, planning an attack with his entire war party for the next day. His objectives: devastate the settlement and kill or capture its leaders, in particular, members of the Committee of Safety.

The warriors strained to see more clearly the men parading on the green next to the farmhouse; a company of soldiers, it seemed, was going through morning military drill. *"Colonel Campbell has his house well guarded, I perceive,"* Brant said. "But no troops are supposed to be in Cherry Valley. I must find out."

Circling his scouts around the settlement, Brant stationed them near the main road to the Mohawk River, about a mile north of the compound. "Hide here." He then concealed himself behind a large rock to await someone passing by with the intelligence he needed.

That same morning militia Lt. Matthew Wormuth and his dispatch bearer, Peter Sitz, rode into the compound with messages for Colonel Campbell. The young officer saluted and handed over a sheaf of papers, dispatches. "Sir, I have the honor to inform you that Colonel Jacob Klock will arrive here tomorrow from the Mohawk with part of his regiment."

"It's about time. You can see our 'troops' over there on the green."

Wormuth laughed. Cherry Valley's young boys were marching in formation, attempting to execute complicated drills.

"Don't they look fierce with their paper hats and wooden guns."

"Absolutely. Are any of those yours, sir?"

"Yes, two. William, my oldest, who's one of the sergeants, and James, who's merely a private but fancies himself a general."

That afternoon the two soldier boys were allowed to have tea with their parents and Wormuth. While the adults conversed, Willie and James sat munching cookies and staring at the lieutenant's ash-colored velvet uniform. As soon as their guest rose to leave, they hopped up to bring him his cocked hat.

"Thank you, boys." He turned to Jane and Sam. "Your gracious hospitality has refreshed me, and I feel ready to face the rigors of our ride back to the Mohawk."

"Good, but remember," Sam warned, "Brant's reported to be in the neighborhood."

"Never fear. Sitz and I have fast horses."

Jane took his arm. "Just the same, please be careful." As she led him toward the front door, James grabbed her skirt.

"Mama, will you make me a uniform just like that?" He pointed to Wormuth.

"Really, dear, not now. Let go." She tried to free herself from the boy's grasp.

"Boy, if you mind your mother, perhaps you'll get a uniform like mine."

"You think so?" His big blue eyes bulged with excitement at the thought. "Yes, sir." He released the skirt.

Jane straightened her dress and shawl, trying not to show her annoyance. "Thank you, Lieutenant. I'm sure from now on James will be a perfect soldier."

He patted the boy's head. "And now, madam, we must be leaving; it's getting late." He called from the open doorway to Sitz, his burly companion who was tending their horses. "Have you secured the dispatches for Colonel Klock?"

"Yes, sir, both sets. I put Colonel Campbell's false report about the garrison near the top of one saddlebag. But I've hidden his true account in the secret compartment."

"Very good." With a gallant sweep, he kissed Jane's hand, saluted Sam and both boys, then joined his companion. About to mount his horse, he paused, turned and tossed his traveling bag to one of the colonel's slaves. "Mind this for me; I'll pick it up tomorrow when I return with my company." The bag was heavy and every pound counted.

A crowd of onlookers gawking at Wormuth and his velvet uniform followed him to the gates of the compound, then stood to watch him gallop off. "Safe trip. God be with you."

"Thank you. See you tomorrow." He waved good-bye.

As the stockade disappeared from view behind a hill, Wormuth and Sitz neared Brant's ambush.

The chief sprang from behind his rock. "Halt!" He fired a warning shot into the air.

"Make a run for it," Wormuth shouted.

A volley of musketry erupted. Sitz' mount fell dead; painted Indians leaped out and seized the soldier. The lieutenant, wounded, fell from his horse; the animal bolted off.

Brant, rushing up to the officer, tomahawked and scalped him, then curious, he glanced at his victim's face. "Wormuth! And here I thought you were *a good King's man*." As the chief hitched the trophy to his belt, he

36

moved toward Sitz and signaled the Indians to release him. "Soldier, hand over dispatches."

The prisoner struggled, his big hands fumbling with the saddlebags; at last the bindings gave way. He surrendered the false papers.

Brant read them, shaking his head in disbelief. "Troops, how many?"

"Better part of a regiment, I reckon. You've seen my information."

"Yes, but I've heard to the contrary." He glared at Sitz, trying to make him break.

The soldier stared back in icy-faced silence, never lowering his eyes.

"All right, I'll accept this dispatch as true." Brant turned to his scouts. "We can't chance an attack now or any time soon. Do with the Rebel as you wish."

The Mohawks slapped red and black paint on Sitz' face, marking him as their captive. Then they pinioned him, drawing his arms up behind his back and binding them around a stick. They encircled his neck with a rope and led him off.

Brant and his party vanished into the wilderness. The chief had decided to postpone his attack on Cherry Valley, but vowed to return later in the campaign season.

At the compound, before the crowd had even dispersed, they heard a distant volley of musketry, then an alarm from the sentry. "Riderless horse approaching. Open the gates." The animal galloped in, its saddle stained with blood.

"That's Wormuth's horse. Brant and his warriors are here!"

Campbell called for volunteers. "Quick, a search party." He led out a group, but darkness soon forced them to return.

At dawn the party again set off. This time they found Wormuth's body and Sitz' dead horse; both had been stripped.

"Someone has to alert Colonel Klock and notify the lieutenant's father." Sam glanced around. "Who's willing?"

"I'll go," said his nephew, Robert Dickson.

The colonel looked toward the strapping fifteen-year-old and shook his head. "No, Elizabeth would never forgive me if anything happened to her son."

"Please, Uncle."

"Well, all right."

That afternoon the compound greeted militia Colonel Jacob Klock, his men and Robert Dickson with shouts and cheers. Sam saluted

"Congratulations" to his nephew before welcoming the new arrivals. "Glad you're here at last, my friends." He made a quick head count, 150, more or less, then demanded of Klock: "Where are the rest of your men?"

The colonel's face reddened to his ears in anger. "They're all I can spare. Sam, you've got to realize Cherry Valley is not the only settlement threatened."

"And damn it to hell, Jacob, you've got to realize Cherry Valley is the first line of defense."

Jane took Sam's arm. "Dear, we must be grateful for even these few men."

"Thank you, Mrs. Campbell; I'm glad you understand." Klock smiled in relief, then peered around. "Your husband's preaching almost made me forget Lt. Wormuth's father, old Peter."

"Oh, is he with you?"

"Yes, over yonder."

"That poor man." Jane rushed to him, took his hands in hers, giving them a sympathetic squeeze and led him to the mutilated body of his only son.

Devastated, the father collapsed, crying out, *Brant, cruel, cruel Brant!* Oh God, why?"

Silence and tears enveloped the compound. Jane looked toward her own sons and wept.

6

Fort Alden

George Washington's orders finally arrived: Construct the fort in Cherry Valley.

The inhabitants began hewing logs into sharp posts for a stockade to enclose their church and its burying ground. The site was on the southern edge of the settlement, about a mile from Sam Campbell's farm. The church would serve as troop headquarters, storage for their valuables and refuge for all. Building even this primitive fort, however, would take time.

Meanwhile, in early July, news reached the settlement of a "massacre" in Pennsylvania's Wyoming Valley. Swarms of Old Smoke's warriors and Colonel John Butler's Rangers had ravaged the area and destroyed eight forts. In one battle the attackers had ambushed 400 Rebel soldiers; they took 227 scalps and only five prisoners. Families were separated, husbands from wives, mothers from children. Old and young alike were carried off by the Indians. Those who were lucky enough to escape capture fled toward older settlements, but many became lost in the wilderness and died from exposure and fatigue.

Soon excruciating stories flooded Cherry Valley. Blood-drenched Indians had herded women and children into houses, setting the buildings afire with flaming torches. "Queen" Catherine Montour, an infamous French-Indian squaw, had led her fiends in a frenzied dance around the burning prisons. As they gyrated wildly, the savages relished the agonizing screams of their victims . . . . The tales became more dreadful with each retelling.

Cherry Valley's settlers worked feverishly against time to finish the fort before a similar fate struck them.

Not long after, Sam galloped into the compound, hot and dusty from his ride back from a militia meeting on the Mohawk, in Canajoharie. He tossed the horse's reins to a waiting slave and dashed into the house. "Jane, Jane. Good news at last."

"What do you mean?"

"Washington has ordered Continentals to man our fort. Lafayette was right."

"Thank God." Jane threw her arms around Sam, hugging him in joy. "Cherry Valley is saved!"

"I hope so." He gave her a kiss. "But I am a mite concerned."

"Oh, why?"

"Well, the troops are from Massachusetts, Colonel Ichabod Alden's Seventh Regiment. They may be trained to fight the King's army, but I'd have preferred Yorkers; they're experienced Indian fighters."

July 24, 1778.

> "Arrived at 4 P.M.," Lt. William McKendry, one of Alden's officers, wrote in his diary. "Had a heavy rain. The regiment was received with much joy, with firing a blunderbuss and one round from the militia and inhabitants."

Sam Campbell sloshed through the mud and downpour toward Lt. Colonel William Stacy, the second in command. "Where's Colonel Alden? Why isn't he here?"

"Delayed a bit. But he'll be along. Never fear. After all, the fort's not yet finished."

"But Indians are still prowling the area."

"Now that we're here, those cowardly Indians won't dare strike." Stacy smiled knowingly. "You'll see."

Since the new fort was indeed not ready for occupancy, 250 soldiers moved into the Campbell stockade already crowded with Klock's militia. The Continental officers, on the other hand, chose to live more comfortably, lodging with local families, principally Robert Wells', whose house was only 400 yards from the fort.

No longer so terrified, many inhabitants returned home, taking the precaution, however, of storing their valuables in the church. Some refugees from outlying farms remained in Sam and Jane's compound; others continued onward to the surer safety of Canajoharie, Schenectady or Albany.

July 30, 1778.

Colonel Alden, followed at a respectful distance by an aide and several baggage-laden horses, cantered into Cherry Valley and up to the gate of the stockade.

Stacy was already waiting to greet his commander. "Welcome, sir; we're glad you're here."

"Thank you." The stolidly built officer jumped down from his horse, wiped the perspiration from his bald forehead, placed a hand upon his sword and strode inside. "Show me around," he called back. "I'd like to inspect my fort. Of course, I've decided to call it Fort Alden." By the time the commandant reached the church door he was in a towering rage. "Why are these things lying around? General Washington sent me to command a military fort, not a storehouse."

"They're here for safety's sake, sir. And I thought. . . ."

"Well I'm in command now. And I don't want to be responsible for all these goods and chattel. See to their removal. At once."

"Yes, sir." Stacy saluted obedience.

That afternoon Colonel Alden called upon Robert Wells. "I need suitable quarters. Yours might do."

"Well then, my family and I should be most honored to have you."

"Good." The colonel did not notice the supercilious tone of Wells' voice.

"I fear, however, you may be somewhat cramped with so many of your officers already here."

"That doesn't matter. I will be joining my staff. Show me around."

Wells straightened the ruffles on his shirt and adjusted his waistcoat and jacket before answering. "Very good, sir; let me fetch my walking stick." After the tour, he led Alden outside to survey the house and grounds. Several women were sewing and having tea on the lawn while children were running and playing. A bean bag whizzed past the officer's head. "Careful, boys, you almost shot down our new commandant."

"Mr. Wells, don't tell me all those brats live here, too."

"I assume, Colonel, you are referring to the high-spirited children. No, only three live here; my fourth is away at school. Come, let me introduce you to my family and guests." He took Alden over to the group of women. "May I present my wife."

Mrs. Wells, a handsome woman with greying hair, looked up from her sewing and flashed a warm smile. "I do hope you approve of our new fort."

"I will as soon as I can whip it into shape. All those goods stored there."

Wells quickly interrupted. "My mother-in-law, Mrs. Dunlop."

"Welcome to Cherry Valley. Dominie and I look forward to entertaining you at dinner."

"Thank you. Good home-cooked meals are this officer's delight."

"And now," said Wells, drawing the colonel away from the elderly lady, "my sister-in-law, Miss Dunlop."

"How do you do." Betsy Dunlop looked up shyly at Alden, to find him eyeing her. Embarrassed, she retreated into her needlework.

"And lastly, I present my own dear sister, Miss Wells."

"May I offer you some tea and my own special shortcakes, Colonel?" Jane Wells asked. Her plain face radiated good-heartedness. "I do hope you like them."

"I'm sure I will if you made them." Alden sampled the teacakes. "Excellent, so delicious they've persuaded me to move in." He smacked his lips. "After my long spell of camp life, I'd almost forgotten the pleasures of hearth and home." He turned and scrutinized the property and ladies once more. "No question, Mr. Wells, your place suits me just fine."

"At your service," he replied, bowing.

"In fact, I'm even going to make it my headquarters."

"Oh?"

"Yes, I've decided." The colonel gulped down his tea. "I'm moving in this evening."

"As you wish."

"I'll see you anon. Miss Wells, save me a piece of shortcake." He left without awaiting her reply.

Wells took his cane and in defiance raked the cakes off their plate and into the bushes. "That's that."

"Indeed. I wish I could get rid of the colonel as easily."

"Yes, sister, it's so-called leaders like Alden who will force us to flee to Canada."

His wife sighed deeply, shaking her head. "I can't imagine life away from Cherry Valley, from Betsy and Mother—or Father."

"It'd kill Dominie, and myself," Mrs. Dunlop murmured.

"Robert, dear, do you really think we should leave?"

"Yes and no. Cherry Valley is home, and I hate the thought of giving it up, possibly forever. Yet I deplore the madness of separation from England."

"It's all madness." Jane Wells looked around at the playing children. "Why, oh why can't we be left alone?"

"Until today I thought we could remain quietly neutral. Instead, our house has suddenly become regimental headquarters, a prime target of attack, and from none other than John Butler and the Johnsons, our own Tory friends."

The next morning soldiers erected a tall pole in the center of Robert Wells' front lawn and raised the colonel's flag for all to see.

And the settlers, summoned to the fort, had to retrieve their possessions. As Sam Clyde was departing, he met Major Daniel Whiting, sent by Alden to check upon the remaining valuables. "Your colonel's got a hell of a nerve; after all, we built this place."

"True, but he's in command."

Clyde spit a stream of tobacco juice into the dirt. "So we've discovered."

7

Indian Humbug

August 5, 1778.

"The troops moved from Colonel Campbell's to the fort," Lt. McKendry wrote in his diary. *"We left behind 150 militia in the compound."*

Eleanor Cannon stood in the doorway with her grandchildren to watch the Continentals depart. "Now maybe we'll have room to breathe." The elderly woman put a plump arm around Elly, her namesake. "And the two of us might even have time for a little needlework."

August 7.

"Began to build the redoubt [the inner fortification] *at Fort Alden,"* McKendry noted.

All during August with monotonous regularity friendly Oneidas brought warnings to the settlement: Brant is preparing to attack, and soon.

"Indian humbug," Colonel Alden always said. Meantime he encouraged his officers to organize regimental horse races and field days.

Everyone else in Cherry Valley despaired over such pointless frivolity.

Sam Campbell went with Clyde and Willson to Alden. "Those Indians have never lied to us."

"Well, there's always a first time."

Jim Willson peered over his spectacles. "And what if they're truthful?"

"I'd know it." The colonel shook his finger. "My garrison is always on the alert. I send out scouting parties, round up Tories 'n other notorious villains and in general take quite sufficient precautions. Furthermore we have artillery to protect the fort."

Clyde leaned forward, looking straight at Alden. "That's all very well and good, sir. But in addition, build up stores of ammunition and food in case of a surprise attack."

"Surprise? We'll never be surprised. Reliable, and I repeat, reliable, white spies will always give us a timely warning. In Massachusetts . . . ."

Sam Campbell jumped to his feet. "But, Colonel, Cherry Valley is in New York, on the Indian frontier!"

"My cannon and Continental troops will scare off any Indians before they even dare plan an attack. Good day, gentlemen."

Harvest time, 1778.

Sam and the other Cherry Valley farmers took some cheer; plentiful crops would fill their barns to overflowing that winter. Klock's militia, however, impatiently guarding the settlement instead of tending to their own harvests, marked off days until September 17, the end of their enlistment period. Then every last man marched home.

Cap'n Cannon turned to Sam. "Those farmers might not be Continental soldiers, but sure as shootin' they were Injun fighters."

"And knew about frontier warfare."

"Grampy, do you and Papa think me an' my troops could help?" Willie asked. "We're still here."

"Thanks, son." Sam gave the boy a half-hearted pat on the shoulder. "After all our efforts, Cap'n, we're right back where we started."

The militia had hardly departed when nearby Mohawk Valley settlements erupted into flames; Brant's forces burst upon the warpath. They killed or drove off farm animals and burned grain-filled barns, gristmills and houses; the efforts of a summer, of a lifetime, were destroyed. At least the inhabitants escaped death; forewarned, they had fled to the safety of nearby forts.

Meanwhile on Pennsylvania's northern frontier, Continental troops were burning Tioga and a few scattered Indian settlements in retaliation for Wyoming. Although intending to push farther into Iroquois country, they had retreated when scouts reported the approach of Captain Walter Butler with 300 Tory Rangers and Indians. The captain and his forces were on their way to Tioga, where they would join more Indians massing for an assault, the last of the season. Butler wanted to strike Cherry Valley, but the chiefs would make the final decision.

At the same time other Continental troops from New York laid waste Unadilla and Onaquaga, then announced to Governor Clinton, "The frontier has been *sufficiently secured . . . from any further disturbances from the savages at least this winter . . . .*"

* * *

Winter came early to Cherry Valley. The first week of November a cold, sleety rain began falling the length of the western frontier. When it turned to snow, everyone assumed the Indians had gone home for the hunting season.

At the Campbell farm Sam came in from his morning's farm chores, stomped his boots to get rid of the snow and mud, then headed for his favorite chair beside the fireplace.

"Papa, me." Samuel toddled over to his father and crawled into his lap. Matthew ran to join them.

Sam laughed, then bouncing the boys on his knees, called out, "Who'll fetch me a glass of bitters?"

"I will," Jane replied. "I'm readying them this very moment."

"All r-r-right," he teased, trying to burr the R . . . . Although his wife had been only nine when her parents left Ulster, at thirty-four she still retained traces of the family's Scottish accent.

"Here you are," Jane said, handing Sam his drink. "These should warm your innards." Seating herself near the fire, she picked up some sewing.

"What are you making now?"

She held up a cap. "I've copied this pattern from Jane Wells' new cap. It'll look much prettier once I've put the lace on it."

The two boys hopped off their father's lap to inspect her handiwork.

"Chillun," Lain called out from the doorway, "it's time fo' yo' dinner." The black mammy took them by the hand and marched them off.

Sam waited until the boys had left the room, then went over to Jane, took away her sewing and pulled her close. "I love you." He kissed her tenderly, then put an arm around her shoulders and guided her to a window. Together they looked outside at the new-fallen snow.

46

"My dear, Sam Clyde and I both have a funny feeling about the Indians; we don't think they've headed home. Catherine feels it even stronger. She keeps dreaming about her old friend Molly Brant, that the squaw is trying to tell her something. But Catherine always wakes up before she can hear the message."

"From Molly Brant? Do you suppose it's a warning to flee?"

"I don't know." He paused. "Perhaps you should take the children to Schenectady; I could stay here."

"No, never!" Jane put her arms around Sam and looked up into his eyes. "We're fighting together."

8

More Indian Humbug

Outside Fort Stanwix a friendly Oneida padded up to the edge of the woods, hooted like an owl and waited for the sentry's reply. Signals exchanged, the sally port opened, and Saucy Nick passed into the fort. No stranger to the men of Stanwix, he often carried messages from Indian Territory to Colonel Gansevoort.

"*O Sa'-go* [Greetings]," Major Robert Cochran led the Oneida into the commandant's office. "Our brother the colonel is away. Give me your message."

Saucy Nick reached for his tomahawk, drew out the paper hidden inside the handle and handed it to Cochran.

The major read the message, then hastened to his writing desk.

"Orderly," he called, "dispatch this to Colonel Alden in Cherry Valley. Send it express. Yes, express." He turned to the Indian. "*Hi-ne-a'-weh* [Thank you]. Your intelligence has saved the inhabitants of *Ka-ri-ton'-geh* [Cherry Valley]."

Midnight, November 7, 1778.

The express rider galloped up to the Wells house. With sleep-laden eyes Alden read the dispatch:

Fort Stanwix, November 6, 1778. Sir: A friendly Oneida has just informed us that yesterday an Onondaga had been present at a great meeting of Indians and Tories at Tioga; the result of their council was to attack Cherry Valley. Young Butler will head the Tories. I send you this information that you may make some preparations for their reception . . . .

P.S. It is expected that you will be attacked very soon.

"More Indian humbug." Colonel Alden passed the message to his visiting superior, General Edward Hand.

The general, a red-haired Irishman and the newest head of the northern department, was in Cherry Valley on an inspection trip. He studied the dispatch for several minutes before speaking. "M' good man, I'm not so sure 'tis humbug. Cochran's too experienced in Indian ways to be fooled."

"Well, General, I'm not exactly inexperienced on that subject myself. Ever since I arrived here Indians 've been bringing in warnings of imminent attack. Have we had one? No."

Hand reread the dispatch. "See here, as I understand this message, a hostile Onondaga has betrayed his war council's plans. Why should he pass on false information? No, Colonel Alden, that intelligence must be true. And in view of your lack of provisions, the account is alarming!"

November 8, 1778.

At dawn General Hand reviewed the regiment. "High compliments." He turned to Alden. "You've a splendid lot o' soldiers there and you can be proud of 'em. But even they can't fight very long without more ammunition and food." Hand shook his head, sighing. "I'll find you provisions from somewhere—an' reinforcements, too. In the meantime, Colonel, send out scouts in all directions an' learn just where the enemy is; we want to give those painted scoundrels a hot reception." He looked around the stockade. "Tell the settlers to move in their valuables and be ready to sleep here themselves."

By midday Hand was en route to the Mohawk, where he met with Colonel Jacob Klock. "Send 200 militia to reinforce Fort Alden. Tomorrow."

"Yes, sir. Tomorrow."

The general continued onward to Schenectady and Albany. "Dispatch vital stores to Cherry Valley," he commanded. "Fort Alden is unprepared, and the enemy will attack soon."

Colonel Alden, however, remained unconvinced. And furthermore, he loathed the nuisance of having to reply to Cochran:

49

Received yours of the 6th instant by express informing me of the intelligence you obtained . . . of a large body of the enemy who . . . desire to attack this place.

I am very much obliged to you for your information . . . .

Alden folded the letter and stamped his seal into the wax. "Well, that's the end of that."

November 9, 1778.

No reinforcements arrived at the fort, only frightened farmers and their families. The settlers, encouraged and led by Colonels Campbell and Clyde, streamed toward safety, some in wagons, most on foot. All were heavily burdened with precious possessions, anything and everything from sacks and bags full of personal belongings to farm animals, chests and clocks. At the gate soldiers barred their way.

Campbell marched up to a sentry. "Let us in."

"No, sir. Orders from Colonel Alden."

"Then get Colonel Alden." The guard disappeared into the fort, leaving everyone standing and waiting in the snow, wet and angry.

As Campbell and Clyde paced up and down beside the gate, babies wailed, dogs and children raced hither and thither, adults slapped their bodies to keep warm, neighing horses pawed the ground.

"What in hell's keeping that so 'n so?" Clyde struck the snow from his boots with the butt end of his musket, cursing under his breath. "Sam, doesn't he realize it's blasted cold out here?"

"More to the point, doesn't he realize time is of the essence?"

At length Alden appeared. "Why all this commotion?"

"General Hand told us to move in our valuables," Campbell replied. "He also said, 'Be ready to sleep here.' "

"General Hand's left, and I've rescinded his orders. So get along home."

Clyde gripped his musket and glared at Alden. "Colonel, we wish to store our valuables inside our fort."

"Out of the question. All those goods would only tempt my men to plunder."

Campbell and Clyde persisted. "Colonel, you must see the danger. We've been warned by Major Cochran."

"It's merely another false alarm. I'm the commandant at Fort Alden and I tell you Indians will never dare attack."

"And why not?"

"Because I have disciplined troops and menacing cannon. Furthermore at this very moment my best scouts are out covering all possible approaches; they'll alert me in case of any real danger." Alden whirled round and started to re-enter the fort, then stopped and turned back. "Don't be afraid; I'll give you timely notice when to move in. Cherry Valley is safe as long as I'm in charge." He stalked inside, the gate slamming shut behind him.

Sam Campbell scooped up a handful of snow, squeezed it into a hard ball, then hurled it at the gate. "Damn!"

Jane moved up to his side. "Darling, what do we do now?"

"Obey. We're at the mercy of his stupidity."

In truth, Alden had sent out scouting parties. His commands: "Follow all trails except the old Indian path. No attackers will ever come that way; it's much too overgrown to be passable."

9

As Soon as the Moon Rises

November 9, 1778.
South of Cherry Valley along the Susquehanna River.

Sergeant Adam Hunter and his picket of eight men from Fort Alden dropped with exhaustion. They had trudged the entire day over snow-covered terrain, looking for traces of the enemy and finding none. Now they were cold, wet and hungry. Throwing caution to the winds, they encamped around a blazing fire to cook their supper. Placing muskets beside them, all lay down to sleep, unguarded.

Just before dawn the glow of the still flickering fire attracted an advance party of warriors led by Chiefs Joseph Brant and Cornplanter. The group stealthily surrounded the sleeping soldiers, marking out each man for capture. Then, with shrill whoops Indians pounced and pinioned their startled victims. As if in a nightmare, the scouts saw painted savages everywhere, all armed with tomahawks, muskets and scalping knives.

Brant stepped forward and signaled, "Release the men for questioning," then turned to Sergeant Hunter. "What is the situation at Fort Alden?"

The hulking soldier shrugged his shoulders defiantly and clamped his mouth shut.

Brant asked the other scouts the same question and received the identical response.

Cornplanter gestured: "Use persuasion." His warriors swung their tomahawks, the blades stopping at the prisoners' throats.

Silence.

A Tory officer emerged through the early morning haze. "I'll take over." He waved aside the two chiefs and their warriors.

Sergeant Hunter stared in disbelief at the small, cat-like man; he could never mistake his former cellmate in Albany prison: Walter Butler! Hunter, a one-time Loyalist, had gained his freedom by swearing allegiance to the American cause and joining the Rebel army.

"Well, if it isn't my old comrade." Captain Butler warmly shook the soldier's hand. "How lucky for me; I won't have to persuade you to answer a few questions."

"What do you want to know?"

"The situation at Fort Alden." Butler's dark, piercing eyes seemed to brighten in expectation.

The sergeant, glancing toward his fellow scouts, hesitated, then said, "Troops're quartered there, but the fort's not yet finished. Most of the officers still lodge at the Wells House."

Butler nodded. He knew the family; they were close friends of his father.

"The commandant flies the regimental flag there," Hunter volunteered. "He and his staff go to the fort in the early morning, but some time before noon they gather back at Mr. Wells' for dinner; it's the officers' mess."

"What about the troops?"

"If I tell you, you will spare me, won't you?"

Butler smiled.

"The garrison is expecting heavy reinforcements any moment so they can give you a warm reception."

"They know? When did they find out?"

"Two days ago."

"How?"

"From an Oneida. His Onondaga brother was at your Tioga council."

"Hell-fire and damnation!" Butler turned to the warriors. "Take away the prisoners. No, leave me one; he'll guide us straight to the Wells house."

"Friend, have mercy," Hunter screamed as he was dragged off. "I told you all."

"Mercy for a traitor? Never." Butler whirled round to Brant and Cornplanter. "Convene the council of chiefs. At once!"

Warriors sounded the call, ascending and descending halloos, high-pitched and quavering yalloos. Responses echoed from all directions: the chiefs would hasten with the speed of an arrow.

"Brethren, O Sago," Butler greeted the council. "Attend: Karitongeh has learned of our approach from an Onondaga."

"A brother has betrayed us! Let Rawenio, the Great Good Spirit, the all-powerful king, smite him down."

"Fellow warriors," Butler interrupted, "lend me a listening ear."

"A serpent has stolen into our midst, and we must find him."

"Iroquois brethren, lay aside concerns; you must hear my words. *Dux-e'-a* [leader] is my Indian name; this day and forever I intend to live by its meaning. Remember, it is I who captains the Tory and Indian forces."

Brant and the other chiefs exchanged angry glances. Once again the haughty young Butler had been curt, even insulting in his eagerness for power. They held their tongue, knowing he headed the Rangers but not the Indians, because they alone commanded the warriors.

"Brethren, further attend. Lend a planning ear: The enemy may be expecting us, but has no suspicions we are so near. The moment of assault, therefore, must change. Let us surprise them and attack tonight as soon as the moon rises."

Unanimously the chiefs agreed to the change.

Butler outlined his plan. "One party will surround the Wells house and seize the officers, while the main body of Rangers and Indians will surprise the fort."

Again the chiefs agreed.

"Brethren, harken to my final words: I know your wounds from Tioga, Onaquaga, Unadilla, even Oriskany, are open and grievous. My memories of imprisonment are also bitter. I, too, am shedding tears for my mother and family long held captive in Albany."

The chiefs nodded. "Perhaps he does understand our pain and sorrows."

"Revenge is sweet," Butler continued. "At Karitongeh, glory in battle, even in looting and burning. Send squaws and dogs after you to plunder and forage." He paused to look straight at every chief. "But give me your promise, as you promised my father at Wyoming: spare women, children and non-combatants."

One by one Brant, Cornplanter, Hiokatoo, Little Beard . . . nodded their assent.

"*Hineaweh* [Thank you]. *Na-ho'* [I have finished]. And now, until night, as soon as the moon rises."

But on the night of November 10 the moon did not rise over Cherry

Valley. Instead, a heavy, sleeting rain fell upon the snow-covered ground.

Six miles south of the settlement, Captain Butler gave the signal for the assault to begin. The Rangers sprang to attention.

The Indians did not move. The chiefs sent a message to Duxea: "The day's march tired our warriors. And now the black night's rain discourages them. With no moon showing its face, we must all wait for dawn to gird for battle."

"Damnable insubordination," Butler exploded. "Captain McDonell, Captain Caldwell, Captain Johnston, follow me." He grabbed a torch and swearing mightily, marched over to the Seneca encampment. "Brave warriors, O Sago. I gave the signal to attack."

Not an Indian stirred.

Cornplanter, huddled in his blanket, looked up and grunted, "No moon, only rain and darkness. We wait for break of day."

Little Beard straightened the eagle feather in his scalp lock. "Senecas need light to strip for combat and cover their nakedness with fresh war paint."

Butler turned to Chief Hiokatoo. "Is such a brave warrior as you also discouraged by rain?"

"Soon enough we'll *'sing the song of blood, the soup of warriors which feeds men's souls.'* Until then, Duxea, we are not moving. *Naho!"*

"Leave them be," Captain Johnston said, sensing the futility of Butler's persistence . . . . He was one of the white Indians, Ranger members of the Indian Department, who, disguised and war painted, served alongside the braves in battle and tried to control their sometimes brutal actions . . . . "I'm afraid, Walter, you'll have to change your plans."

"No, order them to obey their Duxea."

"Impossible; you know how independent Senecas are."

"I will not be defied. Come; let's go see Brant."

At the Mohawk encampment everyone was asleep.

"Joseph, Joseph, wake up. What's all this nonsense?"

Brant opened one eye, saw Butler and shut it again.

"Get up and order the attack."

"Why? You know I've only thirty Mohawks." He did not command Cornplanter, Little Beard, Hiokatoo and their 300 Senecas. "Duxea, you'll have to wait till dawn. Naho!" Brant rolled over and pretended to sleep.

Angry, Butler and his officers retreated in the pouring sleet to the

Tory encampment. "Damn those Indians; they've kept me from surprising the fort."

"Surprise may be the right tactic," Johnston said, "but those chiefs don't take orders which make no sense to them, and especially from a white man."

"Then they'll have to learn."

10

November 11, 1778

While Butler's Rangers and the Indians waited for November 11 to dawn, Cherry Valley slept uneasily.

At the Clyde homestead, on a hill about a mile west of Fort Alden, Catherine lay beside her husband. Fast asleep, she once again confronted Mary Brant in a vision; but this time the squaw was silhouetted by a flaming Cherry Valley.

As before, Catherine awoke to find herself sitting straight up in bed. "It's only a nightmare," she convinced herself. A second time she fell asleep; Miss Molly pointed toward war painted Indians waving bloody scalps. Still Catherine hesitated to awaken Sam.

A third time she fell asleep. Now Miss Molly shouted her message: "Indians are upon you. Escape!"

Catherine shook her husband awake. "Go back down to the fort. Beg Alden to let everyone in. Please. It's already dawn and may be too late."

"What do I say? That my wife had a vision from Molly Brant? He'll say I'm crazy."

"Please, for me and the children."

"All right," Clyde finally agreed. "I'll go brook the devil once more. But first, Jimmy 'n I'll have to finish our chores." .... "Jimmy" was James Simons, their sixteen-year-old black apprentice farmer.

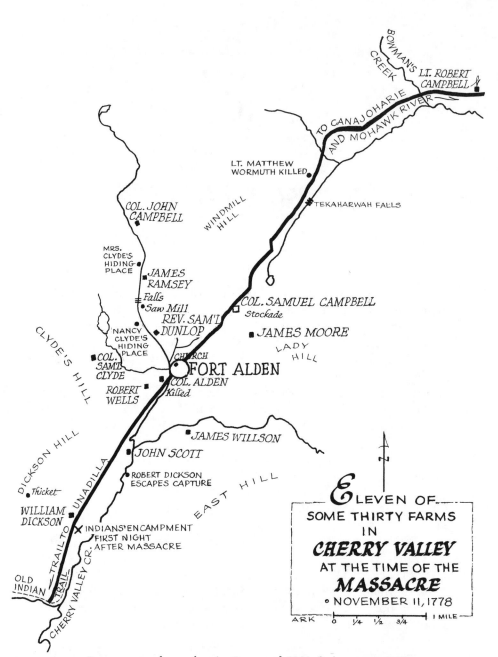

From a map drawn by the Reverend H.V. Swinnerton, 1877.
Lyman Draper Manuscripts. State Historical Society of Wisconsin.

Some two miles south of the fort, on William and Elizabeth Dickson's farm, little Janet sat beside the cabin window, gazing out at the rain falling upon the snow; she was Robert's nine-year-old crippled sister. She watched her father cross the clearing and start into the forest, then turned her attention to her young brothers, John and Samuel, splitting wood for the fire.

A war painted Indian bolted out of the woods and headed toward the door, followed by John, Samuel and their father holding axes high, ready to strike.

Inside, Janet screamed hysterically for her mother and sister Rosanna. They reached her just as the savage burst into the cabin, shouting, "Me no kill. Me good Indian. Me no kill."

The family, now assembled, stared speechless: rings and stripes of red and black colored the Indian's head and body; feathers decorated his black scalp lock; silver ornaments dangled from his nose and ears, adorned his chest and arms.

The warrior strode over to Janet and reached out a painted hand, only to stroke her blond hair. "Good little squaw." He turned back and tapped his leg with his bayonet. *"Indian never forget kindness."*

In astonishment the family recognized him; long ago they had nursed him back to health when he had broken his leg.

"Indian come tell white man run. Bad Indians come; kill, scalp white man; burn house." Whipping out his tomahawk, he began to cut the air with zigzags. "Run like rabbit." Still waving his tomahawk, he rushed out the door.

In frantic haste William Dickson picked up his crippled daughter; called back to Rosanna, "Bring a blanket"; and started out of the house, leaving his sons to support his lame wife, Elizabeth. He led his family through the forest, heading toward a nearby hill where he knew he could conceal them in a thicket of underbrush.

Elizabeth struggled to keep up, not even stopping to retrieve the cap which had covered her flaming red hair. Despite the boys' help, she was slowing down the family. Reaching a rail fence, she collapsed, her whole body shaking uncontrollably from the icy rain, her hair streaming wildly down her face and back. "Look." She pointed toward a fence corner enclosed by overhanging vines and fallen leaves. "I can hide there. Father, take the children and go on. Save yourselves."

"No."

"Leave me," she gasped.

John tried to pull her back up. In vain. "I'll stay here with you."

"Not enough room. Hurry on."

"Oh Mama," Janet wailed, "they'll find you 'n kill you." She threw her arms around her mother, kissing her.

"There, there, my darling. Father and Samuel will come back for me."

The boys placed Elizabeth inside the fence corner, covering the hiding place with more leaves and vines. "We'll be back soon," Dickson whispered. Heartsick, the family left her behind, clambered up the slippery hill and ducked into a dense thicket. "Hide here. Not one sound," their father ordered. Then he and Samuel departed.

"Oh my mama, my papa," Janet sobbed. "We'll all be killed!"

"Shh." Rosanna put a hand over her sister's mouth and motioned for John to cover them with the blanket. Cowering in their icy thicket, the three of them heard Indian hoots sound in the distance, then closer, then all around them; they scarcely dared breathe. Eventually the signals died away.

William Dickson and Samuel heard those same hoots as they lurched back down the hill, tripping against rocks and underbrush. At last they reached Elizabeth's hiding place; it was empty. Horrified, father and son called softly, looking around for clues but finding none; in resignation, they stumbled back toward the thicket, to resume the search when darkness fell.

* * *

Near the old Indian trail about a mile south of the fort.

Robert Dickson had just returned from one of Colonel Alden's scouting parties and was riding toward his father's farm when he spied the advancing Indian and Tory army. Whirling round, he headed for the garrison, but an enemy flanking party stood between him and the fort.

Pressing his body against the horse, Robert determined to pass or die. He rode headlong into astonished Rangers, warriors and their ready bayonets, then through a rain of bullets. Although horse and rider were cut by the flailing weapons, they kept on going and escaped.

As Robert raced by the Wells house, he shouted to the sentries, "Indians and Tories. They're coming! Down the old Indian trail!" He galloped into the fort. "Sound the alarm, the cannon!"

"Colonel Alden, may I get you another drink before dinner?" Jane Wells asked.

"Yes, I'll be persuaded." The officer and his staff were warming themselves by the fire. Several, including the colonel, had taken off their boots.

The sentries burst in. "Indians and Tories, sir, attacking along the Indian trail!"

Alden looked up and yawned. "Probably a straggling party, but call in the guard anyway." War whoops sounded in the distance. "Major Whiting, perhaps you'd better get back to the fort and find out what all this fuss is about."

Whiting and a few other officers rushed out the front door to see the enemy advancing. They raced to the safety of the fort.

The Indians stormed the house, Senecas under Little Beard to the front and Mohawks under Brant around back. The terrified sentries fled as the shrieking Indians bore down on them.

Inside, Alden was struggling with his second boot when war whoops erupted everywhere. "Guards, fire a volley out front." He staggered to his feet, leaving one boot behind. "Stacy, follow me. Out the back door."

61

Brant seized Stacy. "Where's Alden?"

"How should I know?" The officer's eyes, however, inadvertently shifted toward a figure hobbling down the hill.

The chief raced in pursuit. "Surrender. Surrender or else." Alden stopped, turned, aimed his pistol and pulled the trigger. It merely snapped. Brant, enraged, raised his arm and hurled his tomahawk at the officer's head. Alden fell. The Indian unsheathed his knife and rushing over, deftly severed the colonel's scalp as a personal trophy.

In front of the Wells house, the round of gunfire had badly injured three Senecas. Crazed and bent on revenge, the warriors swarmed into the house, tomahawking and scalping twenty-three people, including soldiers, servants, Robert Wells, his wife and three children.

Jane Wells had fled outside to hide behind a pile of wood. But a Seneca had seen her escaping. As the Indian approached, he slowly wiped his bloody knife, replaced it in its sheath and drew out his tomahawk. He pounced, grabbing her by the arm.

"Mercy, mercy!" She flung her free arm across her face.

"Halt." A white Indian raced up. "Halt." It was Peter Smith, a former servant in the household. "My sister. Spare her."

The Indian shook his tomahawk defiantly, raised it and struck her down with one blow. He pulled off her cap and flung it aside. Then grabbing a handful of hair, he scalped her. As he hitched the prize to his belt, he caught sight of the cap, picked it up, examined its lace border and hung it, too, at his waist.

* * *

Walter Butler, meanwhile, with 100 of his Rangers had passed by the Wells house, pausing only long enough to note that his white Indians were burning the regimental flag. Some seventy yards from the garrison, he positioned his men on a slight elevation and began pelting the fort with bullets. The defenders replied with sharp, brisk volleys.

Butler signaled his men to cease firing and stepped forward to yell, "*Surrender, damned Rebels.* Surrender, before we destroy you."

Three huzzahs and a discharge of cannon and musketry answered his challenge.

The attackers resumed shooting down upon the garrison.

Captain McDonell turned to Butler. "We'll never storm the fort from here; we need cannon."

"All right. Move the men around to the other side. Let's explore that flank. To take the fort, we'll have to find a weak spot."

From the Wells house the blood-crazed Indians fanned out into all parts of Cherry Valley. As yowling Senecas surrounded the Reverend Dunlop's house, Ranger Lt. Henry Hare grabbed a fellow soldier by the arm. "Run tell Captain Butler what's happening." Catching sight of Mohawk Chief Little Aaron, he signalled: "Follow me inside."

They discovered the Dominie praying and Betsy lying sprawled over her dead mother, hysterically trying to prevent a Seneca from scalping the body.

"Brave warrior," Hare growled, "move aside."

In that instant Little Aaron pulled Betsy away, grabbed her father and pushed them toward the back door.

"My mother, my mother," she screamed, arms flailing. "We've got to take her away!"

The Ranger seized her. "Come on!"

"No!" Betsy wrenched herself loose and started back. "Help me."

Acquiescing, Hare turned to Little Aaron. "Quick. Let's get the old squaw."

The two men carried the body outside and laid it on the cider press. As Betsy covered her mother's head with an apron and the Reverend Dunlop recited a prayer of farewell, a Seneca dashed up, snatched the minister's hat and ran off. Little Aaron gave a whoop and followed in pursuit.

As if from nowhere, another Seneca appeared, knocked the old man down, jumped on him and seized a handful of hair. To the warrior's astonishment off came the Dominie's wig. Stuffing it under his belt, he kicked his victim aside and departed.

Little Aaron returned in triumph with the hat, speedily painted red prisoner marks on the foreheads of Betsy and her father, then sent them away with a group of his Mohawks.

*　*　*

Colonel Samuel Clyde had scarcely entered Fort Alden earlier that morning when cannon thundered their alarm across Cherry Valley.

Catherine Clyde threw a shawl around her stout figure, snatched up the baby and gathered the seven older children. Calling Jimmy to tend to their little dog, she sped out of the house. Shrieks, screams, war hoops and yalloos spurred the fleeing group up the hill and into the woods. Catherine caught sight of Indians approaching her deserted house and knew they would soon take up the chase. "Faster," she panted. "Deeper into the woods."

For over a mile the little band fled, staggering, stumbling, slipping and falling, frantically searching for a safe hiding place. At last Catherine stopped and pointed: to fallen trees, hollow logs, thick bushes near rocks, to anywhere their bodies could crawl in and be hidden.

"Hold your hands over the dog's snout," she whispered in Jimmy's ear. "If it barks, we're all dead." Catherine looked for her oldest daughter, but fourteen-year-old Nancy was missing; she could neither call out nor go back for her. Once everyone else was concealed, the frantic mother could wait no longer, but squeezed herself under a vine-covered log, clasping the baby to her breast.

Indians began to pass where the group lay hidden, but the little dog never growled, never barked. Once an Indian even trailed his gun along the log covering mother and baby; the infant remained miraculously silent.

Catherine, peeping out from her hiding place, saw smoke from the burning settlement and heard the distant whoops and halloos of ravaging warriors. Did Sam reach the fort, she agonized, or was it a burning heap? And she prayed the Lord to watch over Nancy.

When Nancy fled the house instead of following her mother's group, she ran toward the fort. Seeing Indians in a field slaughtering her father's sheep, she hid herself under a mass of fallen trees. The enemy often crossed directly over her, so close she could look up and see under their breech clouts. Some had tawny bodies and others, the white bodies of painted Tories.

* * *

The Indians surged toward the farmhouse of Loyalist James Ramsey, who with his four grown children was waiting to greet them at the door. The family waved to the attackers, calling out, "O Sago, brethren."

The warriors paused to listen.

"We are good King's people and we hail your arrival," the Loyalist explained. "We rejoice that Karitongeh feels the might and power of your strong arm."

"Karitongeh, Karitongeh. We will burn and destroy and plunder this hornet's nest. We will show no mercy."

"Brethren, harken," said Ramsey. "We are your friends; hold back your flaming torches from my house and barn. Spare my farm."

"White brother, listen with an understanding ear: This farm must be burned to the ground. Otherwise the Yankees will discover you are loyal. Come with us."

Warriors seized the group, painted prisoner marks on their foreheads and marched them off.

* * *

Lt. Hare's messenger found Walter Butler still on the far side of the fort. "Indians, sir, they're running amok. Little Beard stormed the Wells house 'n massacred almost everybody. Hiokatoo and the other chiefs're raging over the settlement, butchering women and children."

"Savages and their promises. Damnation! Captain McDonell, detach a party of Rangers to try and save people. Get the Indians to bring in prisoners, not scalps."

"And plunder?"

"Of course, encourage them to plunder. Get them to move up their squaws and dogs from the rear so they can pillage and scavenge. But stop the killing."

"What about the fort?"

"I'll move my Rangers back round to the other side and prevent the Rebels from sallying."

* * *

That morning Jane Campbell had risen before dawn to see Sam off to a militia meeting on the Mohawk, in Canajoharie.

"I'll be back by early afternoon, well before dark," he promised, "certainly in time for our double celebration." Elly was eight that very day and James had turned six just two days before. "I hate leaving you all here alone."

"We'll be all right. But do hurry home." Jane, however, was worried, and afraid; she, the five children, her parents and the several slaves were virtually defenseless. Cap'n, who was sixty-one, could hardly stave off an attack singlehandedly. The house was strong, but the surrounding embankment was beginning to crumble.

Nothing Jane did all that morning relieved her fears. She put the final stitches on James' coveted uniform and Elly's new coat. She looked in on Lain making the birthday cake, then turned to Tom, the slave boy. "Fetch some wood;" Lain would be needing more for her baking. She listened to the sleet striking against the window panes, thankful to be inside but uneasy about Sam.

She wandered into the next room. Willie sat in the corner,

memorizing a passage from the family Bible as part of his school work. The other children had gathered near the fire, around their Grammy; Eleanor Cannon was re-telling the Parable of the Good Shepherd and his lost sheep.

Cap'n Cannon blustered into the kitchen from outside. His thin, sharp nose sniffed appreciatively. "Apple cake." The words were barely out of his mouth when alarm cannon thundered at the fort: Boom! Boom! Boom!

"Everyone, help secure the house," Jane commanded. "Bolt doors and shutters." She snatched up Samuel. "Quickly, hide in the back room."

In the semi-darkness she counted figures; Willie was missing; he had disappeared! Also Lain. In fact all the slaves had vanished. Jane was alone with her mother and four children.

Cap'n, meanwhile, had grabbed a stock of muskets and Sam's cartridge box. "Tom, come along outside with me. Boy, you load 'n I'll shoot." The two had barely stationed themselves behind a tree before they heard war whoops and yalloos. The horde was swarming up the hill.

"We'll make those divils pay dearly," Cap'n shouted as he let one shot fly after another. "By God, they're slowing down." A musket ball struck his leg. A Seneca rushed forward, seized the weapons and pounced upon Cannon. With a daub of blood-red paint he marked man and boy as his captives and dragged them down the hill.

The attackers surged forward and over the embankment. Reaching the house, they pounded and battered and rammed the doors and shutters. Suddenly with a deafening crash, the fiends swarmed into the house, wild and hideous, dripping water, paint and blood. The feathers in their topknots drooped from the sleeting rain; red and black war paint had dribbled over their half-naked figures; bloody knives dangled from their chains and still bloodier scalps hung from their belts. The savages seized Jane and the terrified little group clustered behind her, dragged them outdoors, then slapped on prisoner marks.

Jane watched helplessly while whooping Indians spread over the farm to plunder everything from pots, pans and quilts to Sam's precious pocket watch. They drove out the livestock before setting fire to the house and well-filled barns.

Frantically Jane looked for her boy to escape from the fiery inferno. "Willie! Lain! . . . Willie!" An Indian rushed up and silenced her, brandishing a tomahawk at her throat.

William and Lain had not heard Jane's screams. As the first war whoops sounded, the slave had grabbed "Massa" Willie and the Bible and raced upstairs to the attic where they cowered behind a large pile of flax.

Lain saw flames! "Quick, chile. Follow me." Still clutching the Bible, she led the boy back down, only to encounter a war painted Tory at the foot of the stairs.

"Why Mr. Lottridge," Willie exclaimed.

"That is not my name, but here, pass out this way." He led child and slave outdoors. *"Run to the woods."*

In the forest behind the house the two found a hiding place among thick bushes beneath a rock ledge. They hoped it would conceal them from the keen eyes of prowling Senecas.

* * *

Sam Campbell was riding home from Canajoharie when he heard gunfire and cannon in the distance. He spurred on his horse to full speed.

Reaching the edge of his own woods he stared in horror: his farm was ablaze and wildly whooping savages swarmed inside the flaming compound. All of a sudden, with a triumphant yell the Indians left, prodding his family and cattle down the hill. Sam drew his sword, about to race to their rescue, but caught himself, realizing his inevitable death would also seal his family's fate. Weeping in anguish, he retreated into the woods.

Just before darkness Campbell surveyed the smoking ruins of his farm. A wobbling colt ran toward him, prancing and kicking up its heels, then fell dead at his feet.

Two slaves emerged from the woods, calling out, "Massa, Massa."

"Yes. I'm here but by the grace of God."

* * *

The incessant rain and sleet continued. The main body of Rangers stayed at Fort Alden until late evening, preventing the defenders from sallying and thereby enabling their forces to burn and plunder the settlement uninterruptedly. Under McDonell's influence, however, the Indians did take prisoners, not scalps.

By the time Captain Butler signaled retreat, most of the houses and barns had been burned and much cattle slaughtered or driven off. "Damn those Indians," he cursed, looking straight at Captain Johnston, "they're demanding every prisoner."

"Yes, and you've got to comply."

"I know. Otherwise the savages will kill all seventy of them."

Butler watched while the Indians divided their captives into groups. With the help of Joseph Brant and another chief he furtively drew aside the Reverend Dunlop, Betsy and twelve Loyalists, and sent them to the Tory encampment not far from the settlement.

The Indians drove their prisoners two miles down the valley to their encampment, the hill on William Dickson's farm. The glaring light from a great central fire kept them from seeing Dickson and his son Samuel peering from among nearby hemlocks. In the inky night the two had ventured down from their thicket to continue the search for Elizabeth. As they recognized many friends and relatives staggering in, they took hope.

Cap'n was standing with Tom beside the great fire when his wife, Jane and the four children stumbled up to join them. Eleanor Cannon, exhausted by the ordeal, collapsed in her husband's arms, then drew back, seeing his bloody and torn trouser leg.

"It's nothing. The shot merely grazed my leg."

Nevertheless his wife tore a strip from her petticoat and bound the wound.

"Father," Jane whispered, "where's Willie? Have you seen him?"

An Indian loomed up. "No talk, white squaw. No talk, white man. Kill!" He swung his tomahawk, stopping at Cannon's mouth; then motioning with it, he pointed to a rock. "Go there."

* * *

Willie and Lain crouched in their hiding place until nightfall, fearing even to raise their heads. When the gunfire stopped and the war whoops died away, they emerged, warily. Lain wrapped the Bible in their one blanket and hid it behind a fence. Then, with her arm around Massa Willie's shoulder, she guided the boy past the smoking ruins of their house and barns, and set off through the woods toward Canajoharie and the Mohawk. "We dasn't use de trail 'cause Injuns 'n Tories might find us."

"The forest's so quiet and dark. The bears'll get us." He stopped. "Oh Lain, I'm scared."

"No!" She took his hand, praying he would not realize she was equally frightened. *"Less go on."*

"But I'm cold, 'n starving." He stopped again. "I'm so tired. Let me lie down."

" Neva, we'll soon git somewhar."

They groped their way through seemingly endless trees and underbrush.

"My papa's gone. My Mama's dead. My brothers an' sister 're dead." Willie threw himself into the slave's arms. "Oh please, please, please let me die, too."

Lain held him lovingly until he could stop crying. *"When good massa come home and find* [all dat trouble], *oh how glad he be to find Massa Willie alive! Come den now, less go on; we'll soon git somewhar."*

* * *

Thick sleet drenched the captives crowded around the central fire. Stripped of coats and cloaks, without food or shelter, they huddled together for warmth, teeth chattering and bodies shaking uncontrollably in slowly freezing clothes. In the distance they watched occasional flames burst forth as gusts of wind relighted the smoldering ruins of Cherry Valley's once prosperous farms.

Surrounding them painted Indians squatted beside many small watchfires, their faces glowing in the flickering light. They were examining and distributing their plunder. A warrior dangled a gold pocket watch by its chain to catch the reflection of the dancing flames.

"Sam's watch!" Jane Campbell bit her lips to silence herself but could not control the angry tears.

Other warriors were counting scalps and fastening them onto poles. Suddenly to the accompaniment of an exultant yalloo, a scalp with long flaming red hair was raised on high. All the warriors gazed in admiration and envy at the magnificent trophy.

From their hiding place among the hemlocks, William and Samuel Dickson sickened with horror.

Jane Campbell also recognized Elizabeth's red hair and shuddered in dread; would Willie's be next? Or Sam's?

Night crept slowly on and silence descended. From time to time the stillness was shattered by an Indian's prisoner whoops; the high-pitched, unearthly sounds signaled the arrival of yet another captive.

"A nightmare. Please, dear God," Jane prayed, "let me wake up." But it was no dream.

Not Jane, not her family, no one slept that night. They were too terrified, not by the fear of death but by a much more horrible fear: excruciating Indian torture.

11

Down the Cherry Valley Creek

November 12, 1778.

At last dawn broke upon the encampment.

"Quah, quah, quah!" [Hail, hail, hail!]

At that raucous call the Indians leaped to their feet, ready for action. The sleepless prisoners, benumbed with cold, struggled to stand, their sodden clothes now almost frozen stiff.

Seneca warriors swooped down upon the cluster of Continentals seized at the Wells house: Colonel Stacy, three other officers and ten privates. Within minutes they had been stripped naked except for boots, their clothes thrown to squaws. Then waving tomahawks and with gleeful whoops, the Indians drove the men down the hill and into the valley.

Jane, her family and the other captives watched dumbly until they themselves were prodded to move; the still painted Indians separated them into small companies and dumped heavy sacks of plunder at everyone's feet. Even Elly and James were expected to carry their share.

Matthew began to whimper.

"Stop that," Jane snapped. "Take Elly's hand." Then knotting two ends of her shawl to make a sling, she picked up little Samuel.

Eleanor Cannon, meanwhile, was struggling with her load. Although she had placed the flat, braided carrying strap, a tumpline, across her forehead, she was unable to hoist the sack onto her back. Her squat body simply refused to comply. "Oh Jane, what'll I do?"

"Lean farther over and bend your head down."

"But now I can't see where I'm going."

James took her hand. "I'll guide you."

"Jog'-go," [Get going] called out their Seneca commander, "joggo."

Jane adjusted her tumpline one final time to balance the load on her back and shuffled forward, Samuel in front and the heavy plunder behind.

Cap'n watched with Tom as Jane and her little group stumbled off and at the bottom of the hill turned south along the Cherry Valley Creek to disappear from view. "Damn the Injuns. And damn this pesky leg."

"Yo' needs a cane." Before Cap'n could stop him, the boy had darted to some wood piled beside the now smoldering fire and begun searching.

A warrior dashed over. "Slave, get away. We kill."

Tom grabbed a stick, then waving it on high, scuttled back.

"Joggo," shouted the leader of their company. "Fast joggo."

The two heaved up their sacks, tottered down the hill and also headed south, Cap'n leaning hard on his walking stick.

* * *

James, Matthew and Elly plodded along with Grammy, helping her over rocks, icy patches and roots. Even so she slipped and staggered, often falling to her knees. The children would silently help her up, then continue onward.

But Grammy's load was too heavy and the march too rapid. Now she fell more and more frequently, pulled down by the swaying sack. Jane could only look on helplessly as she and her family trailed farther and farther behind.

"Fast joggo." A Seneca struck the flat head of his tomahawk against his musket. "Fast joggo or kill slow white squaw."

"Leave us, children. Fly ahead. Samuel and I'll stay with Grammy." Jane and her mother quickened their pace but still dragged behind.

Eleanor Cannon turned her ankle, lost her balance and fell backward. "Jane, I can't. I can't get up."

"Please, Mother. I'll help you." She pulled. She pushed frantically as the hollow warning of tomahawk striking musket sounded once again. "The Indian's coming. Mother, get up!"

"I can't." She took off her wedding ring. "Here."

72

The Seneca thrust Jane and Samuel aside, knocking them down as he seized Eleanor Cannon. He raised his tomahawk and struck, then grabbed her hair and quickly ripped off the scalp with his knife. He began to strip the body but suddenly stopped, turned to Jane and slapped her face with the bloody trophy. "Joggo."

Vomiting, she clutched Samuel to her, shouldered the sack of plunder and fled foward. She clenched her jaws to keep from screaming.

Minutes later the Indian was shadowing her. "Fast joggo, fast." He zig-zagged his blood-stained tomahawk through the air, only stopping when Jane caught up with her children.

"Mama, your face," Matthew shrieked. "Bloody!"

Elly clapped her hand over his mouth just as the Seneca rushed up from behind. But he passed by and instead snatched a squalling infant from another mother's arms. Seizing the baby's feet, he swung and smashed its head against a tree, then cast the body aside.

Jane flattened Samuel against her bosom, encircling the child in a wild effort to conceal him. Another warrior came up, grabbed him and disappeared into the forest.

"Mama, Mama, Mama . . . ."

She fought to hold back her sobs. *"That Indian's more merciful than the other one,"* she tried to console herself. *"He's taken my boy so far away I can't hear his* [dying] *screams."*

All the rest of the day Jane and her children marched on, stunned with grief.

*   *   *

At nightfall Jane and her company staggered into the encampment already established by an advance group of Indians. Dropping her sack, she slowly righted herself, shook her head and peered around. There, by the fire was little Samuel!

The child was seated on the warrior's lap being fed, all the while laughing and toying with the Seneca's silver ornaments. At the sight of Jane his face lit up. "Mama."

The Indian beckoned her over. Taking Samuel into her arms, she covered him with kisses, then flew back to Elly and the boys.

Soon Cap'n, aided by the ever-faithful Tom, limped up to the campfire and looked around anxiously. "Where's Grammy?" he mouthed.

74

Jane began to cry, raised her hand and pointed to her mother's ring.

He grasped Tom's shoulder for support, moaning. "She's dead." Tears rolled down his cheeks.

Other companies straggled into the campground. Last of all, Colonel Stacy's group dropped by the fire, bloody and battered but once again in uniform; the squaws had merely been given their clothing to safeguard it.

An Indian doled out a cupful of dried corn per person and gestured toward some icy mud puddles, as if to say, "There's your water. Lap it up." Another Indian tossed out blankets, one to a prisoner. Elly nudged her mother and pointed to a scarlet and green quilt which had just landed at the feet of a soldier; it was one of theirs.

Snow began to fall as Jane and her family, exhausted and benumbed, dropped off to sleep. No more did she fear for the morrow; already sufficient unto that day was the evil thereof.

12

The Only Remaining Building Amidst the Ruins

November 12, 1778.

While the Indians goaded their prisoners down the Cherry Valley Creek, soldiers from the fort slipped out to retrieve the body of Colonel Alden. Major Daniel Whiting, now the garrison's senior officer, ordered his commandant buried *"under arms with firing three volleys over his grave."*

Sam Clyde watched the ceremony, barely able to conceal his angry thoughts: May Alden roast in Hell! He brought down this bloody massacre on us all.

Scarcely had the farewell volleys sounded for Alden than Catherine Clyde stole from her hiding place and checked that her family was safe. Cautioning them not to come out, she then roused Jimmy, directing him to take the dog, go to the next hill and see if the American flag was still flying at the fort. If so, he should try and get there. "If Colonel Clyde's inside, tell him where we're hiding. God speed."

In the meantime, Walter Butler dispatched Captain McDonell and sixty Rangers, as well as Joseph Brant with fifty Indians, to complete the destruction of Cherry Valley. He stationed himself at the fortification with the main body of Rangers in order to prevent the defenders from sallying. In addition, his men patrolled the settlement, gathering information about Rebel activities.

The garrison, cooped up within its breastworks, watched in frustration and fury. Suddenly spying Jimmy with the scampering dog, they shouted, "Faster. Faster!" As the two approached, the men cracked open the sally port and pulled the boy inside, the animal at his heels.

"Massa Clyde."

"Jimmy!"

"Massa, come wid me. De missus and de chillun, they be's safe."

"Praise the Lord." The colonel pulled out a handkerchief and blew his nose loudly, trying to conceal his tears. He sought out Whiting. "Major, help me rescue my family."

The young officer drew back in surprise. "Why no, I can't send out any men with the enemy roving the settlement; it's far too dangerous."

"But my family! How can you leave them out in the woods? To be captured or die of the cold. It's inhuman."

"Well," Whiting muttered, scratching his unshaven chin, "I guess I could ask for volunteers."

Fourteen men answered "Here" to the call.

Jimmy led Clyde and the soldiers back to Catherine's hiding place and whistled. The family crept out, their bodies benumbed and their clothes frozen, but they were alive.

Sam put his arms around his wife and baby. "Thank God you're safe!"

"Is Nancy at the fort?"

He shook his head.

Catherine stifled a moan, took her husband's arm and began stumbling down the hill.

Stealthily the small band trudged past James Ramsey's smoldering house and on past the falls where only the day before Cherry Valley's sawmill had stood. Outside the Dominie's house, gruesome red things were dangling from the branch of an apple tree: parts of Mrs. Dunlop's mutilated body.

Finally only a creek in an open meadow separated the group from safety; a log served as a bridge.

"Injuns," a fort sentry shouted, "Injuns."

Clyde's soldiers whirled round to cover the family's flight. The children nimbly threaded their way over the bridge, then darted into the fort, but Catherine, still numb with cold, could not. As she inched her heavy body along the log, musket shots struck the tree trunk, joggling it; she kept her balance and lurched into the waiting arms of her husband and

Jimmy. They raced into the fort, the two men half carrying her.

The volunteers had scarcely retreated to safety when Nancy emerged from her hiding place. She sped down the hill, braids flying, bullets peppering her path. At the log bridge she glanced up toward the ramparts and saw red-clad figures. "Oh no, Indians! They've seized the fort." She turned to flee.

"Nancy, Nancy Clyde, come back," the figures shouted. *"Run! Run! For God's sake run!"*

She stopped, then raced into the fort, unharmed, thankful that the "Indians" were merely sentries wrapped in red blankets against the sleet and bitter cold.

Hardly had Nancy arrived inside the fort than Rangers and Indians made a direct attack. Whiting's cannon drove them back. Next, Butler tried to draw out the garrison but suspecting an ambush, the commander refused the challenge. Once more the Rangers probed and poked, seeking a way to storm the fort, but without cannon of their own a frontal assault was not feasible. The captain gave up and resumed his support of McDonell's and Brant's marauders.

When Butler finally retreated from Cherry Valley, only one building stood amidst the ruins: Fort Alden.

13

Pawns of War

"Quah, quah, quah."

At the Indian encampment the warriors and their captives awoke to the same squawking call of the day before, now muffled by a pall of snow.

Walter Butler, Captain John Johnston and Joseph Brant strode into the encampment and signaled for the prisoners to congregate. "In the name of His Majesty the King, greetings," Butler called out in a honeyed voice. "For humanity's sake I am induced to permit the women and children, and certain men among you, to return to Cherry Valley."

Everyone gasped in disbelief; Jane and her father exchanged glances.

"The winter weather, plus your naked and helpless condition, might otherwise prove fatal to you. With the assistance of Captain Johnston here I have been able to persuade the Indians to agree."

"Mama, is he saying we're going home?" Elly whispered.

"Nevertheless," Butler continued, "I am also retaining some prisoners, in particular Mrs. Samuel Campbell and her family."

Jane groaned. She reached out to touch Elly but dared not look at her father.

"Let it be noted that I am sending back Colonel John Campbell with his wife and their grandchildren. Unlike his brother, Colonel Samuel, he did not give aid and shelter to infinite numbers of Rebels by fortifying his house; nor did he fight at Oriskany.

"Furthermore, I am keeping Mrs. James Moore and her three

daughters to answer for James and John Moore's infamous support of the Rebels."

"Mercy, Captain Butler," Mary Moore cried out. "My girls and I've done nothing. Mercy!"

"Hold your tongue, woman." Butler pointed toward Matthew Cannon. "As a member of the Committee of Safety, you, too, will remain, your just reward for traitorous activities against the King."

"And damn proud of them," Cap'n growled under his breath.

"In sum, the Samuel Campbell and James Moore families, plus Matthew Cannon, are to be my personal hostages, my pawns of war." Butler's eyes blackened in anger. "For three years Rebels have kept my father's family in Albany. At long last I can see to their release and transfer to Canada; I propose an exchange of the before-named prisoners for my family. If that cannot be arranged, and promptly, too, I fear you captives will spend the rest of your lives in the land of those Senecas."

All heads turned toward the painted warriors checking and adjusting their trophies, scalps waving on poles.

"It goes without saying," Butler continued, "that good King's men are welcome to join my forces and help fight for the Loyalist cause. Since I am in the presence of Rebels who might betray you, I decline to mention names."

The captain inadvertently looked toward the Ramsey family; they tried not to react. James Ramsey had decided to send his children on to Niagara: the two girls would stay at the fort for the duration of the war, and the two boys would join the Rangers. He himself planned to return to Cherry Valley with the prisoner group, take care of some business and then flee to Niagara.

"As for the Continentals, you, too, are welcome." Butler laughed. "And so are men and boys captured in arms. I'm sure, when you arrive at the Indian villages, you will be given a most interesting reception." He waited for their cries of mercy, but no one uttered a word.

Brant broke the awkward silence. "Let all prisoners here assembled understand one important fact: we are not warring against slaves." He turned toward twelve black men, women and children huddled together. "You people have no evil deeds to answer for and consequently will not suffer any punishment. But you will continue the march, that is, all except the two of you owned by the Dominie. Since you both are too old to work, we'll return you to Cherry Valley."

Several slaves shouted and jumped for joy at the thought of a new life.

"Yes, rejoice. For soon your masters will be loyal officers or noble Iroquois."

Two or three other slaves wailed, frightened by the prospect of spending the rest of their lives with the Tories or in an Indian village.

Amidst the confusion Cannon heard Tom's voice: "I wants to stay wid my Cap'n."

Butler motioned for silence, then took out a paper and waved it high in the air for all to see. "This is a letter to General Philip Schuyler, proposing the aforesaid exchange of my father's family.

"Colonel John Campbell, take this letter and deliver it to Fort Alden. Tell the commander to forward it to Schuyler with extreme dispatch; many lives are hanging in the balance, awaiting a reply.

"And now, returning prisoners, you are dismissed. But move quickly, before the warriors change their minds."

Butler called to the waiting Indians. "Naho!" They sprang into action. With tomahawks they prodded the remaining captives into new groups and again dropped heavy sacks of plunder at their feet.

"Fast joggo! We kill."

* * *

Back in Cherry Valley later that same morning of November 13, Colonel Jacob Klock and his long-promised reinforcements arrived at the fort in the midst of pelting sleet.

From the safety of the ramparts four blanket-clad officers surveyed the devastation: Colonel Klock, Major Whiting, Colonel Clyde and Captain William Harper, the newly arrived Magistrate for the Mohawk District.

Klock shook his head, his unruly hair sticking up like an Iroquois topknot. "Whiting, I'm mighty sorry, but I can't help you. You need a regiment of Continental troops, not my 300 militia. Your needs are way beyond me 'n my men."

"Perhaps so, but surely you can give us some relief. I think . . . ."

"Look here, Jacob," Sam Clyde interrupted, "at least help us bury the dead and collect any remaining goods 'n cattle."

"Impossible. My men were called up to be reinforcements, not grave diggers 'n cattle hustlers." Klock drew his blanket more closely around him. "The enemy's left and we've got to get back home before he strikes somewhere else."

"Stay; we're desperate!"

"No, Sam, I can't. Look, even now Butler may be attacking and burning farms along the Mohawk."

The pleas were of no avail. Klock *"did not stay above two or three hours,"* Harper reported to Governor Clinton. He *"warmed himself, and turned about, marched back without affording the distressed inhabitants the least assistance or relief."*

Late that afternoon Colonel Frederick Fisher arrived from the Mohawk with his militia and a few wagons loaded with the first provisions the fort had received in weeks. Whiting greeted the painfully thin officer at the gate with Harper and Clyde: "Thank God you're here. We're destitute; we need men, food and ammunition."

"Glad I could help with provisions." Fisher turned to a sergeant. "Hurry up with those sacks. Time's a-passing."

"What's that mean?" Captain Harper growled. "Aren't you going to stay?"

82

"No. I wish we could, but we've got to march right back. On the other hand, looks like this sleet isn't going to let up any time soon." His whole body shivered perceptibly as he studied the sky. " 'N besides, it's getting dark. We'll just encamp here and leave at dawn."

Even as the colonel spoke, a group of people appeared outside the gate. Those whom Butler had secreted in the Tory encampment were returning: the Reverend Dunlop, Betsy and the Loyalists. They had an astounding message. "Tomorrow the rest of the women and children will be coming back."

"I for one don't believe it," Fisher announced. "Butler's too much of a devil."

"A devil yes," Clyde agreed, "but a practical one. All those women and children would slow down his retreat."

"Of course they would." Harper grabbed Colonel Fisher by the arm. "So send out a party to meet them. My sister and her girls could even be among them."

"Ridiculous. They're not coming back."

"Then stay 'n help us bring in the dead and bury them."

"No. Tomorrow my troops 'n wagons have to be back on the Mohawk to defend the living."

"Colonel Fisher," Whiting asked, "I assume your wagons will be empty?"

"Yes, of course."

"Then why not fill them with some of the distressed people who've come into the fort."

"No, we could be ambushed and everyone killed. I don't want that responsibility."

"Responsibility be damned," Clyde roared. "In the name of Christ, carry them off."

Fisher sighed in resignation. "All right, if you insist."

"Yes, by God, we do!"

November 14, 1778.

The next morning, Fisher and his caravan had hardly left when Butler's returning prisoners, some forty men, women and children, staggered into the fort. John Campbell, his clothes ragged and wet, a mane of white hair falling over his haggard face, went directly to Whiting's office.

The major looked up from his desk at the exhausted militia colonel.

"Come in and sit down."

"I never thought we'd make it back."

"Nor did we."

"Butler's sent a letter proposing an exchange of prisoners; I have it here." Campbell seemed to find new strength as he continued speaking. "My brother's family and all the remaining captives can be saved if our authorities act at once. You must help."

Whiting, himself red-eyed with fatigue, seemed bewildered. "Ye Gods, what more am I supposed to do now?"

"Dispatch Butler's letter as soon as humanly possible."

"All right, the moment I can spare a soldier to deliver it."

Whiting set the letter aside where it lay untended almost three weeks. Not until December 2 did he send it off, and then not to General Schuyler, but to Captain William Harper, who had returned to his magistrate's duties on the Mohawk.

Harper immediately forwarded Butler's letter to Governor Clinton and added his own report:

> As with the first group of prisoners, a considerable part of them are Tories, or strongly suspected and such as ought to be sent back to him again . . . . [Even so] I am sure you will do everything in your power to relieve our distressed friends from worse than devils . . . .

> Sir, Mrs. Moore is my sister, and duty and nature binds me to entreat her exchange and her three daughters who are all women grown, for whom my heart trembles, lest they who were worse than brutes should treat them with worse than death.

Back in Cherry Valley soldiers and survivors searched the bloody ground to recover mutilated bodies of their friends, families and comrades. Heartsick, they dug a deep trench and there, in a common grave, laid most of the slain to rest. In all, nearly fifty people had been killed: twenty-nine women and children, three civilian men and at least sixteen soldiers.

The destitute survivors bade farewell to Whiting and his men who would remain at Fort Alden until the following June. Then, mournfully, the refugees wended their way through the now deep snow to the Mohawk River and on to Schenectady, abandoning their once flourishing farms to roving animals and the returning wilderness.

PART II
KANADESAGA

14

Sold!

"Fast joggo. We kill," the Indian repeated.

Jane had no need to be reminded; she, her family and the remaining captives were already reaching for their packs, terrified of being struck down if they lagged behind.

Colonel Stacy sidled over to young James and patted him on the head. "You're a brave little soldier."

The boy replied with a worshipful gaze.

All at once, several warriors swooped down upon the officer, threw him to the ground and stripped him naked except for his boots. Instead of pulling them off, they flipped him over and dragged him on his stomach, making a bloody trail in the snow all the way to Brant, the commander of their party.

"Mercy, Brother Brant! Spare a fellow Mason." Desperately Stacy gave the secret clasp with his hands. "Spare me!"

"Perhaps a Mason." Brant fingered a scalp hanging from his belt. "But a Rebel, no."

"Save me, or else." The colonel made other signs, showing Brant how he would be punished if he refused to help his masonic brother. "Your vows are sacred."

"Warriors, halt. Wrap the prisoner in a blanket and sell him to the British." Almost as an after-thought he sneered, "Demand a goodly price."

James, watching and listening, could hardly keep back the tears. "Mama, will Colonel Stacy be all right?"

"Sweetheart, let's pray so."

Before she could say more, an Indian came up, tapped her and each child on the shoulder, then pointed to himself. "Me guard. Me *Ga-no'-geh*."

Jane was surprised to recognize him as the one who had cared for her baby; to her, all painted warriors looked alike: he was thickset, however, and appeared older than the others.

After handing around some parched corn and scraps of meat, Ganogeh whisked away Samuel to carry him on the day's march.

The boy laughed and waved, "Bye, bye, Mama."

"He's a nice Indian, isn't he," Elly whispered.

"Yes, he is now." Jane adjusted the tumpline and hoisted her huge bundle. "Time will tell."

Again the pace was swift, the attackers still fearful of pursuing soldiers as they sped down the Cherry Valley Creek. Reaching a fording place they waded across and joined a branch of the Susquehanna to snake in a southwesterly direction along its banks.

Jane and her children, joined by Mrs. Moore and her three daughters, staggered clumsily through the snow. Backs and necks ached from the heavy loads; icy clothes crackled and scratched; bruised and swollen feet shot waves of pain with every step.

Mary Moore tripped over a snow-covered rock and lurched to the ground. "Help me. I can't get up. Help!" Her daughters and Jane Campbell rushed over. They pulled and pulled, trying to right her unwieldy body while keeping their own balance. All to no avail.

An Indian guard waved Jane and the girls onward with his tomahawk. "Joggo." He turned to the cowering woman. *"Prepare for death."*

"No, no. Please!" She burst into tears.

"You too slow joggo."

"Butler, carry me to Butler. He'll have mercy and he'll give you many dollars."

"Dollars?" He paused, slapping the flat of his tomahawk against her sack. Suddenly he rehung the weapon on his belt, picked up his captive, trotted off and dumped her at Walter Butler's feet.

Mary Moore clutched the captain's boots, wetting them with her tears. Looking up, she pleaded with him through disheveled hair. "In the name of your own mother, have mercy. Save me."

"Let the Indian kill you and have the benefit of your scalp." He kicked a foot loose from her grasp. *"You are old enough to die. What do you wish to live longer for?"*

"Mercy! In Christ's name have mercy!"

"Never." With a scalping motion Butler turned away and began speaking to one of his sergeants.

The warrior jerked up his captive by the hair and raised his tomahawk to strike.

"Halt," commanded the sergeant. "I'll buy the prisoner. How much?"

"Eight dollars. Yes?"

As the soldier counted out his money, the Indian let go of Mary Moore's hair and she collapsed in a heap.

Gently the sergeant pulled her upright, then half dragged her to his horse. "This here's a mighty fine animal. I got it in Cherry Valley."

Butler laughed. "And you're wasting it on an old hag."

That night Jane and her group shuffled into the newest encampment, numb with exhaustion and despairing, not knowing Mary Moore's fate. They were greeted by Samuel, playing happily on Ganogeh's lap. With an affectionate pull at the boy's blond curls, the Indian handed him over and signaled for everyone to go to the central fire.

Elly pointed to a kettle sitting in the coals. "Mama, what do you 'spose is in the pot?"

"I don't know. Probably hunks of beef."

Painted warriors were placing similar pots on the fire, squatting down and waiting for the food to cook. As their bodies warmed, the air began to reek of dried blood, bear's grease and smoke.

Matthew grabbed his sister's skirt and covered his nose. "They stink."

"Yes." Elly started to gag.

"Cough," Jane whispered as she and the rest of the group began to retch; they had nothing in their stomachs to vomit.

Cap'n limped into the encampment with his company, Tom by his side. His leg, thanks to the cane, seemed much better. Indian guards abruptly seized the two, led them close to Jane's group, pushed them down onto some scattered pine boughs and lashed their arms and legs to long poles. Then they looped their necks with ropes which they attached to trees.

"I wonder what the Indian did to Mother," Abigail Moore blurted out; she was fifteen and impulsive. "Do you suppose?"

"Shhh." Jaynie grabbed her sister. "Don't suppose anything." Although only four years her senior, she looked and acted much older. "And be quiet. Or they might come get you—and us."

"Jaynie, don't be so gruff." Young Mary, their middle sister, put her arm around Abigail. "If we're going to survive, we've got to obey the Indians and not attract attention."

The water in the kettles had scarcely come to a boil when warriors began pulling out slabs of beef and hacking off huge pieces to stuff into their mouths. Blood and grease oozed down their chins and dripped into the snow. In a roar of laughter someone threw Cannon and Tom two chunks which landed on their faces. Ganogeh motioned for Jane and Elly to go feed them and take portions for themselves and the others.

"Vile-tasting," Cap'n muttered, "worse than the maggot-filled stuff I used to get on shipboard." Nevertheless the entire family choked down everything, too hungry to be squeamish.

15

Cauche Quando

Dawn, the next day.

Warriors grabbed Cap'n and Tom, cut their bindings and prodded them into a standing position. Jane and her little band struggled to move, their bodies ever racked with pain from the relentless journey and half frozen from sleeping on pine boughs in the now deep snow.

"Joggo!"

The captives swung up their burdens and staggered forward. News of Mary Moore's rescue was soon whispered about. Abigail looked at her sisters and sang out, "Oh, Mother's saved! Thank God."

"Yes, thank God, but be quiet or you'll be scalped," Mary hissed.

Jane Campbell's spirits also lifted to rejoice in her friend's good fortune, but quickly sank again into the nightmare of reality.

The march went on and on, left foot, right foot, left foot, right, their feet often sinking into the deep piled snow. Clothes, stiff and ice-caked, caught on low-hanging branches and tore. Shoes wore out and soles separated from tops; Jane and the girls ripped petticoats into strips and stuffed or bound together the families' shoes. They saw barefooted companions plodding through the snow, their swollen, frost-bitten feet cut by rocks, brushwood and ice.

November 19.

Suddenly the Indians stopped and painted their prisoners' faces and hair with vermillion and black, then resumed the march another few miles.

"Halt! Drop sacks!" *Sha-whi-ang'-to* [now South Windsor] was near.

Warrior after warrior began sounding the prisoner whoop, high-pitched quaverings and hallooings to inform the town of the number and natures of their captives. "Listen, Shawhiangto," they howled. "Count. Braves are returning from the warpath."

In terror Jane drew the young children together, her arms encircling them. The Moore girls clustered behind as Cap'n and Tom inched toward the family.

Snarling dogs swarmed toward the new arrivals, followed by men, women, even children all shrieking and waving clubs and knives. The place exploded in a frenzy of hatred: they were avenging the destruction of their neighboring town, Onaquaga; it had been burned to the ground by the Continental Army only the month before. Although most of Onaquaga's inhabitants had fled to villages farther west, a certain number had settled in and around Shawhiangto.

Ganogeh seized Cap'n and Tom by the hands and started running. "Fast. Fast joggo," he called back to Jane and her group. He zig-zagged them all through the raging horde to a distant hut, jerked back the bearskin curtain-door and pointed inside. In the pitch darkness they found each other and held on desperately.

Matthew broke their silence. "Listen. I hear a noise."

"A sentry," Abigail whispered.

"I'm scared." He started to whimper.

"Stop that," Cap'n snapped. "Indians demand courage."

From the distance wave after wave of tortured screams pierced the air. They listened, hardly daring to breathe.

Tom gripped Cap'n's arm. "I's so 'fraid. Sir, I'm glad I be's wid yo'."

Dawn.

Ganogeh drew back the bearskin curtain, surveyed his prisoners and pointed to Tom, then toward the outside. *"Cauche quando."* [Come out.]

A squaw entered the hut. "Cauche quando," she repeated, catching the black boy by the ear and pulling him toward the doorway.

"Massa, Massa Cap'n!"

"God be with ye, my friend."

The bearskin curtain dropped and darkness again shrouded the group; the boy was gone forever.

James tugged at his mother's sleeve. "Will they take me away, too?"

"Hush. Don't say that."

The curtain lifted. Ganogeh reappeared in the doorway; this time he spoke to everyone. "Cauche quando. Joggo." The prisoners found themselves consolidated into a smaller company; others besides Tom had disappeared.

As before, the trail often narrowed to the width of a person's body. Twisting and turning with the contours of the land, it followed the Susquehanna, sometimes at water's edge, other times along the hilly ridges but always through unbroken wilderness. As Jane, her family and all the prisoners filed along the path beaten down by their captors, eyes burned and teared from looking down into the bright snow. Even worse, the swaying sacks of plunder rubbed raw sores into their backs, or catching on jagged branches, caused tumplines to wrench around and burn their foreheads.

At least the Indians had slowed to a less frantic pace, having traveled too far to be concerned about enemy pursuit. And they no longer pinioned Cap'n at night, for escape now meant only death in the frozen waste. Ganogeh even allowed his group to speak among themselves.

"Father, look over here." Jane grasped her mother's wedding ring and started to take it off. "You should have it."

Dogs barked in the distance, signaling the captives' approach to another Indian village.

"No, Jane, the ring's safer with you. Who knows what the Injuns'll do to me."

Each settlement meant more face-painting for the prisoners, another dash among snapping dogs and swinging clubs, and the all-night whoops and halloos of the celebrating Indians. But it also meant Ganogeh would lead the family to shelter for the night. Even a lean-to or a hut was a godsend; their tortured bodies needed rest, out of the snow and cold.

16

Captain Montour

At Tioga, the Indians quit the Susquehanna and chose a northwesterly course, leading their captives along the Chemung River.

"Halt."

As Indians rent the air with their wild, piercing shrieks and halloos, Ganogeh brought Samuel back. Taking out his small paint sacks, he quickly daubed more red and black onto the faces of his charges while the little boy giggled with delight. Reaching Cannon, however, he took great pains to recolor swirls and circles, and redesign others to suit the prisoner's unshaven stubble.

Cap'n spit a mouthful of caked paint into the snow. "Foul stuff you divils use."

A warrior rushed over, threw him to the ground and stripped him naked. "Yankee, Yankee." He kicked him to get up. "Joggo!" Then with the butt of his musket he goaded his victim forward at a fast trot. Suddenly he stopped and disappeared.

Ganogeh ran up, threw a blanket over Cap'n's shoulders but did not return his clothes. *"Chemung."* He pointed to a town in the distance.

Here, as before, packs of watch dogs surged toward the approaching prisoners, followed by hordes of people who thronged out of the town and closed in on the new captives. Young and old alike brandished sticks, whips and hatchets.

Clutching Samuel more tightly, Jane looked anxiously at her frightened children. "Courage, my darlings; don't let the Indians see you

94

cry. Courage means life and . . . ."

"Damn it," her father interrupted, "tell 'em never show the divils we're all scared like Hell."

Ganogeh drew Jane and her little group aside and signaled, "Drop packs. Stay here and watch." Grasping Cannon by the arm, he steered him to an area with several other male captives.

The children clustered around their mother. "Is Grampy going to run the gantlet?"

Jane choked "Yes, I'm afraid so," at the same time keeping her eyes on her father.

"Courage, courage," Cap'n muttered to himself. "Dear God, give me courage!"

Some thirty townspeople, all armed with weapons, ranged themselves loosely into two long lines, leaving a wide pathway between: space for their clubs, sticks, knives and tomahawks to swing at a prisoner running the length of their course. "Let slain warriors be avenged," they screeched. "Butchery and death to white cowards; life to the brave, fleet-footed, agile, for they should join our Iroquois ranks."

Ganogeh pointed to a red-painted post about forty yards away and clutched himself. Cap'n understood: to survive, he must run there and catch hold of it as quickly as possible.

Cannon burst forth, throwing his nearby attackers off guard. Half-way and still unharmed. He leaped; he zig-zagged around flailing sticks and swinging clubs. He stumbled, twisted and righted himself. Still he kept on going, pell-mell. In one final, desperate explosion of energy he escaped to the safety of the pole, unhurt.

The crowd roared approval, then turned its attention to the next prisoner's trial.

"Let go of the pole," a warrior commanded in good English. "Get up and come with me." At a nearby hut he handed over the captive to a squaw. "She'll give you clothes and serve you tonight, Captain Cannon."

"How do you know my name?"

"I took you prisoner at Cherry Valley. I'm Captain Montour."

The next morning.

"Grampy, Grampy," the children exclaimed.

"Bet you never thought you'd see me again. And I'm all in one piece, too; even my bald head is untouched."

"Oh, Father, thank heavens!"

"Do you know what's happened? I've been adopted by the smelly divils. An' even worse, guess who's my captor: none other than 'Queen' Catherine's lad."

"The son of the Fury of Wyoming?"

"Yes."

From Chemung [town] the Indians and captives continued their northwesterly course along the river until they turned to go due north. As Indian settlements became more and more frequent, the prisoners began wondering if their destination were near. But each time the captives tramped onward, leaving village after village far behind.

November 26.

"Halt." Ganogeh pointed to a distant town. *"Shech-qua'-go."* [now Montour Falls]

Jane and Cap'n looked at each other; they knew Schechquago was Queen Catherine's town.

As dismal and blood-curdling whoops and halloos proclaimed the

96

warriors' arrival, Captain Montour reappeared. "I'm taking charge of you," he said to Jane and her band, then turned to Cannon. "Come here." Taking out some vermilion and black, he plastered another thick layer upon his prisoner's face and hair. "Now follow me. All joggo."

Past angry throngs the warrior led his group to the council house. A tall, elderly squaw, elaborately dressed in blue and red with many dangling silver and bead ornaments, emerged from the building: Catherine Montour herself. After scrutinizing each captive, she pointed to Cap'n and demanded of her son, *"Why did you bring that old man a prisoner? Why did you not kill him when you first took him?"*

"A brave warrior deserves . . . ."

"I wish to hear no more. Brave warrior indeed!" Queen Catherine whirled round and stalked off, snarling: "Guard, take charge of that old man."

"Joggo, Yankee." The Indian gave him a fierce kick. "Joggo!"

A wince of pain crossed Cap'n's face. He spat upon the ground, straightened up and marched off, never turning to look back.

"God protect you," Jane murmured as he disappeared into the forest, then reached out toward the children clustered around her. "At least we're still together." She wondered, "But for how long?"

17

Schenectady

In Schenectady that same day, November 26, 1778, Colonel Samuel
Campbell, Captain James Willson and Quorum Justice John Moore
presented General Edward Hand with an urgent petition:

> We, . . . at the request, and in behalf of the poor distressed
> inhabitants of Cherry Valley, who made their escape in the
> conflagration thereof . . . humbly sheweth that, by reason of the loss
> and destruction of their all, [the survivors are] left in a doleful,
> lamentable, and helpless condition, destitute (many of them) of
> meat, money, and clothing, either for back or bed.
>
> We . . . humbly pray your Honor to take the distressed condition of
> these people into your serious consideration, and grant such supplies
> of provision, and wood, to those settled in and about Schenectady . . .
> and also advise, or devise some ways and means . . . whereby those
> distressed people may be supplied with some clothing to cover them
> from the inclemency of the weather . . . .

* * *

After the Massacre Sam Campbell, with his two slaves, had fled to
the safety of Canajoharie, where he waited, desperate for word concerning
his family.

Friends brought in his Bible, its leather cover and pages still wet
from rain and sleet. "We found it lying beside your fence, all wrapped up
in a blanket."

"How on earth? I saw those Indians."

"Someone in your family must have escaped."

"That's too much even to pray for."

Other refugees from Cherry Valley, including Sam's recently widowed brother-in-law Jim Willson, also reached the town, but they hastened eastward to Schenectady.

Just when Sam despaired of ever hearing news, Colonel John Campbell arrived in Canajoharie. "Jane and all the children except Willie are captives. And Walter Butler has proposed to exchange them for his family."

"The Lord be praised!" Smiling for the first time in two weeks, Sam clasped his half-brother's hand. "Thank you."

"I may be old enough to be your father, but I'm not too old to help. You can count on me."

"I'll remember your promise." He paused. "You said Willie wasn't with Jane and the others?"

"Correct."

"John, someone saved our Bible. Do you suppose Willie's still alive, too? But where could he be?"

*　*　*

Willie and Lain, despite the freezing rain, had wandered through the forest all night long. At daylight the bedraggled pair came to a clearing and discovered a hut enclosed by a log fence.

"Please. Let's go in. Please."

"An' iffen dey be Tories?" his black mammy asked.

"I don't care. I'm so tired."

"Aw right, chile. Lemme go knock. Yo' hide in de bushes. Run if I screams."

As Lain climbed over the fence and stumbled toward the hut, the owner cautiously opened the door and thrust out a shaggy head. "What do you want?"

"We's from Cherry Valley. Injuns, they done 'tacked us. Kin yo' help?"

"Sure." He opened the door wide.

"Massa Willie, come out. He be's a friend."

"Of course we're friends." The settler's young wife took Willie's arm. "Come in, both of you. Go warm yourselves by the fire an' I'll bring something to eat."

99

Willie gulped down a bowl of hot soup. "Thank you, Ma'am." He looked about. "Excuse me, sir, but where are we?"

"In Ames."

" 'N whar be dat?" Lain asked.

"A few miles south of Canajoharie."

"Oh that's where Papa goes to militia meetings."

"And who is your papa?"

"Colonel Samuel Campbell. Do you know him, sir?"

"Why, everyone knows of him. He led off our men at Oriskany." The settler put a hand on the boy's shoulder. "Tell you what, son, soon as I think the danger's passed, I'll ride into town an' try to find out about him. Meanwhile, you stay here with us."

Several days later the settler went to Canajoharie and straight to militia headquarters, Goosen Van Alstyne's house, where he found Colonel Campbell. "Sir, your son Willie 'n his black mammy. . . ."

"Willie!"

"Yes, sir, he's with me 'n my wife in Ames."

"Thank God." Sam swallowed hard, trying to control his emotions. "Let's go."

When the two men arrived, Willie was asleep on the floor beside Lain. Sam knelt down and lovingly stroked the boy's hair.

"Papa?" He rubbed his eyes. "Papa, Papa!" Willie threw himself into his father's arms.

Silently father and son clutched each other and wept.

"Massa, we be's so glad to see yo'."

Sam reached out to touch Lain. "Thank you."

* * *

Sam Campbell and Willie, with Lain and the other slaves in tow, left Canajoharie for Schenectady, then joined Jim Willson and his family in nearby Niskayuna. Together perhaps the two now-motherless households could pool their few remaining resources and survive for the duration of the war. They had both lost almost everything; yet most of the other refugees were even more destitute.

Thus it was that on November 26 Sam and Jim, with John Moore, were petitioning General Hand *"in behalf of the poor distressed inhabitants of Cherry Valley . . . in and about Schenectady."*

"Truth to tell, gentlemen," Hand replied, his usually amiable face darkening, "under our present laws, Cherry Valley survivors don't qualify for relief. Therefore, I'm powerless to grant you any emergency supplies."

100

Sam pounded the table. "Then bend the laws!"

"I'm sorry. I deeply wish I could."

"General, our people can't eat sympathy."

November 28.

Not willing to take "No" for an answer Sam Campbell and John Moore rode to Albany, where they called upon Mayor Abraham Yates, Jr., to enlist his support. They also delivered another petition for food and supplies, this time to veteran General James Clinton, the governor's older brother.

"All right, Sam," the balding Clinton finally agreed, "I'll order the commissary in Schenectady to issue you one week's provisions."

"Good. And then what?"

"We'll have to wait for the legislature to consider your plight."

"But General, I don't believe Congress meets any time soon, does it?" Moore asked. As a former Assemblyman he was aware of legislative schedules.

"You're right; it's the second Monday in January."

"Six weeks without food and clothing?" Sam leaped to his feet and leaned across Clinton's desk. "By then the Cherry Valley refugees will all be dead."

"My friends, I myself can do no more." His face brightened into a smile. "But I can ask the governor to see what he's able to do. Perhaps he can relieve you in the meanwhile."

John Moore sighed. "I guess we must be patient. Now then, we'd like to talk with you about getting our families back from the Indians."

"That's General Schuyler's department, as Commissioner for Indian Affairs; his office is just down the hall." Clinton walked out the door, followed closely by Sam. Moore limped behind, dragging his club foot.

Philip Schuyler listened attentively, then looked down his long nose, perplexed. "What letter, Sam?"

"Walter Butler's proposal to exchange my family."

"And my brother James' family."

"For Colonel Butler's."

"I've never received it." Schuyler turned to Clinton. "Have you seen it?"

"No." He shook his head sorrowfully. "Today is the first I even heard of it."

"Can't you act without it?" Sam pleaded, looking first at the

101

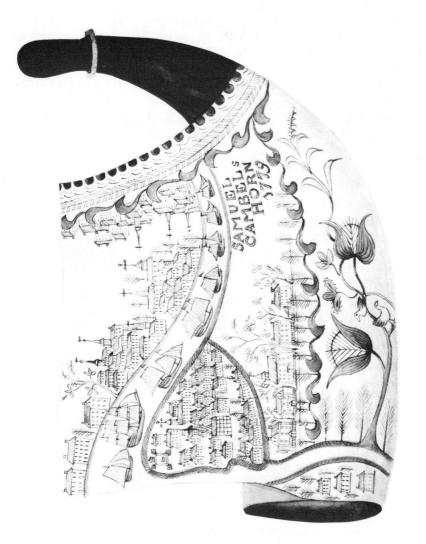

The engraving on the horn reads: SAMUELS CAMBELN HORN 1779

commissioner and then at the general.

"Impossible," Schuyler replied. "We must have it in hand or we're powerless to do anything."

"Look, my friends, Butler called for immediate action, and two and a half weeks have already passed. Indians don't wait forever."

Schuyler took Sam's arm. "I can give you only my word of honor: when the letter arrives, we'll do all in our power to bring about the exchange."

"And," Clinton added, "as quickly as possible."

Before the week was out, Governor Clinton ordered provisions to be released for Cherry Valley's *"unhappy sufferers,"* promising to defray the expenses himself if Congress disapproved of his action. And Sam had volunteered for duty at Fort Stanwix; from there he thought he would be in a better position to fetch his family home from Indian territory.

But still Walter Butler's letter concerning the prisoner exchange remained undelivered.

18

Kanadesaga

As Jane and her little band watched Cap'n disappear from sight, tears trickled down their stony faces.

"Joggo!" Once more Ganogeh took charge. Without being asked Samuel ran to his outstretched arms.

From Shechquago, Catherine's Town, the Indians and all their prisoners continued north a few miles to the head of Seneca Lake [now Watkins Glen]. Ganogeh paused a moment to look around, but Jane and her group, perpetually bent over by heavy burdens, had no strength or spirit to straighten up; readjusted tumplines and sacks reopened sores to merciless chafing.

Still the trail led them northward, following along the eastern shore of Seneca Lake for some forty miles to its end. There, they crossed a rickety bridge over the outlet, passed along the tip of the lake and stopped at the foot of a long hill.

"Halt! Drop sacks."

Jane obeyed, too quickly; everything turned a dizzying black. Only a nearby tree saved her from plunging headlong into a pile of snow.

Ganogeh brought Samuel back to his family and pointed. *"Ka-na-de-sa'-ga."* [now Geneva].

"What's Kanadesaga, Mama?" Elly asked.

"The Senecas' biggest town."

The warriors began their now familiar prisoner whoops, much louder and longer than ever before. "Ah–a–a–a–ah! Ah–a–a–a–ah! Ah–a–a–a–a–ah!"

Silence.

They repeated the calls. "Ah–a–a–a–ah! Ah–a–a–a–ah! Ah–a–a–a–a–ah!"

In the distance piercing halloos echoed and re-echoed Kanadesaga's answer.

Seemingly satisfied, the Indians opened their paint sacks. While Jane and the children watched, they colored their tomahawks bright red, then with the dull edge of their scalping knives, they scraped off all their old war paint and began applying fresh colors. Ganogeh traced a streak along his nose, swirled circles around his eyes and curved stripes onto his cheeks. Next, he and a fellow warrior re-braided and painted each other's scalp-locks. Upon completing the decorations with eagle feathers, they went over to one of their sacks of plunder, dug around and brought out a mirror.

Abigail exploded. "Mother's wedding mirror."

"Hush." Through clenched teeth Jaynie hissed: "Don't make a scene. They can still kill us all."

"Come here." Ganogeh lined up the Moore girls, Jane and her children to repair their smeared paint and plaster on yet another layer of dots and swirls. He handed over the mirror so they, too, could admire themselves.

Moments later he snatched it away; several squaws were approaching from Kanadesaga. The women carried huge bundles which they deposited beside a distant tree. As soon as they departed, the warriors picked them up and disappeared into the woods.

Elly pulled at Jane's ragged skirt. "What are they doing?"

"I don't know. We never saw anything like this before."

"Maybe this is where they're taking us." Mary's hollow voice was barely audible. "I can't go on much farther."

Ganogeh and the warriors emerged from the trees, several carrying T-crossed poles with billowing scalps. Jane clutched Samuel; the other children darted behind her. "Don't show them we're afraid. Remember how brave Grampy was."

From head to toe all the Indians were arrayed in fine new outfits, having wadded their old clothes into bundles and left them on the snowy ground. "Go fetch," they signaled, pointing toward a tree in the distance; the captives knew "braves" never carry anything except weapons and trophies of war.

Samuel started toward Ganogeh.

"No!" He waved the child back, as if to say, "I am no longer a friend."

105

"Mama!" The boy burst out crying.

Jane and Elly rushed to his side. "Hush."

"Joggo."

Jane and all the prisoners shouldered their burdens and lurched forward, prodded from the rear by muskets and tomahawks. With scalps waving on high, the procession started up the hill to Kanadesaga.

Abruptly the pace changed. The leaders slowed to a ritualistic march: they stepped, lifting high one knee, then stamped down the foot, heel first, all the while howling their prisoner and scalp whoops.

Men, women and children surged down the hill to escort the procession into town. "Long life to the victors," they shrieked, brandishing clubs, sticks and knives. "Vengeance and death to the vanquished!"

Warriors and prisoners marched and paused, marched and paused; at the council house each passing brave gave a great whoop and buried his tomahawk blade into a wooden post. Onward, around and around a roaring bonfire they paraded the captives, the plunder and the scalps.

Suddenly squaws seized the packs from Jane and her little group. Caught off balance, the prisoners pitched to the ground. Before they could scramble up, snarling dogs had leaped upon them and were tearing at their shredded clothing.

Ganogeh ran over and with flailing musket sent the animals fleeing, then led his charges to a hut, pulled back the bearskin and pointed inside. Before departing, he stationed an Indian to guard the entrance.

The group stood dazed and bewildered in the shadowy darkness, their eyes blinking and tearing from the thick smoke.

Elly coughed and choked her way to a bunk along the wall. Crawling in, she discovered a bearskin and pulled the fur around her, only to feel things creeping up her neck. Bugs!

"Mama, Mama," Samuel whimpered. Jane groped around dumbly, only to find the boy at her feet. She picked him up, staggered over to give him to his sister, then leaning down to kiss him, lost her balance and fell onto the dirt floor.

Concerned, James and Matthew rushed to put their arms around her. "Mama, we'll take care of you."

She shook her head, as if to clear her mind. "I'm all right, my darlings, just lightheaded for the moment." Noticing a few feebly burning coals inside a circle of stones, she waved her hand. "Go over there and get warm."

"I just want to dry off." Abigail Moore spread out her skirts.

106

Jaynie slipped down beside her sister. "Snow! Twenty days, two or three hundred miles of nothing but snow."

From outside came the sounds of whooping yalloos and halloos. Frenzied shrieks, wails, screams filled the air as Kanadesaga grew ever wilder with joy. Its glorious warriors had returned home with captives and plunder and scalps.

Jane saw the bearskin curtain move and drew back in terror. It was only a squaw carrying a kettle; she padded up to the fire circle, set it down among the coals and left.

As everyone clustered round, James peered in. "Hair. Looks like Injun dog to me."

"I don't care." Mary dug her hand into the pot. "I'm hungry."

19

Goahwuk

The next morning, shortly after dawn began to filter through cracks in the bark hut, Ganogeh returned. He looked around the room, then beckoned first to Mary, then Abigail and finally Jaynie Moore. "Cauche quando." He drew aside the bearskin.

"Oh, Mrs. Campbell, they're taking us away!" Abigail found her sisters' hands and held them tightly as the three stumbled toward the door.

"Pray for us," Mary wailed.

"Fast cauche quando, fast joggo."

Jane and the children clung to one another in terrified silence.

Five painted warriors filed into the hut. "To the middle of the room," they signaled. Whipping out knives they scraped the prisoners' faces and hair, repainted them blood red and departed.

The curtain opened again and Ganogeh ushered in many solemn-faced squaws who poked and prodded the captives as if inspecting cattle. Hardly had they left than Ganogeh returned with three of them. "Choose," he indicated with a sweeping motion.

Matthew. James. Elly. The Indians dragged them out.

"Oh no! My babies. No!"

"Mama, help! Mama, Mama, Ma!"

The curtain closed.

Frantic, Jane swept Samuel into her arms. "My darling, my little sweetheart, at least I have you." She kissed him and rocked him with her body.

A warrior approached and grabbed for the boy.

"No, no! Leave me my baby!"

He tore the child away and flung him over his shoulder.

"Mama, Mama," Samuel shrieked, tears pouring down his cheeks. Red-painted curls fell over his face. "Mama." He stretched out his arms to be rescued. "Mama, Mama . . . Mama . . . Mama . . . Mama . . . Mama . . . ."

Jane listened to her baby's piercing cries until they were lost in the distance, then collapsed, sobbing. "Oh God, let me die. Let me die!"

She lay there, benumbed, robbed of all emotion.

"Cauche quando." An elderly squaw with long, stringy black hair led Jane outside and into a nearby longhouse. There she marched her through a windowless corridor of bunks and partitions, and around smoky fire circle after smoky fire circle. "Halt. Sit," she motioned, pointing to a bearskin on the dirt floor.

Within minutes Jane was surrounded by squaws, their matted hair exuding the stench of bear's grease. As a chorus the women raised their voices, crying out, howling and moaning in agony. Tears streamed down their faces, and hands twisted in grief.

Jane sat terrified, expecting at any moment to be tortured to death. At the same time she was strangely at peace: "Thank you, God; you're sending death to release me."

Instead the ceremony continued. The wailing squaws slowly quieted, only to become serene, their faces radiating happiness. Jane looked on in shock; "When does the torture begin?"

All at once the chorus filed out, and the ceremony seemed over. Jane was left alone with the elderly squaw and several young girls. *"Go-ah'-wuk,"* she heard them say as they embraced and kissed her.

"Goahwuk," the woman repeated, then patted her hollow chest *"Noh-yeh'."* She pointed to five pig-tailed girls: *"Kah-yah'-dah."*

Nohyeh drew Jane to a tiered, double bunk, covered her with a blanket and made signs that the top part was hers to share with one of the girls. Next, she pointed directly to the opposite wall; the four other girls shared those two berths.

Squinting in the dim light, Jane noticed that other double bunks adjoined the family's; together, they seemed to make one long cubicle separated from the next by a small partition. In the middle of the compartment, beneath a hole in the ceiling, sat a number of kettles warming over some coals. She gestured across, as if asking, "Whose are all those?"

109

"Another family's," they signaled back, indicating they shared the room and the cooking fire.

"O Sago!" An elderly warrior with two red-painted slashes angled across his cheek bones appeared in the open doorway of their cubicle. "Me father, *Hah'-nih*. You wel-come."

All at once it dawned upon Jane: she had just been adopted, taking the place of a dead relative the chorus had been mourning. Nohyeh **was** her mother and Hahnih, her father, the young girls, their grandchildren. She was their daughter, Goahwuk.

Jane's eyes flitted from the old woman to the five girls, then rested on the painted warrior. "This, my family? Oh God, help me!"

20

Fort Niagara

December 8, 1778.

Fine snow whipped the faces of Captain Walter Butler and his returning soldiers as they filed north on the Niagara River trail to Lake Ontario. "Only a few more miles, only a few more miles," they kept repeating. They trudged onward, bent nearly double against the swirling snow, barely able to put one foot in front of the other.

Finally a great tower and parapet loomed ahead: Fort Niagara.

Later, at headquarters, Lt. Colonels Mason Bolton, the commandant, and John Butler greeted the weary officers.

"Congratulations on the expedition." Bolton was seated behind his desk, a blanket wrapped around his thin, sickly body. "We read Captain Butler's account of your *success* at Cherry Valley when Lt. Hare delivered it last week.

John Butler strode over to shake hands with his son; the two men had the same dark eyes and short stature, but the colonel was considerably heavier. "Now we're eager to hear your report in more detail."

"Except for the damned fort," Walter began, "Cherry Valley is entirely desolated, nothing but ruins. Furthermore, Colonel Alden is dead and twenty-seven soldiers besides. Lt. Colonel Stacy is our prisoner with thirteen officers and privates."

"And our losses?" his father asked.

"Not a soul killed; only our fife major, one private and three Indians wounded."

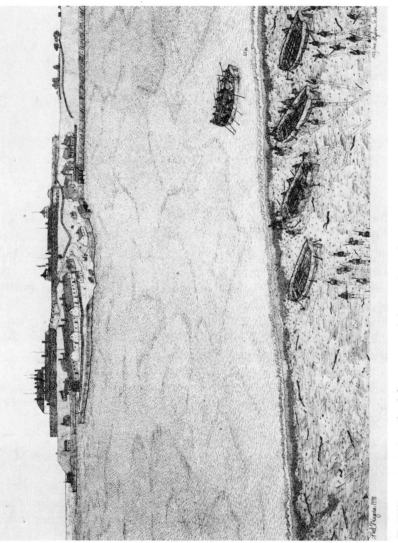

Fort Niagara, 1778. Reproduced from an original drawing by Stephen G. Strach.

"Remarkable. How'd the men come through it all?"

"*In better health and spirits than could be expected*, considering the many hardships and the beastly weather." Walter turned to Colonel Bolton. "As leader of the expedition I'd like to mention Captain McDonell's *activity and spirit*, but I'm also most pleased with the *alertness* of all my fellow officers. In truth, I'm much indebted to everyone."

"I will pass on your comments and commendations to His Excellency General Haldimand in Quebec. Thank you, Captain."

Walter cleared his throat, glanced at John Butler, then turned back to Bolton. "I'm also gratified to say I've found prisoners important enough to exchange for my father's family in Albany and I have written such a proposal to General Schuyler."

"Well, well, that's excellent news. Yes, excellent news!" Colonel Butler, when excited, often repeated his words. "Thank you, son. Are they here now?"

"No, the Indians prevented me from taking them along."

The commandant rapped his hand on the table. "If you don't mind, gentlemen, we'll discuss that subject anon. Please continue with your report, Captain."

"Yes, sir. Personally I have many regrets. *Notwithstanding my utmost precaution and endeavors to save the women and children, I could not prevent some of them falling unhappy victims to the fury of the savages.* Many were carried off prisoners, and many more were killed."

"Yes," his father broke in, "the Wells! *I would have gone miles on my hands and knees to have saved that family.* Why, oh why?"

"Because they provided quarters for Colonel Alden and his principal officers. Why did Wells do that?"

"Robert probably had no choice, but what a price to pay. Their death is one of the tragedies of war. A tragedy!"

"That may be, Colonel," said Bolton, "but Captain Butler, you should be pleased with your achievement; certainly General Haldimand, even Lord Germain in London, will be. Just remember, your success in Cherry Valley has distressed the Rebels, has beaten down their will to fight. Nothing else matters so much."

January 1, 1779. Headquarters, the Stone House.

For one day Fort Niagara put aside thoughts of war.

"Happy New Year." Colonel Bolton welcomed his festive guests to the Great Hall. He himself felt less than festive, however; for the past several weeks he had been bedridden with violent stomach and leg cramps,

113

and each handshake sent a shock of pain through his rheumatic fingers.

"Sorry we're late, Colonel," said John Butler, as he and his Rangers filed past the commandant. "You know how it is, rowing over from Butlersbury against snow and strong winds." The new settlement of Butlersbury [present-day Niagara-on-the-Lake, Ontario] was an extension of Niagara, directly opposite the fortress, across the Niagara River.

Walter Butler paused before entering the Great Hall to view himself in the mirror; for the first time he was wearing the new Ranger uniform, a dark green jacket trimmed in scarlet, and buckskin leggings.

"Yes," a voice murmured, "very handsome."

He turned to find Lyn Montour, Catherine's twenty-year-old daughter. "Ah, my love." Walter gave her a warm kiss before stepping back to display his outfit. "I wore it in your honor."

"Duxea, you're just saying that."

"No, not at all." He took Lyn's hands, drawing her close to look into her dark, almond-shaped eyes.

His father appeared in the doorway. "Walter, come along and greet Colonel Bolton."

"Yes, sir." The captain glanced appreciatively at Lyn in her red, beaded over-dress and skirt and dangling silver ornaments. "Take my arm; we'll greet the commandant together." As they crossed the room, he whispered, "Everyone is looking at us. See the faces of some of those stuffy officers' wives? And are their husbands jealous of me; I'm escorting the most beautiful girl here."

"Happy New Year." Colonel Bolton shook hands with Walter, then smiled at Lyn; the young officer was not the only one paying court to a squaw. "I'm sorry," he said catching John Butler's arm to steady himself, "but I'm feeling rather poorly. Would you please give the toasts in my behalf."

"Yes, of course." Butler stepped into the center of the room and raised his glass. "To His Majesty, King George III. To his loyal forces. To us all."

Walter murmured in Lyn's ear, "Especially to those we love."

"And may the next holiday season find us in the warmth of our own homes, in the embrace of our own families."

A sadness fell over the group, for nearly everyone had close relatives still among the Rebels or a dear family far away.

Walter began a rousing song, and others joined in; the New Year's spirit returned. As everyone danced some and drank more, couples soon found at least fleeting pleasure in a warm embrace. Before long men paired off with squaws or wives of luckless officers serving at the far outposts.

Walter drew Lyn close and brushed her lips with a kiss. "My dearest love." His fingers slowly traced the outline of her mouth, caressed her hair, played with an earring. He pressed her to him, feeling her warm body against his. "Come." He put his arm around her waist and together they hurried out of the room.

21

Letters

Mohawk District
Tryon County
2 December 1778

To His Excellency, Governor George Clinton:

Sir, [wrote Captain William Harper] I send you enclosed a letter
from Walter Butler which he sent in by [Colonel John Campbell]. I . . .
forward it to you, as I conceive the exchange of inhabitants is more
properly your province than General Schuyler's. . . . I am sure you
will do everything in your power to relieve our distressed friends
from worse than Divels. . . .

* * *

Poughkeepsie
December 23d 1778

To William Harper, Esquire, Tryon County.

Sir, [replied the Governor] I this day received your letter of the
2d instant, with that of Walter Butler enclosed. I feel most sensibly
for the sufferings of the unfortunate inhabitants of Cherry Valley
and particularly for those who are in the hands of a savage enemy. As
my residence renders it impracticable for me to execute the business,
I have requested of General Schuyler (to whom I have sent Butler's
letter) in conjunction with my brother General Clinton, to take such
steps as may be most likely to bring about an exchange of our Cherry
Valley friends, and as I have referred the matter altogether to them, I
doubt not that they will do everything in their power to effect the
desired exchange. . . .

116

To Captain Walter Butler or any other British officer to whom it may be handed.

Sir, [wrote General James Clinton] A letter dated the 12th of November last . . . is come to hand . . . . His Excellency Governor Clinton . . . has authorized me to make the exchange [of Mrs. Campbell, Mrs. Moore, their children, and Captain Cannon for Mrs. Butler and her family].

[But] I am at a loss to know [not only] where to direct [my reply] to you, but also to what part of the country the unhappy prisoners taken from this state have been carried. I therefore send the bearers [Colonel] John Campbell and [Jacob] Newkirk, with a flag [of safe conduct] to carry this letter to any place, where they may learn [of] you or [of] any other officer who can effect the exchange in your absence . . . .

Clinton paused to re-read the concluding remarks of Butler's letter:

I have done every thing in my power to restrain the fury of the Indians from hurting women and children, or killing the prisoners who fell into our hands, and would have more effectually prevented them but that they were much incensed by the late destruction of their village of Onaquaga by your people. I shall always continue to act in that manner.

I look upon it beneath the character of a soldier to wage war with women and children. I am sure you are conscious that Colonel Butler or myself have no desire that your women or children should be hurt. But, be assured, that if you persevere in detaining my father's family with you, that we shall no longer take the same pains to restrain the Indians from prisoners, [including] women and children, that we have heretofore done. . . .

"Damned impertinence! I won't be bullied and I won't ignore Butler's impudence."

Do not flatter yourself, Sir, [Clinton wrote to the young captain] that your father's family have been detained [in Albany] on account of any consequence they were supposed to be of, or that it is determined they should be exchanged in consideration of the threat contained in your letter. I should hope for the honor of civilized nations, and the sake of human nature, that the British Officers had exerted themselves in restraining the barbarities of the savages. But it is difficult even for the most disinterested mind [not] to believe . . .

117

the British force was sufficient to have restrained [the Indians], had there been a real desire to do so. . . .

The enormous murders committed at Wyoming and Cherry Valley would clearly have justified a retaliation. That your Mother did not fall a sacrifice to the resentment of the survivors of those families who were so barbarously massacred, is owing to [their] humane principles . . . [something to which] their enemies are utter strangers. . . .

22

One Can't Always Die When One Longs for Death

January 1, 1779. Kanadesaga.

Jane fought back the tears. "Today is my 35th birthday, but what have I to celebrate? My children are taken away. Sam and Willie are dead for all I know. And here I am, alone and lost among these savages.

"Dear God, why don't you just let me die?" Jane buried her head in her hands, sobbing. "Why am I condemned to a living death?"

She heard herself repeating: "The Lord is my shepherd; I shall not want. . . . Yea, though I walk through the valley of the shadow of death, I will fear no evil. . . ." Jane became calm, resigned. *"One can't always die when one longs for death."*

* * *

One morning Jane saw Nohyeh and her granddaughters puzzling over a length of cloth. "Cherry Valley plunder," she wondered, "or British bribery." She saw an opportunity. Digging down under a raveled petticoat, she brought out her sewing kit, so precious she always carried it hidden in a deep pocket. "Nohyeh, Kahyahdah." She opened up the kit.

"Ot Ka-ya-son?" [What do you call this?] The squaws had never seen a thimble, scissors or a metal needle.

119

Jane picked up the cloth. Taking Nohyeh by the waist, she draped and tucked, gathered and folded, all the while indicating how she would turn the material into a new skirt.

The women broke into broad smiles.

Jane's reputation as a seamstress spread throughout the longhouse. Soon she was making garments for the neighboring families, who paid her with corn and venison. Her family, however, was too needy to provide her with cloth. She had to make do with her filthy rags, for otherwise they would have no food. She prayed the children were better off than she.

With her sewing Jane became her Indian family's main support, taking over from Hahnih, who had grown too old to hunt or go on the warpath. All day, every day she toiled, perpetually confined to the longhouse. Seated as close as possible to the fire circle, she strained to catch the rays of light filtering through the smoke.

"O Sago." Hahnih bent over her shoulder and Jane shrank back, ostensibly to wipe her tearing eyes. Despite the weeks of living in a bunk directly above him and Nohyeh, his rank smell still nauseated her whenever he came close.

"You cry," he said in the limited English he had learned once upon a time. "Why?"

"Smoke." She dared not admit she was also weeping in wretchedness; to the Indians tears showed intolerable weakness.

"Goahwuk good. Joggo. In Kanadesaga," he emphasized. "Come back; eyes better."

"Me go outside alone? Thank you—hineaweh." Jane smiled, elated that she had finally earned enough of her family's trust to be given some freedom.

Emerging from the longhouse, she drew her blanket more closely against the winter wind gusting down the hill toward Seneca Lake. Once outside the entrance, she paused. Above the doorway was a red painting, a turtle, her family's clan. Of the eight Iroquois clans this one was the most important.

Nearby were other longhouses, each displaying a similar red animal painting over the doorway, and all facing the town's central clearing. Not far away a brook meandered.

A large, log building caught her eye: the Great Council House. Directly in front of it stood a post ten or twelve feet high. Carved into the wood were perpendicular red marks, red crosses and red X's with a head or dot. "A war post!" Jane recoiled, knowing instinctively the slashes recorded battles and raids, numbers of scalps and prisoners taken; the brightest red marks probably represented Cherry Valley, perhaps even Sam and Willie.

Horrified by that thought, she whirled about and quickly chose a path leading downhill toward the lake. Kanadesaga's buildings almost formed a circle. Most longhouses were bark, but she did notice a few log ones. More people were in those few acres, she reckoned, than in all Cherry Valley.

Part way down the hill she arrived at the town's main gate and a large, dilapidated blockhouse; obviously the Senecas did not worry any more about enemy attack. She paused to look at the view. Fruit trees were everywhere, apple, peach, pear. . . .

All at once Jane heard popping sounds. In the distance along the snow-covered lakeshore, uniformed men were shooting at targets outside several barracks: "Butler's Buildings," the colonel's main staging area which Sam had mentioned so often.

Not far from Butler's Buildings, on the other side of what was probably a cornfield in summer, stood an impressive house of hewn logs: Old Smoke's, she figured. Hahnih had said the war chief was some sort of Turtle relation and lived close to the lake.

When Jane returned to the longhouse, Nohyeh was busily stirring something in the kettle. "Here," she gestured, handing over her only spoon and pointing inside to the frothy scum.

Floating deer hide and entrails! Jane retched, then clapped a hand over her mouth.

As soon as the stew was ready, Hahnih took the spoon and piled his family's one broken plate full of food for himself. After finishing, he licked the utensils clean and with a flourish, presented them to Jane.

"Hineaweh." She tried to seem appreciative as she slowly lifted the spoon to serve herself.

The squaws could wait no longer but dug their hands into the now lukewarm stew to eat their share.

"Noyheh," Jane said in a mixture of her best Seneca and sign language, "I know many special ways to cook venison and corn. May I prepare them for you?"

"If that would please our Goahwuk, yes."

Jane smiled. Now she could take over the cooking and at least make sure the food was clean. Next she would figure a way to serve herself first. She pushed aside misgivings about Hahnih and his solicitous concern for her. And when she learned enough Seneca, she vowed to ask what had happened to her children.

121

23

Letters into the Wilderness

In January 1779 Colonel John Campbell was a youthful sixty-three, but hardly young enough for an arduous trek into Iroquois Territory. Nevertheless, he volunteered to carry Clinton's letter, and also one from General Schuyler to Captain Walter Butler; his promise to help his brother Sam was sacred.

Waving a white flag of safe conduct, John Campbell and his companion, Jacob Newkirk, tramped forth on snowshoes, heading west into the almost unknown wilderness of Indian country. Their instructions: "Carry the letters to any place where you may learn the whereabouts of Walter Butler or of any other officer who can effect the exchange in his absence." Contrary to usual procedure, their heavy packs included guns in order to hunt game since they did not know how long their mission would take.

In time the two men reached the friendly Oneidas' chief town where they were escorted into the meeting-house. Soon elders silently filed in to seat themselves cross-legged in a circle around the council fire. Their leader lighted the pipe of peace, took a few thoughtful puffs and passed it onward for his neighbors, one by one, to share in the same manner.

The ceremony completed, John Campbell solemnly rose to his feet. "Brothers, friends of our great American cause: O Sago." He nodded to each of the assembled chiefs before continuing. "Our mission is urgent, for we carry dispatches from Generals Schuyler and Clinton to Captain Butler."

With great dignity the Indians' leader also arose, then slowly folded his arms and blanket across his chest. "Brothers of Albany: Welcome to *Kä-na-wa-lo'-häle* [present-day Oneida Castle]. You seek Duxea, but he is not here. 'He is at Fort Niagara', thus say our enemy kinsmen, the other Iroquois."

"Brothers of Oneida, thank you for the information, hineaweh," Campbell replied. "Now, we pray you, open a helping ear: The distance is far, and the trail difficult to follow; we need a warrior to guide us to Niagara."

"Brothers, attend: All that is true, so very true. Yet would you arrive in safety? That is the question. Let our chiefs call a council to decide. But first we must dispatch runners to obtain information. Naho!"

Campbell turned to Newkirk. "We've no choice; we have to wait. Time is precious, and look at us, forced to sit around till they decide, only God knows when. Damn!"

After seemingly endless days, the chiefs summoned the two envoys to appear before the council fire. "Brothers, friends and honored guests of the Oneidas, harken to our words, for we have made our determination: It is impossible for you to proceed because a great council is now sitting at Cayuga."

Campbell jumped to his feet. "But we must proceed!"

The leader raised his arm for silence. "Continue to give a listening ear: Those chiefs do not understand the nature of a flag; they might treat you as enemies and kill you."

"Then so be it. Newkirk and I will not be deterred by fear." John Campbell gravely bowed to the elders. "Hineaweh. We thank you for your advice and hospitality. Nevertheless, we must and will push forward."

Campbell and Newkirk proceeded west to *Gä-nagh'-sa-rä'-ga,* [present-day Sullivan], virtually the last Indian town friendly to the American side. Once again they pleaded their case before the assembled elders, requesting a guide to lead them to Niagara, and once again the chiefs called a council.

"Brothers, brave warriors from Albany," the Indians at last replied, "now attend: Listen to our final judgment. '[We] *can not be answerable to the American chiefs for any misfortune that might befall* [you. . . We] *would very justly incur the displeasure of* [our] *brothers, the Americans, if* [we] *permitted* [you] *to proceed, when* [we] *know the consequences that would ensue.* [We] *therefore insist on* [you] *to return.*' "

John Campbell bowed his head in defeat. "Brothers wise and brave, your words have touched my mind and I will obey. Beforehand, however, open a kindly ear: I pledged myself to deliver the letters to Captain Butler;

can you do nothing to help?"

"Our ears have been opened to your plea. We promise we will forward the letters to Duxea, and with more speed and safety than if you went yourself. Naho!"

"Oh Chiefs: Hineaweh. I will have faith. In consequence of your promise, Jacob Newkirk and I bid you farewell and do return to Albany. Naho!"

24

The White Dogs

"Saturday, January 30, 1779." Jane dug another notch into her calendar stick and turned to Hahnih, saying in English, "Tomorrow, Sabbath, always special to my Great Spirit. Goahwuk not sew; go joggo."

"Tomorrow, day Great Spirit get New Year Message from White Dogs."

To Jane's surprise, he took her hand and squeezed it, then led her to the fire circle and pointed upward to the smoke curling through the hole in the roof. Suddenly Nohyeh entered the cubicle; Jane breathed a sigh of relief.

Acting as if nothing had happened, Hahnih continued, "Smoke message. Nine day frolic."

"Hineaweh." She still did not understand but pretended she did for fear of another hand squeeze.

Early the next morning, Jane started to reach for the old matted bearskin Hahnih had given to her, but then hesitated, wondering if the present were really a kind, fatherly offering. She threw it around her shoulders anyway, knowing she would freeze without it.

This day, she wandered in the opposite direction from the lake, looking for a place where she could be alone to pray. At the northern edge of town snow-covered corn fields and vast orchards greeted her. Following a leftward trail, she passed an enormous mound six or seven feet high, the town's burial place. And maybe hers as well. She hurried on.

The path led toward a giant elm in the midst of a corn field: the Seneca's Great Council Tree. Jane stopped to admire it.

Continuing onward, she soon discovered a grove of maple trees and wandered inside. Maples were home and sugaring, Sam, the children and so many happy memories. She smiled, content. From now on this grove would be her sanctuary.

Upon returning to town, Jane heard sounds of gunfire and hastened toward her longhouse. Outside the Great Council House she met a crowd all staring up into the air and murmuring, "Beautiful. The Great Spirit will be pleased." From atop a tall pole dangled two dead white dogs decorated with red paint, ribbons, feathers and a string of white wampum.

Now Jane understood Hahnih and the reason for the shooting; the White Dog Festival had begun.

She had hardly reached her family's cubicle and stowed away the bearskin before a man appeared at the entrance; he was naked except for a breech-clout, war painted, and carrying a shovel-like paddle. Aghast, Jane tried to retreat into the shadows, but Nohyeh's beady eyes caught sight of her.

"Goahwuk, come here." The squaw beckoned for Jane to stand between herself and her granddaughters.

Hahnih stepped forward. "O Sago, honored member of the festival committee. My family and I welcome you to our humble abode."

"Hineaweh." The nude warrior scooped up fine ashes from their fire circle and flung them about the room, scattering them everywhere. While the cloud of grey dust settled, he removed the old coals and other debris, only to rekindle the fire and wordlessly move onward to the next cubicle.

As soon as their visitor had disappeared from sight, Jane and the family shook themselves, making yet another powdery grey cloud. They were still coughing and sputtering when shots rang out.

"No fear, Goahwuk," Hahnih hastened to reassure Jane. "Guns say this longhouse now have new fires. All Kanadesaga do same."

The second day.

Next morning, Jane pulled her bearskin closer, trying to keep out the extreme cold, as she and her family and the rest of the townspeople gathered near the council house to watch the ceremonies. The festival committee, still painted but now clad in bearskin leggings as well as breech-clouts, was dancing about or waving baskets and guns. Presently, the leader rubbed a tortoise shell rattle along the entrance to a nearby longhouse; at his signal the group fired shots into the air and disappeared inside the building.

Nohyeh put her hand on Jane's shoulder. *"Sä-da'-che'-ah* [Morning] welcomes the committee into our longhouse. *O-na'* [Now], dear Goahwuk, come with us to enjoy more dancing."

By the time they arrived at the Great Council House, spectators were already lining its walls. In the center of the room sat two performers droning religious verses and accompanying themselves with turtle shell rattles. Presently Jane heard the beat quicken as a long column of some twenty braves, trailed by several squaws, filed into the building and began dancing slowly around and around the room. The noise of their knee rattles nearly drowned out the music of the two singers.

The dancers gestured with their arms, often contorting their bodies into incredible positions. Rattles beat and shook more and more wildly as heels lifted and pounded ever faster. The figures writhed and twisted, never stopping to rest, forced to drop out only by exhaustion. Then in one final frenzy of sound and fury the dance ended.

The following day.

The committee called upon Nohyeh's longhouse, the leader's rattle clacking against the bark walls to announce its arrival in her cubicle. Hahnih shoved a wad of tobacco leaves into Jane's hand just as the visitors entered. Snake-dancing their way around the room, they paused in front of each family member.

"O-yeh'-gwah-ah'-weh [Tobacco], or anything else." They poked smelly baskets under everyone's nose. "Give incense for the sacrifice. The Great Spirit needs our tidings for the new year."

"I wonder just what message the incense is supposed to waft upward," Jane thought as she dropped in her offering, hoping Hahnih's generosity would always be that fatherly.

Two more days of frolic with singing, dancing, rattling, blasts of gunfire.

"Joggo, Goahwuk." Nohyeh took away Jane's ever-present sewing. "Come outside with your family." It was time to laugh.

Disguised in false faces of woven cornhusks, committee members were running and jumping about, amusing the onlookers with crazy antics and absurd masks. From time to time they stopped to bedaub themselves

128

with dirt, snow and mud, then passed their baskets again for another donation of incense.

A basket jabbed into Jane's stomach.

"No tobacco. Nothing."

Hands smeared her face, hair and clothes with slimy mud as the crowd guffawed. Jane stood motionless, her eyes glaring hatred.

Stifling tears of rage, she marched back to the longhouse. She grabbed a blanket to cover herself, trying not to befoul it with the muck while struggling to undress. "May that Indian monster rot in Hell!" she kept muttering. "And to think everyone laughed." She scrubbed herself and her garments with the icy water from the family's storage pot, then for hours shivered beside the smoky fire, turning the damp clothes in a vain effort to speed their drying. Cleanliness might be next to godliness, but in the future she would just as soon be less godly.

Several noisy days later. Dawn.

Once again the family insisted Goahwuk accompany them outside. When they arrived in front of the council house, the white dogs were nowhere in sight, only a blazing wooden altar.

"Ah—a—a—a—a—a—ah!" At that exploding whoop Jane saw the committee process from the Great Council House, four of them bearing the dogs upon a bark litter. They marched once around the pyre, halted to face the rising sun and then with great ceremony laid the dogs upon the altar to be engulfed in the flames.

The leader raised his arms in prayer. "Quah, quah, quah. Oh Great Spirit, listen now with an open ear: The White Dog Spirits, wafted upward in the smoke of the incense, are bringing the people's New Year Message."

"To-ges'-ke, togeske [Very true]," the people chanted.

"Quah, quah, quah. Continue to listen." The leader threw more tobacco leaves into the fire. "Hineaweh. The people are sending you their thanks for the blessings of the past year. As the dog is faithful to his master, so, too, the Iroquois commit themselves to remain faithful to thee, Oh Great Spirit, our creator and preserver. Naho!"

The ninth and last day.

Nohyeh took Jane's hand. "Come. Now all Kanadesaga shares a dinner so elegant that you, dearest Goahwuk, must have the privilege of carrying our spoon and plate."

Near the council house people were crowding round several enormous kettles, either scooping out food with small dippers or eating directly with a spoon. "Suc-co-tash and meat," Nohyeh said as she gazed hungrily at the stew. "But first, my husband must enjoy the feast."

Hahnih took the plate and spoon from Jane and disappeared into the crowd. Upon his return, he carried a mess of food—but not for the family. With a nod of his head and a grunt he told Nohyeh and the grandchildren to go take their fill. As soon as he assured himself the squaws were out of sight, he lifted his right foot, scrubbed the spoon on the sole of his moccasin, placed it in the stew and gallantly handed the plate to Jane.

"But," she protested in Seneca, "the honor is entirely too great."

"No, never; not for our favored daughter."

"Hineaweh." She eyed the meat and succotash, and then the spoon, blanching.

"Goahwuk, you are hesitating."

"This gift is not deserved."

"On the contrary."

Trapped, she took a mouthful and swallowed it in one gulp.

"Slowly. Savor the delicacies. Not until the sun goes to sleep will dancers rage in the whirlwind of war, then be still, and finally tread down the pathway of peace. Afterwards, leaders will smoke the pipe of peace and put the festival to sleep for another year."

Little did Hahnih or Jane or anyone know that the White Dog Festival would never again re-awaken in Kanadesaga, for the town was destined to be destroyed, burned to the ground.

25

A Promise Kept

At Niagara, soldiers passed the winter weeks endlessly drilling or repairing the fort and its fortifications, while officers planned the spring and summer campaigns against the frontier settlements. And day after dreary day Walter Butler waited, forever wondering when he would receive an answer to his letter proposing the exchange.

At last, true to their word, Indians delivered the dispatches entrusted to them by Colonel John Campbell.

Young Butler immediately replied to General James Clinton:

18th Feb. 1779

SIR:

I have received a letter dated the 1st January last, signed by you, in answer to mine of the 12th November.

Its contents I communicated to Lieutenant Colonel Bolton, the commanding officer of this garrison, & by whom I am directed to acquaint you, that he had no objection that an exchange of prisoners . . . should take place. But not being fully empowered by his Excellency—General Haldimand—to order the same immediately to be put in execution, has thought proper I should go down to the Commander-in-chief for his direction in the matter.

In the mean time, Colonel Butler . . . will make every effort in his power to have all the prisoners . . . in captivity among the different Indian nations, collected and sent in to this post to be forwarded to Crown Point. . . . Colonel Bolton desires me to inform you that the prisoners shall receive from him what assistance their wants may require, which prisoners have at all times received at this post.

131

The disagreeable situation of your people in the Indian villages, as well as ours amongst you, will induce me to make all the expedition in my power to Canada, (Quebec) in order that the exchange may be settled as soon as possible. For the good of both, I make no doubt that his Excellency General Haldimand will acquiesce in the proper exchange. . . .

Walter Butler gazed out the window at the frozen wilderness of Lake Ontario, lost in thought. General Clinton's accusations of cruelty angered him. Returning to his desk, he wrote:

It is not our present business, sir, to enter into an altercation, or to reflect on the conduct of either the British or the Continental forces, or on that of each other. But since you have charged . . . the British officers in general with inhumanity, and Colonel Butler and myself in particular; in justice to them, and in vindication of his and my own honor and character, I am under the disagreeable necessity to declare the charge unjust and void of truth, and which can only tend to deceive the world, though a favorite cry of the Congress on every occasion, whether in truth or not.

We deny any cruelties to have been committed at Wyoming, either by whites or Indians. . . .

[Concerning Cherry Valley,] the prisoners sent back by me, or any now in our or the Indians' hands, must declare I did every thing in my power to prevent the Indians killing the prisoners, or taking women and children captive, or in any wise injuring them. Colonel Stacy and several other officers of yours, when exchanged, will acquit me; and must further declare, that they have received every assistance, before and since their arrival at this post, that could be got to relieve their wants. I must, however, beg leave, by the bye, to observe, that I experienced no humanity, or even common justice, during my imprisonment among you [in Albany]. . . .

I am,

Your very humble servant,

Walter Butler,
Captain Corps of Rangers.

26

A Gift of Venison

Giving a deep sigh of resignation, Jane picked up her sewing and began jabbing the needle in and out, in and out.

Hahnih entered the cubicle. "O Sago. Outside, good weather begins to chase away the cold of winter." He started to approach Jane but veered off when he noticed his wife poking around the remains of the fire.

The two women stared at him, astonished, for he usually gave no greeting whenever he came in.

"Good weather," he repeated. "Maple sap is running."

Nohyeh tossed a blanket around her threadbare clothing and rushed out.

Hahnih switched to English, as he often did when they were alone. "Sugar, squaw work. But Goahwuk stay. We talk white man's tongue. You do needle and get food."

Jane obeyed; their supply of venison and corn had dwindled to almost nothing. Despite her constant sewing, the family often went hungry.

"Goahwuk like Indian syrup, Indian sugar. Make all food taste good, even weeds of springtime."

"At home, my husband has many maple trees, and my children love. . . ."

"No, Goahwuk, this home." The old warrior pointed to the fire circle. "You no husband; you no children. You daughter of Hahnih, Nohyeh."

Appalled, Jane laid down her sewing. "I go watch family make

133

syrup." At the sugar house squaws were pouring maple sap into hollow logs, alternately dropping in red-hot stones and removing cooled ones. She wondered why they did not they use iron kettles to boil down all that liquid, the way Sam did with the children back home.

Sam. The children. Home. If Hahnih refused even to admit that she had another family, so would Nohyeh and everyone else. "How can I ever find out what happened to my children?" She fought back tears.

Several days later a messenger from Chief Old Smoke delivered a whole deer, a present from relatives on the Genesee River. Just in time, for the family had been reduced to a fare of sugar-coated ground nuts and roots with occasional kernels of corn.

Nohyeh drew Jane over to the carcass. "Goahwuk, you must have the honor of preparing our feast."

"Hineaweh." Jane began hacking at a leg. "Honor?" she wondered. She always did the cooking. Did this present mean something special; she knew Indian families often gave one hint of future plans. Perhaps they intended to send her to the Genesee, but why? She looked toward Nohyeh, who, contrary to her usually impassive face, smiled back enigmatically.

In a flash Jane understood: Nohyeh had arranged to marry her off, to get her away from Hahnih. And the gift sealed the contract.

"No!" She raised her knife and stabbed the venison. "No, a thousand times no! I already have a husband, Sam."

27

The Lace Cap

Spring 1779.

Jane looked up from her needlework, sensing the presence of a strange Indian staring at her. Finally he pointed to the cap covering her hair and asked in English, "Why do you wear that? *Indians do not do so.*"

"It's the custom of my countrywomen."

"Well, come to my house, and I will give you a cap."

Once inside his cubicle, he reached up behind a beam and pulled out some lace, grey from the smoke of many fires. *"I got* [this] *in Cherry Valley."* He handed it to her. *"I took it from the head of a woman."*

She examined the Indian's gift; it looked familiar: Jane Wells' cap. It was spotted with blood and had a cut in the crown; only a tomahawk could have made the slit. This man had murdered her friend!

Jane retreated from him in horror. She ran frantically, blindly, until she reached the town brook. With tears streaming down her face, she knelt at the water's edge and began washing the cap.

"Excuse me, Ma'am."

She looked up to see a white man on horseback. "I'm sorry," she said, wiping her eyes with the back of a hand and trying to compose herself.

"Ma'am," the man repeated, "Fort Niagara heard there's a white woman at Kanadesaga who needs clothing, and I. . . ."

"You're from Niagara?" She struggled to her feet.

"I have a bunch of old clothes for her." His eyes traveled from the matted strands of hair hanging beneath Jane's cap, to her tattered and darned dress, and finally to her shoes bound together with rags. "I guess that's you." Dismounting, he untied a rolled bundle from behind his saddle. "Here."

"Thank you so much." Jane looked imploringly at the man's impassive face. "Please, maybe you know about my children, my father."

"Who are you?"

"Mrs. Samuel Campbell, Jane Cannon Campbell from Cherry Valley."

"My God, Butler's whole Corps of Rangers is looking for you and your family!"

136

28

Yes!

From: His Excellency, Sir Frederick Haldimand, governor in chief of the Province of Quebec and commander in chief of His Majesty's forces in that province and its frontiers.

To: Lieutenant Colonel Mason Bolton

Quebec the 8th April 1779

SIR:

. . . In consideration to [Colonel] Butler I shall allow the exchange of the prisoners to take place, as by this act he is in expectation to recover the liberty of his family. . . .

Also on that same day, Haldimand wrote to John Butler:

SIR:

. . . I derived great pleasure in seeing Captain Butler who has given me a very satisfactory detail of his expeditions last summer [and fall] . . . . The prospect you have of recovering the liberty of your family is sufficient motive for me to acquiesce in the exchange you propose. . . .

General Haldimand, a confirmed bachelor and a native Swiss who had fought his way up to high rank in the British army, was not pleased *"to acquiesce."* Prisoner exchanges were contrary to his liking; he feared *"the perfidy of the enemy we have to deal with."* He further worried that other Loyalists would begin *"clamoring for the same consideration."*

He finally agreed only because Colonel Butler was a faithful servant to the Crown and to the Indian Department and should, therefore, be rewarded.

29

News

April 1779.

For the first time since her captivity Jane's heart was light and her steps happy as she returned from the maple grove; now she could dream again. "The Rangers will come and get me. They'll find the children and father, too. And then some day, somehow, we'll all go back to Cherry Valley with Sam and Willie."

Nearing the sugar house, she was surprised to see a throng of people, for sugaring season had passed. She was even more surprised to see a thin, white man dressed in Indian clothes standing quite alone at the edge of the crowd. Cautiously she sidled up to him. "Hello. Who are you?"

"I'm Luke Swetland from Wyoming Valley. No, now from *Kendai'-a.* And you?"

"Jane Cannon Campbell from Cherry Valley. Kendaia? Where's that?"

"About a day's journey south, near the eastern shore of Seneca Lake."

"Quickly, before the Indians separate us, tell me why you're here."

"Last week Kendaia heard that Yankees from Fort Stanwix had devastated Onondaga country and might be headed our way. So we all fled." Swetland glanced quickly from side to side, turning his hawk-like head. "At the moment we're staying here but we're really heading for Niagara."

"Niagara?"

"*Es-te qua-to*" [Go away], a voice commanded. "Joggo."

Back in her longhouse cubicle, Jane hardly felt the gnawing pangs of hunger; Luke Swetland's news tumbled through her mind: "He said our army invaded the Onondagas. Will it push this far, into Seneca country? Will the Indians flee and take me with them?"

"Goahwuk," Nohyeh called, interrupting Jane's reflections, "the family has no more venison, only sugar water for leaves and nuts."

"Yes, I know. I will soon finish sewing this."

"No matter. Kinsfolk on the Genesee want to welcome my daughter. Their son is a good provider, a good hunter. Naho!"

Jane wanted to scream out: "You can't send me to another family. Not now!" Instead she bit her tongue to keep silent. Her thoughts, however, raced on: "Nohyeh mentioned a son; Indians still marry off young men to older, experienced women. Like me."

"Dear God, let Butler's Rangers take me away from here before Nohyeh . . . . How monstrous! The Rangers destroyed my whole world and now I expect them to rescue me."

30

Butlersbury

Walter Butler was elated as he rowed across the river from Fort Niagara to Butlersbury. His mission to General Haldimand had been a success and now he could reply to General Clinton. Furthermore, within the hour he would be holding Lyn Montour in his arms.

Official duties first, however:

May [c. 14,] 1779

SIR,

Agreeable to my letter directed to you of the 18th of February last I wish to acquaint you of His Excellency General Haldimand's determination of the proposed exchange of prisoners: I am so happy as to have His Excellency's direction to inform you of his assent thereto, and that the same may take place by way of Crown Point . . . next [year] . . . .

I have by this opportunity wrote Mrs. Butler and transmitted her some money, in order to enable her and family to come to Canada, which please permit to be delivered to her. If the season will admit, it will oblige me, and particularly the younger part of the family, their being allowed to come immediately to Canada, as the children [Thomas, William Johnson, Andrew and Deborah] are to go to England in the first ships.

I am, Sir, your most obedient and very humble servant . . . .

Walter Butler laid down his pen, smiling. "Now that the exchange appears settled, I can begin to think about my own future. Should I really ask Lyn to marry me? I'm not so sure she's worthy of me; after all, she is a squaw."

A knock sounded and Walter raced to the door. Lyn was standing there, shyly peeping up at him in the Indian manner, from under her black eyebrows.

"My love, I thought you'd never arrive. What kept you so long?" He embraced her while tenderly placing a finger over her lips. "Don't answer. You're here; that's all that matters."

He shut the door and turned to caress her, softly, gently. "Some day we'll be together for always." He brushed her ear with a kiss, then bit it.

Seizing his hair, Lyn pulled his face, his lips to hers. In a frenzy of passion she kissed him.

Their bodies merged into one.

31

Fear

The next Sunday as Jane was passing the sugar house, she again met Luke Swetland; his beak of a nose seemed more prominent than she had remembered. "You're still with us? Why?"

"Quiet. Can't talk here."

"Follow me. I know a place." She scuttled off, not stopping for him to catch up until well inside the maple grove. "Why are you still in Kanadesaga? I thought you'd be almost to Niagara."

"My Indian relatives heard the Yankees had returned to Fort Stanwix; so they decided not to flee. Instead, they went back to Kendaia and left me here in Kanadesaga." Swethand looked around nervously. "If the Lord spares me, I'm going to run away."

"That's suicide. You'll be caught."

"Perhaps, but I think I can escape."

"And if not?" Jane reached out and took his arm, as if holding him back. "You know what happens."

"Indeed I do. Why just the day before yesterday I heard the prisoner whoop and went to see who, no, what they brought in: two prisoners taken near Wyoming." He shook his head. "Were they *some bloody*, especially the second."

"They survived?"

"Yes." He lowered his voice to a whisper. "They told me General Sullivan is collecting an army on the Susquehanna. He's going to come and destroy the Indians once and for all."

"Good Heavens!"

"This could mean deliverance, Mrs. Campbell."

"Or death."

May 23, 1779.

A red-painted messenger appeared at the entrance of Jane's cubicle. "Goahwuk, come, so commands Chief Old Smoke."

Trembling, she scrambled to her feet, straightened her cap and skirt in a vain effort for time to calm herself, and followed the Indian. "No doubt about it," she decided, "Old Smoke is going to tell me I'm being married off and sent away to the Genesee."

At the Great Council House a stocky officer in a green Ranger uniform stood silhouetted in the doorway: Colonel John Butler himself. "Ah, Mrs. Campbell, I've good news, yes, good news. You're to be exchanged for my wife and family."

"Dear God, I must be dreaming. Did you just say I was to be exchanged? What about my children?"

"We're still hunting for them." He hesitated a moment. "But don't you worry; we'll find them for you. Yes, yes, we will."

John Butler took Jane's arm, escorted her inside and introduced her to Chief Old Smoke. Although she had never before been presented to him, she had seen the tall, portly warrior several times; once again she was struck by his commanding presence.

"O Sago, Goahwuk. It has been agreed around the council fire that our white daughter will be given up. As a token of consent, *Su-gan'-tah* [Colonel Butler] has given me this string of wampum."

"But what about Nohyeh and Hahnih? They're preparing to send me to kinsfolk on the Genesee."

"The plans must be stopped. Go back to your longhouse and send your parents to me. Sugantah and I will change their minds."

Within a short time the couple returned to the cubicle, their eyes blazing with anger. "Goahwuk, you open a dutiful ear." The elderly squaw spit out her words. "All good daughters obey their wise mothers who plan what is best for them. And what is best?" She pointed a finger straight at Jane. "That our precious child go to live with her Genesee family. Their young son is skilled in war and the hunt; and they need an experienced daughter like Goahwuk, trained in sewing and cooking."

Hahnih seized Jane's arms, almost shaking her in his fury. "And you further attend: Sugantah proposed to pay us if we would release our favored daughter to him. How dare he? One never sells family. No, never, never, never! Naho!"

145

The next day Chief Old Smoke appeared at Jane's longhouse. "Cousins, bury the hatchet of anger and harken: Deliver Goahwuk into the outstretched arms of Sugantah, for he is a good man and worthy of your sacrifice." Without allowing Nohyeh and Hahnih time to protest, he said, "Yes, your Goahwuk is indeed an experienced and good squaw, but is she irreplaceable? No! Let your Genesee kinsfolk, therefore, find another.

"Cousins," Old Smoke continued, "listen with an accepting ear: so much does Oneonta, our Great White Father, the good King George, treasure the well-being of his Sugantah that he wishes to present noble gifts of food and money to this little Seneca family. He begs you to accept them and release Goahwuk. Naho!"

"Great cousin, Chief Old Smoke," Hahnih replied, "open a sorrowful ear: In Goahwuk lives a precious spirit, the dead child of our late years. How can we sell her?" He glanced at his emaciated wife. "And yet, the Great Good Spirit who supplies men with all the comforts of life also knows we are hungry, nearly starving; we must, therefore, accept his generosity. We have no choice but to release Goahwuk."

"Hineaweh." The chief bowed. "Sugantah thanks you, as does our great Oneonta."

Hahnih slowly raised his hand. "Further harken: Our consent is not the final voice; that belongs to the Genesee cousins. Dispatch a messenger westward to deliver persuading words. Naho!"

"I myself will be that messenger," Old Smoke announced. "And I myself will deliver the persuading words. Let no one expect me back, however, before the beginning of the next moon. Between Kanadesaga and the Genesee River are swamps and lakes, high grasses, forest and rolling hills. Rattlesnakes, bears and wolves will challenge my right to pass.

"Furthermore, when I reach my destination, let everyone remember I must summon the council. This problem must be considered under a new light: can the Genesee family who are not in need sell Goahwuk, who glows with the spirit of a deceased relative; and in so doing, will they bring down the wrath of the Evil Spirit upon their longhouse?"

* * *

"What if the council says no?" Jane pushed aside the torturing question by immersing herself in the family chores. Fetching water one day, she met Andrew Piper, an elderly Kanadesaga prisoner also from the

Mohawk Valley. "Why, hello. What are you doing here in front of the council house?"

"Waiting for an Oneida. I heard he was in town," Piper replied; his weather-beaten face lit up expectantly. "I want him to take a message back to the Mohawk."

"Oh," Jane exclaimed, "do you think he could do the same for me?"

"Brother, *you wished to see me,*" the Indian interrupted, speaking English in a very grave tone. *"I have come. What do you want?"*

"When you return, will you go to my family and tell them I'm alive?"

Jane spoke up. "Could you try and find my husband, too?"

"Is that all?" The Oneida turned to Piper. *"I supposed you wanted me to conduct you back to your home."*

"I don't dare leave. I'd surely be recaptured and this time killed."

At that very moment Colonel Butler emerged from the council house, saw the little group and drew back to listen to their conversation.

"You are mistaken, Piper," the Indian replied. *"I can lead you safe, by paths which they do not know."*

"Thank you, but I'll take my chances on being exchanged." He sighed in resignation. "No, I'm too old to try and escape."

"Escape, never." Butler stepped forward and seized Piper's arm. "Guards, arrest this man; send him to Niagara right away. Right away. And catch that Oneida, too."

The Indian had already disappeared.

June 1, 1779. Early in the morning.

"Yoho, yoho, yoho, yoho, yoho!"

Kanadesaga was jolted awake by that cry. Instantly Jane and all the townspeople assembled to hear the news. "A body of Yankees is advancing and before nightfall they will reach Cayuga. The Oneidas must have showed the enemy a new route; our scouts just now discovered them."

Cayuga was only a long day's journey away.

June 5, 1779.

The alarm [John Butler wrote to Colonel Bolton] proved to be without foundation. The report of the enemy's advancing was [merely] occasioned by some tracks. . . . The Indians . . . took it for granted that they were those of an enemy and set the whole country in motion. . . .

Once aroused, however, Kanadesaga remained panic-stricken.

Each day more scouts confirmed Luke Swetland's news that a large Rebel army was massing on the Susquehanna, preparing to invade Iroquois Territory.

And each day hordes of hungry refugees streamed in from Onondaga, telling tales of destruction and devastation from the Yankees' April raid. They expected to be fed, but no corn would ripen for another six weeks.

Kanadesaga faced starvation.

32

June 18, 1779

The same red-painted messenger as before entered Jane's cubicle. "O Sago. Cousins of Old Smoke, attend: The great chief has just returned to Kanadesaga. He wishes to inform Mrs. Campbell that she is now free. Also he takes pleasure in delivering the promised supply of food and gifts, enough to wipe away forever her family's tears."

Jane struggled to keep from singing out for joy. Instead, she said solemnly, "Please inform the chief that I am deeply grateful for his efforts in my behalf." She longed to ask how Old Smoke had persuaded the Genesee council but dared not. Looking at Nohyeh's and Hahnih's impassive faces, she wondered about their feelings; as with all Indians, they had been trained from childhood to show no emotion.

"Hineaweh." They dismissed the messenger.

Nohyeh walked quickly over to the mound of food. "Goahwuk, prepare us a feast." Then, gathering a small quantity of corn, she handed it to Jane. "We'll share this gift with our dear child. Pound it into meal and make cakes for your walk to Niagara."

A few days later Chief Old Smoke himself appeared at the family's cubicle. "O Sago. I have come to bid you farewell and to wish you success on your journey."

"Thank you." Jane flushed with excitement, knowing this visit signaled her immediate departure.

"You are now about to return to your home and friends; I rejoice [for you]. You live ... many days' journey from here.... [If I] live to the end of this war, ... I will come and see you."

"Oh Chief, you will always be welcome. Until my dying day I will

remember your efforts in my behalf. Hineaweh."

Old Smoke departed, never able to fulfill his wish.

Jane turned to her Indian family, not knowing how to take her leave.

"Goahwuk," Nohyeh said, "you will forever remain our favored daughter, the true spirit of our departed child."

"Hineaweh." Embarrassed, Jane continued. "May the Great Spirit be generous to you. Until the end of my time I will pray to my God to keep you in safety." She glanced at the granddaughters, then looked at Hahnih. "Farewell."

The elderly warrior folded his arms across his chest and said in careful English, "Good-bye, my daugh-ter."

Jane grabbd her packet of journey cakes and fled the cubicle.

In front of the council house Colonel Butler was pacing fitfully back and forth. "Mrs. Campbell, at last they've released you."

"Yes, thank God."

"And this is Mr. Secord, who will take you to Niagara." He presented a tall, thin Ranger with hair braided into a pigtail.

"How do you do, Mr. Secord," Jane quickly murmured, trying to be polite, then asked, "Before we leave, Colonel, have you any news of my children or my father?"

"None, I'm sorry to say, but perhaps Niagara knows something by now."

"Oh, I hope so."

"On the other hand, I do expect Mrs. Moore and her family to be released in a few days."

"Mrs. Moore? Why I thought she was rescued a long time ago by a Ranger."

"That could have been, but now she's with the Indians at Little Beard's Town on the Genesee [present-day Cuylerville]. And her girls aren't too far away."

Secord spoke up. "In fact, Mrs. Campbell, we'll be passing through *Canandaigua* where her daughter Mary is living."

"Are we going to take her with us?"

Butler pointedly ignored Jane's question. "Upon reaching Niagara, you must go directly to Lt. Colonel Mason Bolton, the commandant. You'll remain under his protection at the fort. Tell him, if there is not a more convenient place, you may stay at my house."

"Thank you very much. By the way, what is today's date?"

"Friday, the 18th of June 1779. Why?"

"I want to remember it forever."

151

33

The Central Trail

"Ready, Mrs. Campbell?" Secord asked.

"Ready? Of course. Whenever was I not ready!"

Jane, Secord, two Ranger scouts and their Seneca escorts swung up packs, setting off for the 150 mile journey west to Fort Niagara; they would follow the Iroquois' great Central Trail.

At twilight, just as they reached Fall Brook, the heavens opened, but within half an hour the Rangers and Indians had built a hut with bark stripped from nearby trees and kindled a fire. Everyone crowded around, trying to dry off while journey cakes heated in a kettle of water.

As Jane lay down to sleep, she was content, still wet, but not hungry. She was on her way to Niagara, and perhaps to the children and home.

At sunrise the group set off for Canandaigua, Indian file, with Jane in the middle. As the travelers approached the town, the setting sun enfolded the buildings in a pink glow, and back in the distance Canandaigua Lake glistened from the sun's last rays.

"Such an enchanting spot," Jane exclaimed. "Mr. Secord, are we going to pick up young Mary Moore and take her with us?" She deliberately repeated the question Butler had chosen to ignore.

"I'll find out tonight 'cause the colonel's ordered me to make final arrangements for her release. Trouble is, all of a sudden her family's turned downright disagreeable and refuses to give her up."

"Mary is close to eighteen. Do you suppose they're planning to marry her off?"

"I don't know." Secord stopped in front of a turtle-marked longhouse and dismissed his men. "You're free to visit your favorite squaws. Just remember, we reassemble at dawn. As for us, Mrs. Campbell, we'll spend the night here with some of my Seneca cousins. Come along." He disappeared into the building.

Following after him, Jane passed a slender young squaw adding wood to a central fire. How strange, she thought; she's bending over, not squatting. She paused and turned around for a better look. The girl straightened up. "Mary. Mary Moore! It's Mrs. Campbell."

In a flash the girl put a finger to her lips for silence. Motioning Jane to leave, she vanished into the shadows of the longhouse.

Jane hurried onward, much distressed by the encounter.

At dawn she and Secord rejoined the waiting Rangers and Senecas to continue their journey along a well-worn, narrow footpath.

"Mr. Secord," Jane called ahead, "what about young Mary? Last night I saw her and tried to speak, but she ran away."

"Not surprised. Her family won't even let me talk to her."

"But they will release her, won't they?"

"No. They said she's our daughter; we love her; and we wish to keep her."

"Then she's not to be married off?"

"Apparently not. Only one thing's certain: the Indian Department will have to give her family a fancy ransom or she'll never get back."

"Oh no! I pray my children are spared Mary's fate."

For two days the group marched in stifling heat over gently rolling countryside. Frequently their trail threaded through overhanging forest with only hatchet-marked trees to point the way; at other times it cut across creeks and streams, or passed through grasses taller than Jane's head.

At last they reached the Genesee, where the Indians and Rangers fashioned a raft of logs roped together with long hickory withes— flexible, slender twigs. Once on the other side of the river, the group swung up packs and resumed the march in the still stifling heat.

"About a mile from here," Secord remarked, "we hit *Ga-no-wau'-ges* [now Avon], where my Seneca family lives. So tonight we'll have a frolic with plenty of 'milk'. "

"You and the Indians can call it milk, but I call it firewater."

"As you wish. I'm merely informing you that rum 'll be flowing. I think you should be prepared."

"What do you suggest I do?"

153

"I'll hide you in my family's cubicle and cover you with bearskins. You might be hot, but at least you'll be out of sight. I don't need tell you the drinking bout will last till every drop's drunk."

The frolic began as soon as they arrived at Ganowauges' central clearing. Almost immediately quarrels and fighting broke out among the warriors, their wild halloos reverberating from one end of the village to the other.

Crazed with rum, Indians went charging through the longhouses, often jolting the very bunk where Jane lay hiding. All night long she cowered, praying that the bearskins would not slip off and that the Indians' milk would run dry. Soon!

The sun was shining brightly by the time she dared crawl from under her suffocating covers, but not until mid-afternoon could the bleary-eyed Secord, his Rangers and Senecas manage to depart.

For the next five days the group kept a steady pace, journeying through thick forests or open fields, around marshes, swamps, rapids and falls. Just as they were fording yet another creek, they saw a company of Indians approaching from the opposite bank.

"O Sago, Powell." Secord recognized their leader, a slender, blond man dressed as a Seneca. "Halt a moment."

The white Indian grinned, his blue eyes twinkling as he helped Jane out of the water. "Captain John Powell to your rescue, Madam. And you are?"

"Jane Cannon Campbell, Mrs. Samuel."

Secord interrupted. "Colonel Butler has just managed to get her released from Kanadesaga."

"Ah yes. We've all heard about your plight, Mrs. Campbell. As a celebration may I offer you pigeon for dinner? We've shot quite a few."

"How very kind." Jane smiled, thinking, "Such a charming man; what a shame he's an enemy."

Powell began questioning Secord about conditions at Kanadesaga, obviously not caring whether Jane heard or not. Both men knew she could hardly escape and if she did, she would perish in the wilderness.

"Colonel Butler is trying to preserve calm," Secord said, "but everyone's terrified because invasion is inevitable."

"From where?" Powell wrinkled his brow in puzzlement. "Do we know yet?"

"Not really. Bits of information still need piecing together. The other day a prisoner confessed that General Clinton's damming Lake Otsego."

"Why that's near Cherry Valley," Jane thought.

"He's raising the water level. When it gets high enough, we hear his army of boats will float down into the Susquehanna."

"Raising the water level," Powell exclaimed. "That'll be some feat if he succeeds."

"Indeed yes, if he succeeds. And then other scouts tell us troops are massing elsewhere, especially in the Wyoming Valley."

"What about food and supplies?"

"Disagreeably low. The Iroquois are near starvation. And worse yet...." Secord nodded in annoyance toward the Indians squatting around them. "Butler is obliged to send for more ammunition, all because stupid warriors waste it firing at every little bird they see."

Powell shook his head. "At least I know what we're heading into. Thank you." He turned to Jane and gave a jaunty bow. "And now good-bye, Madam."

The captain and his Indians crossed the ford and disappeared into the forest while Secord and his group shouldered their packs and headed westward.

"Invasion?" Jane asked herself. "Inevitable?" She remembered Oriskany and pictured the American soldiers marching off to face death. Would Sam be among them? She thought of the destruction and vengeance they could wreak. "What'll happen to the children, to Father and even to me? We could be killed—and by our own army!"

34

The End of the Trail

"Hurry along, Mrs. Campbell," Secord called back. "Tonight we reach the Niagara River."

Jane's face brightened. "Does that mean we'll see the Falls, too?"

"Not exactly. Our trail ends a few miles north. Then we head down river to the fort—another day's journey."

Atop the next hill the Ranger halted and motioned for Jane to join him. "See that small, blackish cloud?" He pointed beyond the sea of green trees to just above the horizon. "That's spray from Niagara Falls. You know what it is 'cause it's always in the same spot."

"Really?" She squinted to have a better view. "The falls must be immense."

"Yes."

"How far away are they?"

"Maybe twenty miles."

"And where's the fort?"

"Over that direction, some fourteen miles to the north o' the falls."

Late the next afternoon, as the group rounded the last bend, the sun gleamed upon the massive stone walls and blockhouse towers of Fort Niagara, painting them red in sunlight or black in shadow. Beyond lay the forbidding expanse of Lake Ontario.

Secord stopped to dismiss the Rangers, sending them off to Butlersbury, then turned to release the Senecas. "Hineaweh. Go and wait at *Ne-ah'-gah* [present-day Youngstown] until Sugantah sends for you again." He led Jane and the Rangers to a drawbridge over the moat and waited for the bridge to lower. "The end of the trail at last."

"No, Mr. Secord," Jane said, "for me it's only the beginning."

PART III

FORT NIAGARA

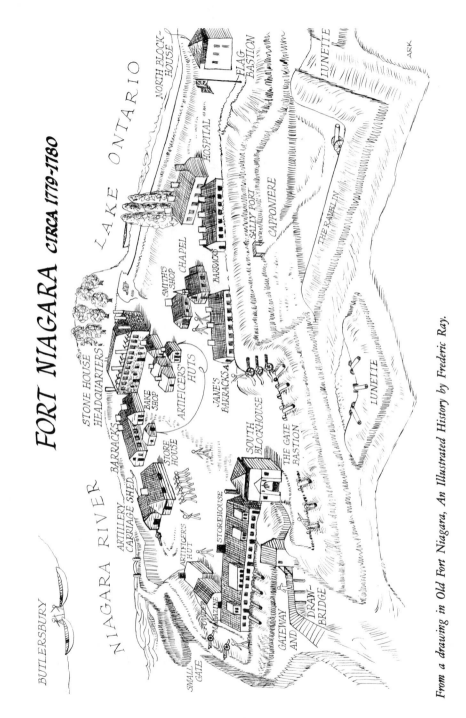

FORT NIAGARA *CIRCA 1779-1780*

BUTLERSBURY

NIAGARA RIVER

LAKE ONTARIO

STONE HOUSE HEADQUARTERS

ARTILLERY CARRIAGE SHED

BARRACKS

BAKE SHOP

STORE HOUSE

ARTIFICERS' HUTS

SMITH'S SHOP

CHAPEL

BARRACKS

HOSPITAL

NORTH BLOCK-HOUSE

FLAG BASTION

CAPONIERE

SALLY PORT

THE RAVELIN

LUNETTE

JANE'S BARRACKS

ARTIFICER'S HUT

MAGAZINE

STOREHOUSE

SOUTH BLOCKHOUSE

THE GATE BASTION

GATEWAY AND DRAW-BRIDGE

SMALL GATE

LUNETTE

ARK

From a drawing in Old Fort Niagara, An Illustrated History by Frederic Ray.

160

35

Guns and Bugles

Secord led Jane over the drawbridge, through a towering blockhouse and into Fort Niagara itself. Far ahead the great Stone House glowed in the last rays of the sun and on beyond stretched the protective barrier of Lake Ontario; all around stood various buildings, some of stone, most of wood.

A cannon boomed. A bugle announced evening chapel.

Jane stopped still, gazing in awe and astonishment: a monstrous English fort in the middle of wilderness!

"Mrs. Campbell, come along. Across the parade ground to headquarters."

"Oh, after eight months I can't believe I'm in civilization again." Jane's eyes lighted on some long, dark wooden barracks. "Do you think I could be put in one of those? I'd much prefer it to staying in Colonel Butler's house; you know, I'd feel awfully uneasy there."

"The commandant 'll make that decision when we see him."

Wherever Jane looked people were milling about: soldiers, a few smartly outfitted, but most in ragged uniforms; women and children wearing clothing almost as bedraggled as her own; and Indians clad in deerskins, shouldering brightly colored blankets. High in the distance sentries picketed the fort's giant walls and guns pointed toward the Niagara River and into the forest wilderness.

Upon reaching the Stone House, Secord paused just inside the door and gestured toward shelves of red blankets, bolts of material, kettles, furs and trinkets. "Our Indian Trade Room."

"Oh, all that wonderful cloth," Jane said wistfully. "For once I wish I were an Indian."

He laughed. "I guess so."

Secord led his charge through a large reception room, down a dark stone corridor and into a long, beamed office where a uniformed figure hunched over a pile of papers on his desk.

"Colonel Bolton, sir, may I present Mrs. Campbell."

"How do you do." As the middle-aged officer struggled to stand, a wince of pain crossed his sunken face; he fell back into his chair.

Pretending not to notice, Secord hastily continued. "Colonel Butler ordered me to bring Mrs. Campbell directly to you. He offered her his house if no other place were available."

"No need, no need. Our provisions may be scarce, but we've room enough here in the fort."

Jane smiled, relieved. "Sir, please, have you any news of my husband, Colonel Samuel Campbell? Or of my children and my father, Matthew Cannon?"

Mason Bolton dropped a gnarled hand upon a stack of papers, drawing it toward him. "Colonel Samuel Campbell is at Fort Stanwix. As for the others, every day some of the Indians' prisoners arrive here, as well as wives and children of His Majesty's own distressed families."

Bolton continued his search among the papers. "Ah yes, here's the prisoner list. February 18th last, encamped outside the walls: James Campbell . . . ; inside the fort: Matthew Cannon from Cherry Valley; Abigail Moore, also from Cherry Valley."

Jane cried out for joy.

"But now they're all gone elsewhere. Matthew Cannon: sent down to confinement in Quebec [City]. Abigail Moore: back in Seneca country. James Campbell: taken off by the Mohawks. I see no mention of your other children."

Tears welled up in her eyes.

The colonel, embarrassed, hurried on. "Mrs. Campbell, since you are now officially a prisoner of His Majesty the King, I will place you in Barrack A with other female captives and their children. Also lodged there are some of the wives and families of His Majesty's own forces.

"Concerning your exchange, you will remain at Niagara until such time as Mrs. Butler and family reach Canada from Albany; then you will be sent back to the Colonies. If any of your children are also found—and the men of the Indian Department are continually searching for them—then of course they will accompany you." He reached for a bell at the side of his

162

desk and rang for the orderly; the meeting was over.

Jane consoled herself: "At least Sam and Father are safe, but my little children. Oh, where are my little children?"

Colonel Bolton interrupted her thoughts. "Soldier, take Mrs. Campbell for the usual interrogation, then see to her immediate needs." As Jane walked out the door, she heard the commandant ask Secord, "What is Colonel Butler's situation?"

"In desperate want for men and at least 200 pounds of battle powder."

In the next room Jane faced her questioner, a pock-marked officer with a tuft of red hair jutting from the middle of his head.

"Mrs. Campbell, do the Indians at Kanadesaga seem loyal to Oneonta, King George?"

"Why, what do you mean?" she asked in mock innocence. "They're your allies, aren't they?"

"Why yes, of course." He paused, taken aback. "Let me rephrase the question. Now that the Rebels are preparing to invade Indian territory, do you think the Senecas will stand up and fight?"

"Well, sir," Jane replied, "I really can't say. I spent all my time sewing clothes for Indian families. I do know my Seneca father won't fight."

"Oh?" He leaned forward, anxious. "Why?"

"Too old."

"Madam, you know full well I'm asking about braves."

"Well, let me tell you about one of those braves! He tomahawked and scalped my defenseless mother because she couldn't walk fast enough." Jane's voice faltered. "I couldn't even help her. I had four small children and was carrying a heavy sack of plunder."

"Mrs. Campbell, if you please, stick to the subject at hand. I want to know about Kanadesaga."

"Certainly. That's where the Indians took my children from me. Every day since then I've prayed to God for their safe return. Have you any children?"

"No." The officer leaped up and jerked open the door. "Orderly, come get Mrs. Campbell. I've finished with her."

The soldier escorted Jane down the corridor and into the kitchen. "I reckoned you'd be hungry."

"I certainly am. How kind of you."

"No," the orderly muttered. "I'm just doing my duty."

Jane watched eagerly as a mess boy ladled thick soup into a bowl, then dropped in a piece of toast.

"Here, ma'am."

"Thank you. These are the most savory-looking victuals I've seen in ages." She took a spoonful and smiled. "I'd almost forgotten food could taste so good."

As soon as she had scraped up the last morsel, the soldier hurried Jane to the Trade Room, where he thrust a bundle of old clothing into her arms. "From now on you'll have to buy cloth and make things for yourself. Anything beyond bare rations you'll have to pay for with good, hard money."

"But I haven't a penny."

"Where you get it, that's *your* problem."

Ushering Jane out the door into the darkness of evening, he led her across the moonlit parade ground toward Barrack A, then pointed. "There's your entrance. This is as far as I go."

"Thank you." Gingerly Jane opened the door to peer inside at a large, stark room lined with twenty or thirty double-tiered bunks.

A woman emerged from the shadows and whispered, "Welcome." She put a finger to her lips, then indicated a number of sleeping forms. "Follow me." They tiptoed to an empty bunk near an open window. "Yours."

Jane dropped her bundle onto the bedding; instead of the expected bugs darting everywhere, fresh straw crackled inside. "I can't believe everything is so clean. Even my bunk smells of new wood." She moved to the window; the roofs of dark, silent buildings were glistening in the white of the moon and a delicious breeze was blowing.

"Such luxury." Jane smiled to herself; "I'll worry tomorrow."

36

Jane Wells' Cap

Jane Campbell awoke shortly before dawn, jumped to her feet, threw a shawl across her shoulders and slipped outside to explore Fort Niagara before the day began. Discovering the chapel nearby, she hurried in. "God is our refuge and strength. . . ." She prayed, perhaps more fervently than ever in her life. "And please, dear Lord, watch over Sam and our family."

At the sound of reveille, Jane scurried back to the barrack, anxious to meet her new companions. ". . . And does anyone know about my children?"

Silence.

She bowed her head in disappointment.

An older woman put her arm on Jane's shoulder. "Mrs. Campbell, many of us here are also prisoners and have lost families. We understand."

"Thank you. I had so hoped."

Everyone did understand. Wives of British soldiers and Loyalists had also lost loved ones in the war. In addition, others were alone, their husbands and sons away serving on the New York frontier or farther west on the Great Lakes.

Jane looked around the barrack room at the sad faces. "How strange," she thought, "whether enemy or friend we feel compassion for one another. We're all suffering from this war; perhaps worse, we're all like pawns, waiting."

She soon found out, however, that her companions were not above gossip, especially about the senior officers privileged to live just outside the fort in houses on the Niagara River:

— "'O' course we're not talking about the few with families. Anyway, they're mostly over in Butlersbury."

"We mean the ones who live in the wharf area near the public house—like Colonel Guy Johnson. He's head of our Indian Department and should be setting a good example. After all he is a widower. But what does he do? Takes in a squaw to cook and wash. And perform 'other services'."

"Mrs. Campbell doesn't care about the squaw's other services. Or for that matter about any of 'the dreadful women' hanging around this fort."

"Of course we earn money, too, but in the gentle way. We sew and mend for the officers."

Jane spoke up eagerly. "In Kanadesaga I sewed for the Indians; surely I could do that for the officers here at Niagara."

"You can join our circle. Incidentally, the best pay is for linen shirts with lots of fine ruffles on the bosom and cuffs."

"How much?"

"Whatever's the going price for a yard of linen."

Jane quickly adjusted to the group's routine. During the day she joined the women sewing outside in the bright sunshine; despite the good light, however, she often had difficulty focusing on the fine stitches.

Being the newest member of the circle, Jane would listen silently to the conversations, particularly those of the complaining British and Loyalist wives:

— "Why're the King's rations so scarce? The traders' *batteaux* [flat-bottomed rowboats] are always brimful of goods."

"But at prices we can't afford. Unless, of course, our menfolk take extra jobs with those miserable traders. And I resent that."

"Me too. My husband's a soldier here at the fort and has a right to the King's rations."

"Only those lazy, shiftless Indians seem to have that right," a woman carried on. "They come to Niagara and are grandly presented with the King's, Oneonta's, food, kettles, blankets, gunpowder. And rum."

"Who says their war services 're so valuable? I say they're doing nothing but taking victuals from our mouths."

"Well, we're going to need their services, valuable or no, once the Rebel army starts to move toward Niagara."

"Ladies," Jane interjected, "I can tell you the Senecas certainly won't stand up to fight. Rather than face the Continental Army they'll flee here for protection."

Jane's words were accompanied by the sounds of hammers and saws as soldiers feverishly repaired and strengthened the long neglected fortifications.

Several days later the sewing circle was once again gathered outside. "Mrs. Campbell, you're from Cherry Valley; you must know the Ramsey sisters."

"Yes, of course. But I haven't seen them since the day Walter Butler sent us all off with the Indians." She paused, remembering. "They're cousins of my friend Jane Wells, who was killed in the raid. Why do you ask?"

"There they are, leaving yonder barrack."

Jane rushed over and threw her arms around the astonished Ramsey girls. "To think we're all still alive and here together at Niagara. What a miracle!"

"Yes, isn't it a miracle," they mumbled awkwardly.

Not registering their embarrassment, she continued. "I've saved something. Let me give it to you." She drew from her pocket the lace cap she had been guarding so carefully. "This belonged to Jane Wells."

The girls stared in horror at the blood stains and tomahawk slit.

"I got it from the Seneca who. . . ." Her voice broke.

Only afterwards did Jane Campbell learn the Ramsey sisters were Tories and had never been prisoners of the Indians; Walter Butler had sent them directly to Niagara under his special protection.

37

A Mystery

Mid-July 1779.

Mary Moore and her daughters, Jaynie and Abigail, finally arrived at Barrack A, weary, their faces drawn and thin. The three were wearing Indian clothes and their hair had once been blackened with bear's grease.

Jane Campbell ran to greet them. "At last you're here. But where is young Mary?"

"Still at Canandaigua," Jaynie replied. "The Rangers who brought us here said Colonel Butler hopes to have her freed very soon."

Remembering Secord's doubts about the girl's release, Jane quickly changed the subject. "Mrs. Moore, we heard you'd been ransomed by a British sergeant; so how did you end up at Little Beard's Town?"

"I was ransomed, yes, but alas, other Indians soon stole me away."

Mary Moore collapsed onto an empty bunk. "If you and the girls want to chitter-chatter, go outside and leave me be; every bone in my poor old body aches."

Jane Campbell and the two sisters strolled toward the lake shore and sat down by the water's edge.

"How pretty the lake is without ice," Abigail remarked.

"Without ice?" Jane Campbell looked puzzled. "Ah, that's right; Colonel Bolton told me you were here last February."

"Yes. My Seneca family came here from *Honeoye* for food and were persuaded to release me. But after a few days, they changed their minds and the Indian Department had to give me back."

"Freed and then given back?"

"Yes, almost worse than being captured at Cherry Valley." Abigail shuddered. "Mrs. Campbell, do you realize the Indians can still take all of us back? You. Me. Jaynie. Mother. That possibilty really haunts me."

Jaynie sat bolt upright, then pointed a finger at her sister. "Don't be so hysterical. Here in Fort Niagara are we really better off as prisoners of the British? In *Cattaraugus* I was free to move about. My family, my Seneca family that is, treated me like their own daughter, and I loved them back, I really did. I already miss them." She undid a silver pin on her over-dress. "See what they gave me; this was their treasure. Mrs. Campbell, at least you understand how I feel, don't you."

"Understand, yes, but I can't agree. My family in Kanadesaga was also kind and generous with what they had, but love them?" She shook her head. "Never. Why I don't even miss them."

Mary Moore and her daughters joined Jane's sewing circle. Although the two girls quickly adjusted to life as prisoners at the fort, their mother had difficulty. "I wish I were young enough to accept my fate, but I keep remembering Cherry Valley." She swallowed hard, fighting back tears, then turned to gaze toward the lake. "I used to be so pretty and plump, and now just look at me: my skin is hanging on my bones and I'm in Indian rags."

"My friend, we're all shabby." Jane held up a section of her own well-worn skirt. "And of course we all remember the past, but we mustn't dwell on it. As for me, I smother myself in work; it helps."

"Don't you ever feel like screaming when you see the raiding parties go out the sally port over there?"

"Certainly. And sometimes I get so angry I accidentally jab my finger with the needle. But the worst of all is when I see children playing among the fruit trees behind the Stone House."

"Yes, if only I knew about my Mary. When will I ever see my lovely daughter again?"

"At least you know where she is; I know nothing about my children."

*　*　*

As further reports of the imminent Yankee invasion arrived, Jaynie Moore became more and more concerned about her Seneca family, about

169

all the Indians. "The Iroquois never wanted to take sides in this white man's war, but the British forced them to. We may be miserable as prisoners here at Niagara, but what about the poor Indians? They're facing destruction of their homeland and where will they find refuge?"

Mary Moore's patience finally snapped. "Of course we feel sorry for those who treated us well, but I certainly don't see how my own flesh and blood can feel sorry for the whole lot of 'em. Not after Cherry Valley." Her voice rose in indignation. "How can you speak of Indians in the same breath with our soldiers or Mrs. Campbell's children or your poor sister Mary?"

"And how can I make you understand?" Jaynie glared at her mother and walked over to the window. "By the way, remember when we arrived, I was interrogated by a Captain John Powell? I know I've never met him before, but still something's vaguely familiar about him."

Mary held up the linen shirt she was making to scrutinize her stitching. "You're just imagining things, dear."

"No, Mother, I'm not. He's much older than me, maybe thirty, and quite handsome, with blond hair and blue eyes. He wears deerskins; so he must be a member of the Indian Department." She laughed. "How could Captain Powell ever pass for an Iroquois? He could never smear on enough war paint."

"Well, he must," said Jane Campbell. "I ran into him on my way to Niagara and he's definitely a white Indian." She paused, recalling the pigeon he had given her. "I might add he seemed quite charming, considering he's an enemy."

"But where could I ever have met him?" Jaynie twisted a chestnut-colored curl around her finger, smiling.

"Now, darling child, don't you go trying to find out. We don't need to have your head turned by an enemy officer, no matter how charming and handsome." As far as Mary Moore was concerned, the subject was closed.

August 1779.

Each day the garrison waited for news, and each day perspiring, breathless Indian runners brought in more alarming accounts:

— "Generals Sullivan and Clinton are assembling their Continental soldiers by the thousands."

The British and Loyalist wives exchanged fearful glances. "Colonel Butler's having difficulty collecting Rangers and Indians even by the hundreds."

— "The Yankees are building up great supplies of food, ammunition and other matériel."

"Our defenders have nothing to gather."

— And then the dreaded words: "The Rebel Army has begun its advance into Iroquois Territory."

Panic struck the fort.

Some of the British and Loyalist families were hastily evacuated to Montreal and Quebec, but most were forced to remain. For Jane and the others left in the sewing circle a new question arose to torture them: "Will the Rebels besiege Niagara?" The fort still needed repairs, more men to defend the garrison, and above all, reserves of food.

Wives of soldiers stationed far away at the Upper Forts also feared for their husbands; if Niagara were to fall, then those western outposts, dependent upon the fort for supplies, would either starve or surrender.

Jane Campbell listened and brooded. Invasion and siege would be dangerous; yet she could be freed. And what about the Senecas and her children? Unless they could flee, invasion would bring them only starvation or death. "Dear God, keep me from despair."

38

Newtown

For three days in mid-August the fort resounded to chants, whoops and drums of an Indian council just outside the walls. While Jane and her circle watched in fascination, important warriors bedecked in colorful trinkets and silver ornaments strode in and out of headquarters. Colonel Bolton, the women learned, was conferring in his office with chiefs from northern and western lands, trying to persuade them to join Butler's forces. On the last afternoon, however, the sewing circle saw the commandant himself limp from the Stone House.

"Do you suppose Bolton's going out to the council?" Jane asked her companions.

"Can't you tell? Look at those soldiers following him. Every one's laden down with kettles and cloth and boxes of trinkets, not to mention the kegs of rum—all gifts from Oneonta to his loyal Indian 'children'. It makes me sick."

"The colonel's desperate for men. He's tried talking; now he's trying firewater and presents."

All that night they heard the rhythmic, frenzied throbs of the war chant, deafening screams and yells, piercing whoops and halloos. "Bolton is certainly trying hard," Jane muttered to herself as she tossed and turned on her bunk. "Thank heavens at this drunken frolic I'm not hiding under a bearskin."

The next morning the sewing circle learned the results of Bolton's efforts. Of the 200 warriors attending the council, only forty-four agreed to join Colonel Butler; the others refused, their chiefs instead asking the commandant to supply them with troops to wage war with a neighboring tribe.

Jane whispered to Mary Moore, "Bolton wasted the King's money." They smiled with satisfaction.

The war council had scarcely broken up before heavy rains and mud forced the circle indoors. With a peremptory jerk Mary moved her chair. "Trust my luck; we've got a leaky barrack. Soon everything will be a soggy, miserable mess."

Jane put down her sewing. "My dear, it's better than a smoky longhouse."

"Why don't you ever complain?"

"Well, as a matter of fact, my eyes are giving me terrible problems. The light is so poor in here, and doing close stitching makes them tear almost constantly. Sometimes I can hardly see my work."

"Well, at least you can still look out the window and keep track of what's going on. That's better than nothing."

And much was happening at Fort Niagara. As soldiers worked furiously to repair defenses for Sullivan and Clinton's expected assault, every day Indian messengers ran in with word of the Rebel army's movements:

— "The invaders are near Tioga on the Susquehanna."

— "They're laying waste surrounding villages."

— "Now they're burning and destroying our crops and orchards."

Then runners announced: "On August 29 Colonel Butler's forces were routed in battle! At Newtown, near Tioga. The enemy almost surrounded us, but we escaped. Warriors are heading home, gathering up our families and fleeing here to Niagara."

39

Reunions

"Routed in battle?" The sewing circle was in a state of shock. What would Butler do? Could he regroup his soldiers and attack? If he were forced to retreat, how long before Sullivan and Clinton's army would reach Niagara?

And Jane Campbell constantly worried about her children among the panicking Indians.

Not many days later a bedraggled band of Senecas approached the fort. Warriors walked erectly, carrying their muskets, tomahawks and scalping knives, but their faces wore the haunted look of defeat. The squaws shuffled after them, bent nearly double under their burden of household goods.

Guards accosting the group pointed to a sodden field. "Go camp there."

One squaw lingered behind to readjust the tumpline boring into her forehead, but the heavy load on her back suddenly shifted and threw her to the ground. As she struggled to stand, one of the soldiers noticed a small girl clutching at the poor woman's skirt. She was eight, he reckoned. Maybe nine, but already bent over with a sack. The child peered up at him from under her eyebrows. "Something's not right about her."

He looked more closely. Her clothes? They were the usual squaw rags. Her hair? It was blackened with bear grease and stank to high heaven. He looked again. "Her hair! That's it. It's too fine for an Injun."

He strode over to the girl and gently lifted off the sack. Taking her by the chin, he tilted her face and saw blue eyes. "You're no Injun. You talk English, don't you."

"Yes, oh yes!" The squaw grabbed her away, but she shook herself free. "I'm Elly, Eleanor Campbell."

Shortly thereafter, Jane glanced up from her needlework to see a Ranger standing in the doorway, holding a dirty little squaw by the hand.

Jane's heart stopped.

"Elly, oh, my darling Elly!" She leaped up, dropping her sewing onto the floor, ran over and threw her arms around her daughter. But she **was** embracing a statue, an Indian trained to show no feelings. Stunned, she drew back.

Elly remained motionless, head bowed. Suddenly her mouth quivered, then her pent-up emotions burst; she threw herself into her mother's arms, burying her head in Jane's bosom and sobbing.

The next morning at chapel Jane's friends and companions, officers for whom she was sewing, the soldier who found Elly, all gathered to hear the chaplain: "O give thanks unto the Lord, for he is good: for his mercy endureth for ever. . . ." A lost child returned to her mother was cause for rejoicing even in the midst of war.

Elly stayed by her mother's side, often clinging to her skirts. "My Indian family loved me, and I loved them back." She put her arms around Jane and nestled in her lap. "But you're my real mama. Please don't ever let anyone take me away again."

After the momentary happiness, once again the specter of invasion loomed. The advancing Rebel army drove hundreds and then more hundreds of Iroquois refugees to the gates of Niagara, where they squatted outside the fort, begging for food and shelter. Warriors reported, "The Yankee army descends like the whirlwind over our land north and west of Tioga. Kanadesaga, Canandaigua, all towns in its path, lie devastated. The enemy set fire to our longhouses and crops, chopped down our fruit trees. Nothing remains standing. No, nothing! Brothers, we barely escaped with our weapons, the clothes we're wearing, and what our squaws could carry."

Jane knew the Americans were avenging the destruction of Cherry Valley and other frontier settlements. But each day also brought the invaders nearer the fort. Everyone prayed and waited in fear and trepidation.

Suddenly runners brought unbelievable news: The Yankees had stopped at the Genesee River; the fires of Little Beard's Town were still burning, but the army had turned back eastward. "Now," they moaned, "it is cutting yet another pathway of woe."

Niagara, however, was saved!

The third week of September, 1779.

Some 5,000 destitute Indians were swarming outside the walls of Fort Niagara, pounding at its gates, their chiefs sending messages to Colonel Bolton. "Brother, attend: We are angry. After all we have done to help our father, Oneonta, in his war, why did he not help us in our time of need? He could have saved our homeland; instead he sent us only a handful of soldiers. He abandoned us to the mighty Rebel army and we lost everything.

"Brother, lend a pitying ear: We are here, but no food have we to feed our starving families, nor clothing and shelter to protect us against the cruelties of the coming winter. We are wretched and helpless. We need your saving hand. Naho!"

In Barrack A, Jane and her fellow prisoners knew Cherry Valley had been avenged. "I can't feel any satisfaction," she said, shaking her head. "After all, the Indians are fellow human beings."

Jaynie Moore jumped to her feet. "You're so right, Mrs. Campbell; they are human beings just like us."

"Daughter, sit down and don't be so contrary. You know full well the Indians brought their terrible plight down upon themselves."

"No, I do not. Possibly you might say that about the warriors, but certainly not about the squaws and children. They didn't want war any more than we did."

"If your father and Uncle John Moore could only hear you now, you Injun lover!"

"Oh Mother, why can't you understand what I'm trying to say?"

Jane Campbell reached over to pat Mary Moore's hand. "Jaynie means that all women and children, and even most men, whether Indian or white, are victims of this war." She paused. "Of any war."

"Yes. And among the pitiful refugees knocking here at the gates of Niagara may be our Mary and Mrs. Campbell's three boys."

A week later.

"Ladies," Captain John Powell called out as he and Lt. Robert Lottridge entered Barrack A, "your attention, please. We are commanded to inform women with missing children that a number of white captives have been delivered up by starving Indian families."

Elly put her arm around her mother. The two clutched each other, scarcely breathing as they listened.

"Go to the Stone House and see if you can identify any of them."

After the officers had walked well away from the barrack, Lottridge confided in Powell. "I saw Mrs. Samuel Campbell among the prisoners. During the Cherry Valley raid her boy Willie recognized me through my war paint; so I pointed a way for him to escape. Do you think it'd do any good to tell his mother?"

"None at all. He might not have survived." Powell held up a gold ring he was wearing. "I got this in Cherry Valley. Took it off a girl's finger."

Meanwhile Jane grabbed her shawl and flew out the barrack door. At the reception hall in the Stone House, a Ranger gave her instructions: "Go in there 'n circle round the room. Look at the bunch carefully. They'll all be sitting on the floor, right in the middle. But don't claim any child unless you're certain."

Jane groaned in despair upon seeing the children: hollow-eyed creatures, gaunt from hunger, clad in dirty rags, black-haired with bear's grease. "That's not my Samuel. Nor Matthew. Or James." She began to sob.

A soldier tapped her on the shoulder. "Say, lady, don't go bawling. Why don't you take another look."

Jane brushed away the tears and began circling the room once more, pausing to study a child's face and moving onward, then pausing again.

"Samuel," she cried out, "my baby Samuel!" She rushed over to pick him up. The terrified child pushed her away with all his might and shrank back.

A soldier took Jane's arm, drawing her aside. "Can't you see he ain't your child?"

"Leave me be. I'll prove he's mine." Kneeling down, she coaxed the boy to her and pointed to his clothes. He stood still. Ever so slowly she lifted his breech clout and exposed his shrunken buttocks. "There, you see, our mark."

"Well I'll be doggoned. I hear'd 'bout settlers branding babies in case Injuns kidnapped 'em. But this is the first I've ever see'd. When did you do it?"

"In June 1777, shortly after he was born. I thought it was barbarous, but my husband insisted. Thank God he did, or you'd have taken Samuel away from me, too." Gently she drew the child into her arms, cooing, "Oh, my precious, precious baby."

40

Jaynie's Ring

By chance Captain Powell met Jaynie Moore near the Stone House. "How's the little Campbell boy?" As he started to bow, the sunlight reflected on his ring.

"Why that's my ring you're wearing. So you're the Injun devil who stole it from me!"

John Powell flushed with embarrassment. He sputtered and mumbled an apology, then cut himself short. "Please allow me." Taking Jaynie's hand, he placed it upon her finger.

"Good." She paused to admire the regained possession. "You ought to be ashamed of yourself."

"Bury the hatchet. Please?" He reached for her hand and held it, pretending to examine the ring. "It looks prettier on your finger." He kissed it, then grinned. "May I escort you back to the barrack?"

"Well, all right." Pointedly she changed the subject. "Tell me, Captain Powell, since you're a member of the Indian Department, you must know some way of helping those poor refugees outside our walls. The thought of their huddling in lean-to's, caves and holes in the ground—it's so cruel."

"We're doing everything we can."

"If only I could do something."

Powell stepped back in amazement. "Miss Moore, I don't understand you. After all, I'm the one who captured you." He cleared his throat. "And I'm the one who turned you over to some of those very Indians you want to help."

Jaynie merely nodded.

"In short, I can't understand why you're so concerned welfare."

"But Captain, I lived among them and came to care for t. squaws and children are innocent victims just like us."

"Well, you surprise me." He took her arm, detouring her towa lake shore. "Frankly," he confessed, "we're overwhelmed. All Iroquois refugees are a disagreeable burden, and unreasonable, too. Da it, the situation is chaos."

"Despite that, your department must have some idea of how to solve the problem."

"Yes, but the Indians reject every suggestion," Powell explained. "They refuse to go back to their lands and rebuild their villages. They won't even resettle west of the Genesee; yet Sullivan and Clinton's army never set foot in that territory."

"Isn't there someplace else for them to go?"

"Yes, of course. They could move on to Carleton Island; that's at the beginning of the St. Lawrence. Since it lies on the direct supply route from Montreal to Fort Niagara, we could guarantee them provisions and care for them. At the same time their departure would ease the situation here."

"And what do they say?"

"No, absolutely no." Powell shook his head. "Why can't they understand it's for their own good?"

"Why? Because they distrust the British. They can't afford to show their anger, for then they'd be biting the hand that feeds. But they certainly can afford to be suspicious."

"Suspicious? Ridiculous. Oneonta is their loving father."

"Then why is Oneonta trying to push them out of his Niagara house?" Jaynie retorted. "And why is he trying to divide his family? Is that love?"

"I never considered the situation in those terms." Powell thought a moment. "Yes, of course; that is what they'd think." He smiled. "Miss Moore, my compliments. You're not only pretty—you're clever. Now then, since you seem to sense the Indians' frame of mind. . . ."

"My mother says I'm wrong to care about them, but she doesn't understand."

"What do you think they really will do?"

Jaynie hesitated a moment, as if the thought were too horrifying to put into words. "They'll take their terrible revenge; they'll set fire to the

ie other."

ined to agree." Secretly, he hoped the food
so simply, by sending out raiding parties; fewer
fewer mouths to feed. Powell took Jaynie's hand,
to face him, and looked into her eyes; he was
nem a deep green. "If your prediction proves true, I'm
bad news for you."

an my sister Mary?"

With thousands of Indians fleeing to Niagara and heaven
ere else, we simply can't keep track of all their captives."

re you saying you don't know where Mary is?"

Unfortunately, yes."

"And all this time we've been waiting to hear she was released and on
er way." Jaynie clasped both his arms and gazed up at him. "Please be
honest with me. Could Mary be just outside the fort and we don't know
it? Or are you telling me she's dead?" Tears welled up in her eyes.

"Take heart; don't cry. — May I call you Jaynie?"

She nodded. "Yes."

Powell put his arm around her shoulder and drew her close, then
catching himself, released her. "I don't believe your sister and her Seneca
family are dead; the Rebel army destroyed houses and food supplies, not
people. Although the Indian Department has found no trace of them here
at Niagara, we do know other captives are with the Indians in the Buffalo
Creek area."

"Could Mary be one of them?"

"I'll try to find out for certain. I give you my word as an officer." He
hesitated. "And as a friend."

"Thank you. With all my heart."

Powell took her hands, slowly drew them to his lips and kissed them,
then let go, breaking the spell. "I'll be leaving soon to search for captives,
including your sister."

Jaynie sighed. "We both know finding Mary is only the first step; her
Indian family has to be persuaded to give her up. She's such a sweet person
they'll want to keep her."

"Well, starvation is a great persuader. But not necessarily. Only this
morning Secord, Lottridge and I went out to one of the nearby Seneca
encampments where we know there are lots of children, including a white
boy of about four or five. But we can't find him, 'cause every time we go
searching, the Indians hide all children."

"Please let me go with you next time. I'd love to help."

"No, my dear Jaynie, never. What did you just say about revenge? You may be an adopted Seneca, but first of all you are an enemy."

"Yes, I suppose you're right; it would be too dangerous."

"However, since you are so concerned, perhaps you'll allow me to report back to you after our next visit."

"Oh yes, please do." She nearly blurted out, "And hurry." She smiled, to herself. "To think just a while ago I'd have gladly killed him."

41

Apple and Pear Seeds

October 1779.

The weather turned hostile; drenching rains and high winds buffeted the fort. For a week Jane Campbell and her friends worried more than ever about their loved ones who might be among the refugees.

Jaynie Moore was also secretly anxious: where was John Powell? He'd promised to come by and tell her about his search for the missing child. Maybe he hadn't gone because of the awful weather. Or maybe he'd forgotten his promise. And her.

The bad weather had nothing to do with Powell's absence; the captain was involved in planning an expedition to avenge the ravages of the Sullivan-Clinton campaign.

By October 19 the weather had cleared and the sewing circle watched as troops under Colonel Guy and Sir John Johnson left Niagara in sailing vessels. Several days later Colonel Butler and a detachment of Indians departed by canoe. Then Joseph Brant led more warriors through the sally port near Barrack A; they were making the trek on foot.

Jaynie drew her sister aside. "Abigail, have you heard where they're heading?"

"Yes, Fort Oswego. From there they'll march against the Oneidas for revenge, 'cause they helped Sullivan and Clinton."

"I wonder if my friend John's with them."

"Your friend!" Abigail's big brown eyes widened.

"Yes, I think so; I hope so."

After the troops departed, Lottridge, Secord and Powell, who had not gone on the raid, resumed their search for the missing boy. Reaching the hovel where they suspected he was living, they were surprised to find the family standing outside, wrapped in blankets and shivering in the cold.

Once again the father grunted, "White brothers, we have no papoose."

Powell grinned. "Of course not, but we'll have a look inside anyway." A brightly burning fire greeted them. "My, that feels pleasant. You'd think everybody'd be in here."

"Yes, it is sort o' strange," Lottridge agreed as he looked around the room. "Sure is nothing here but that pile of animal pelts."

"The family's skunked us again." Secord stalked to the door. "Come on, Powell; let's go."

"Wait a minute. This ground is dry. So why are the skins stacked up instead of being used?" He leaned down to examine a pelt, when a squaw who had been watching from the doorway threw herself onto the furs. "Oh no, you don't. Get up," he commanded.

As the three men tore apart the pile, an emaciated white boy jumped to his feet and darted into a corner of the hovel, cowering. The squaw rushed over, knelt down and clasped him to her. He curled up, putting his arms around her to merge into the folds of her rags while she gently began rocking him.

"You've fooled us long enough." Lottridge tried to separate the two.

"No. He is my son. My son! Brothers, harken: This boy has the spirit of my dead baby. Now he is my flesh and blood. I love him above all things, above myself. Take him and you take my life."

Powell touched her shoulder. "Sister, attend: Lend a loving ear: Have you enough food to feed your dearest child? Show your love by releasing him."

The squaw stopped rocking to ponder his words, then abruptly stood the boy up. Unfastening two pins from her blouse, she attached them to his tattered shirt and turned him around toward the officers. "Brothers, take my son."

The child set his face, silently, showing no emotion as the captain led him away.

Since the route to headquarters led past Barrack A, John Powell impulsively decided to stop there first. "Boy, I'd like to show you to a very nice squaw. Maybe she'll be able to help you find your real mama."

183

When Jaynie Moore spotted the group approaching, she flew to the door. "John!"

"See what I brought you."

Jane Campbell took one look and ran to the boy. "Matthew, Matthew!"

"Ma . . . ." He stifled the cry and stood dumbly.

"My son, you do remember me. Thank God." She dropped down to embrace him. "Sweet little lamb." He did not resist, but his thin face and sunken eyes registered bewilderment.

Colonel Bolton authorized special rations for Matthew, as he had for Samuel, and in time the child's body lost its emaciated look. Nevertheless, his face seemed haunted and he often mumbled to Jane in Seneca, pointing to his two pins and then outside. Manfully he struggled, as his Indian mother had taught him, to show no emotion. At night, however, he would sob himself to sleep.

Jane would listen in anguish, knowing he was too old to forget, and unable to console him; she had to wait for him to accept her as his mother again.

The wait, however, was less than she feared, ending one day when the children returned from gathering fallen fruit in the orchard behind the Stone House.

Matthew presented his share of apples and pears to Jane. "Mama, for you."

"Oh, thank you. We'll save the seeds and take them back to Cherry Valley." Jane kissed him; Matthew did not shrink away.

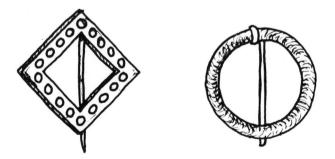

The two Indian trade silver pins. *Sketched from a drawing in Rufus A. Grider's scrapbook, New York State Library, Albany.* Note: the circle pin is now in the Cherry Valley Historical Association.

42

Love

Colonels Johnson and Butler, and Chief Brant, returned from Oswego after barely three weeks, their expedition against the Oneidas cancelled. Sir John and his troops had sailed on to Carleton Island and winter quarters.

Jane turned to her friends in the sewing circle. "Don't you think all that is very strange?"

"Not particularly," Jaynie Moore answered. "Knowing the Indians, I can guess what happened."

Mary Moore jabbed her needle into a ruffled cuff. "You and your precious Indians!"

"Mother, they're not my precious Indians." She sighed, then continued, "Even though most of the Oneidas have sided with us, they're still Iroquois. So I'll bet Oneonta's warriors refused to destroy their Rebel brothers' villages and lands."

Captain Powell on his next visit to Barrack A pointedly avoided any mention of things military. "How are little Matthew and Samuel getting along, Mrs. Campbell?"

"Quite well. Aren't you kind to ask."

"I'm concerned." Nonchalantly sauntering to where Jaynie was sitting, John Powell leaned over her shoulder. "I see your needle is as agile as your tongue."

She peeked up. "Is that a compliment?" Flustered, she hastily returned to her work.

"I don't suppose you'd have any time to sew a shirt for me?"

"Perhaps. Let me take your measurements."

As the tape encircled his chest, John whispered in her ear. "Please go for a stroll with me in the orchard." His lips lightly kissed her lobe.

"Oh!" Jaynie blushed a deep red. "Oh no, I really shouldn't."

"Say yes." He reached for her hand and caressed it an instant.

"All right. I'll go." Never before had she measured so rapidly.

Once outside the barrack Jaynie bluntly confronted the captain. "Exactly what do you do in the Indian Department? I've been wondering ever since I met you."

"You have, have you?" He cocked his head quizzically.

"After all, you're the enemy; I shouldn't be seeing you."

"You really wouldn't want that, would you?" John put his arm around her shoulders. "I guess you have a right to know. But I don't want to offend you."

"Isn't it better to be honest?"

"I wish I could deny that my comrades and I had ever taken part in the Cherry Valley raid or in any other excursions. But I can't."

Jaynie remained silent, waiting for him to continue.

"In my own defense, you must believe that I've always tried to prevent the warriors in my company from killing and scalping innocent civilians. On the other hand, try as hard as we might, we can't make the Indians fight according to white men's rules."

Jaynie twisted the gold ring. "And what about plunder?"

"Well, we do take plunder; that's war." John hurried on. "In recent months my duties have been less disagreeable."

"I should hope so."

"I work among the Indians to see what can be done to relieve their suffering. Meanwhile I try to locate white captives and arrange for their release."

"Like Mary?"

"Yes. And that brings me to a piece of good news. I've finally received permission to leave for Buffalo Creek. My main purpose will be to find your sister."

"And bring her back." Jaynie grabbed his arm. "Oh, thank you."

"Not so quickly, my dear. I'm not even setting off right away. Any moment Molly Brant's to arrive from Carleton Island for a big Indian council."

"When will you be leaving?"

"As soon as it's over. With the Iroquois that probably means their powwow will last three or four days." Powell took her by the shoulders and studied her expression. "Do my answers satisfy you?"

"I think so." Jaynie paused, returning his gaze.

"Good. Now it's my turn to ask questions. Can you look beyond my war time activities, ahead to peace and another life?"

"John, I don't know now."

They had walked through the orchard and along the breezy lakeshore, not stopping until they reached the Niagara River. Putting his arms around Jaynie, Powell drew her tightly to him. They kissed, gently, then fiercely. He caressed her wind-blown hair, pushing a curl from her ear. "I love you."

"I love you."

He stepped back, fighting to control his emotions. "Look over there, across the river. After this war is ended, I hope to settle nearby and raise a family." He turned and looked at her tenderly, then gave her a prolonged kiss. "I want you."

"I love you, too, John, but we scarcely know one another. And you're. . . . It's all too crazy."

"Yes, it is crazy, but's wonderful, isn't it."

Arm in arm they walked silently back toward the Stone House; their love and desire needed no words.

43

Mary Brant

Rounding the corner of the building John and Jaynie saw Molly Brant and a large group of Indians passing through the blockhouse portals. In the center of the drill ground stood Colonels Bolton, Johnson and Butler and their welcoming party.

"Duty calls, my love." John kissed her hand, then hurried off to join the officers.

Wanting time to think, Jaynie did not immediately return to the barrack, but joined a crowd of soldiers and Indians, women and children that had gathered to greet *Deyonwadonti*, Mary Brant. "How can *that* woman be so powerful that they've waited for her to come all the way from Carleton Island to start the powwow?" Fascinated by Miss Molly's many silver ornaments dangling from her ears, by her red skirt and leggings ornately embroidered with quill work, she wondered if the squaw were as wise as she was striking.

The welcoming ceremonies over, Jaynie returned to the barrack.

Abigail whispered, "How's John?"

"Marvelous. I'll tell you later." Casually she took her seat and resumed sewing.

"My dear, weren't you and Captain Powell gone a long time?" Mary Moore asked with biting sweetness. "I trust the stroll was pleasant."

"Yes, it was pleasant, thank you. He told me he'd soon be leaving for Buffalo Creek to look for our Mary and other captives."

"Well, it's about time someone did."

"By the way, ladies," Jaynie raised her voice for all to hear, "did you see Miss Molly arriving for a council?"

"That she-devil," her mother snorted. "I'll never forget how she tried to have Colonel Stacy killed."

"Killed?" The new prisoners looked up, curious.

"Indeed. It all happened while Miss Molly was visiting Niagara last year."

"Oh, let me tell it, Mother," Abigail interrupted, her eyes sparkling with excitement. "After all, I heard it first, when I was here last winter.

"As soon as the squaw learned that Stacy had arrived at the fort, she went to Colonel Butler. 'Give me the Yankee's head. Last night I dreamed my Indians and I were kicking it around the parade ground like a football.'

" 'Impossible, quite impossible,' Butler replied. 'Let me send you a substitute, a small keg of rum.'

"Miss Molly was indignant. 'Why small?'

" 'To look like the Yankee's head. I'll even paint his face on it.'

"No sooner had the Indians drunk the last drop than the thirsty squaw dreamed once more. 'Give me Stacy's head,' she again demanded, 'but mind you, now our football is wearing a hat.'

" 'All right,' Butler said, 'I'll send you a larger keg, big enough to add a painted hat.' Whereupon he rushed Stacy off to Chambly prison near Montreal, for his own safety."

Although the women in Barrack A considered Mary Brant to be a witch, the Indians regarded her as their motherly adviser. Her return to Niagara proved to them she cared not only for her fellow Mohawks, but also for the entire Iroquois Confederacy. Her mere presence lifted their morale.

Guy Johnson stood with Miss Molly, Bolton and Butler before the great council fire, the assembled chiefs waiting expectantly. "Mistress Mary Deyonwadonti and Great Brothers of the Six Nations, O Sago." The pudgy Indian Superintendent raised his hand in greeting. "Oneonta's perpetual love and concern for you, his children, has brought us together. As his representatives, we hold your welfare next to our hearts, suffering in spirit to see our brothers suffering in body.

"Brothers," Johnson continued, "now open an understanding ear: In times past, Fort Niagara's mantle of safety could cover you, but it is no longer large enough; your numbers have become too great. Before the ice of winter, lead your people away. Seek other shelter, other places of refuge. Some of you can go to Carleton Island. Some can return to the villages the Yankees did not destroy. Those of you with strong arms and sharp axes can form new settlements. Only leave Niagara. Like birds, fly away to other nests and survive."

Miss Molly spoke up. "Brothers and Nephews, harken. Again open an understanding ear: Niagara is still a giant eagle able to protect its family. But the family has grown too numerous to feed and shelter in one nest. As many as possible must fly away before the vast cold. Oh great chiefs, I beg of you, send families back with me to Carleton Island; that outpost can provide food for their survival."

"Sister and Brothers of the Great Fort, you also attend," the chief warrior responded. "Lend a contrary ear: To survive, all Iroquois must live together. As one we must remain at Niagara. United we can take up the hatchet and go out on the warpath. If attacked during the snows of winter, we can protect one another.

"Further attend: With the earliest buds of spring, we can seek the blood of our enemies. If it be the will of the Great Spirit, we shall die fighting, but never will we abandon our country. Never again will we flee. Naho!"

Molly Brant departed in defeat, taking with her only a handful of Mohawks.

The refugees surrounding Niagara now numbered close to three thousand.

44

Buffalo Creek

"Captain Powell, do take off your greatcoat and stay a moment."
Jane Campbell started toward him.

"No, Ma'am, I wish I could, but I'm just here to say good-bye. I'm heading for Buffalo Creek to search for missing captives."

"At last." She paused. "We all pray you'll find our children."

"Yes," Mary Moore broke in, "but this time, if you find my Mary, bring her back."

"I'll do my best." John Powell looked around the sewing circle. "Ladies, please remember I cannot work miracles." Turning to Jaynie he asked, "Would you accompany me to the sally port?"

Once outside, he took her hand and entwined his fingers with hers. "I've a confession to make. Thinking of you disturbed my concentration at the Indian council."

"Are you saying, kind sir, that you find me more interesting than Molly Brant?"

Powell looked around, making sure no one was in sight, then kissed her again and again. "Does that answer your question?"

"Yes, darling."

"I love you, Jaynie. When I return, I want to talk about. . . ." He cut himself short; his companion was approaching. John quickly began to study the gloomy November skies. "The cloud over the Falls seems darker than usual. If we don't get snow, we should reach there by nightfall and Buffalo Creek by tomorrow."

"When will you return?"

"We could be back in two weeks." He sighed, gazing upon her adoringly. "An eternity."

"Oh, John, for me, too."

Several days later.

Jaynie stared out the window at the swirling blizzard. "At this rate," she announced, "John will never get back in two weeks—or even in three."

"Last year this time the first snows were covering Cherry Valley." Mary Moore became teary-eyed. "We should have fled long before the Indians came. Oh, where is our dear, sweet Mary?"

"And what about John? Mother, he might be dying out there looking for her and James."

"Now, now, my dear," Jane Campbell reassured her, "he's a white Indian and knows how to survive. So stop worrying about your nice captain."

Mary threw down her sewing and glowered. "Yes, he is nice, but he's definitely not Jaynie's captain; he's an enemy officer!"

"Of course John is an enemy officer now, Mother, but don't condemn him for that. The war won't last forever."

Early December, 1779.

The sewing circle marked the fourth week of Powell's absence. Jaynie watched and waited ever more impatiently, for the weather had turned warmer and melted all snow and ice. "Surely now he'll come back."

Abigail asked impishly, "And who is 'he'? "

"Sister, don't be ridiculous; you know perfectly well I mean John."

"Stop squabbling, children, and tell me where those soldiers and Indians are taking that load of fish."

Jaynie got up to look. "I suppose they're taking them to be salted down. I heard Bolton gave orders to put away as many as possible before winter returns."

"If only that cruel Haldimand hadn't halted all supply ships on the lake last month."

"But Mother, how could he know we'd have a thaw in early December?"

"Don't take up for the British at every turn. Jaynie, you're impossible."

"For heaven's sake. Oh, what's the use."

The women sewed on in silence.

Jaynie suddenly pointed to a solitary figure approaching from the sally port. "Look; he's here. John!" She raced out to meet him and threw herself into his arms. "John, I thought you'd never get back."

He gave her a peck on the lips. "That'll have to do for now. Let's go inside and face your mother and Mrs. Campbell."

As the two walked through the door, Mary Moore cried out, "Where's my daughter?"

"It's good to have you back, Captain," Jane Campbell said. "We've missed you."

"Yes, John, all of us." Jaynie reached out to take his coat.

"Daughter, don't distract him."

"As you see, Ma'am, I've returned empty-handed, but not without news.

"We reached Buffalo Creek just as the blizzard hit." Powell drew up a chair and sat down. "But we were lucky; some refugee families took us in. Being snowbound, we had plenty of time to talk round the fire and question everyone. Finally we gathered enough information to figure that several captives were nearby."

"But did you find my Mary?"

"Yes. And as soon as we could get around on snowshoes, we ferreted her out plus a couple of others, but no young children such as James. Alas, we were never allowed to talk with any of them."

"How is Mary? What did she look like?"

Powell hesitated. "She looked . . . very thin, but all right." He could not bring himself to tell her mother he had seen the girl crouched in the corner of a hovel, shivering under rotting shreds of a blanket.

"Is she still as pretty as ever?"

"Mother," Jaynie interrupted, "how could he tell? John, please go on."

"Each time we asked the Indians to release their captives, they refused. 'We have no captives,' they said, 'only white relatives.'

"I offered them gifts.

"Then they protested, 'Indians do not sell family.'

"So I reminded them they'd be needing seed and hoes.

"That did it; they relented, saying, 'Drop off supplies in early spring. Return after planting season.' "

Abigail asked almost fearfully. "Do you think the Indians will release their captives afterwards?"

"I hope so, I pray so, but your mother will have to keep on waiting." John Powell looked around at the dejected faces which only a month ago had been so full of hope. He stood up, walked over to Jane Campbell and put his hand on her shoulder. "I tried."

"Yes, I know you did. Thank you. My James must be. . . ." Her voice broke.

He turned to Mrs. Moore, who opened her mouth to speak, but instead collapsed in tears.

"Oh, John." Jaynie took his hand and guided him out the door. "How can we ever thank you? You risked your life to find Mary." She reached up to kiss him and buried herself in his arms.

45

Yes, When?

Snow, sleet and winds stormed over Niagara, so freezing cold that the sewing circle could hardly work. Although their fingers turned to ice, the women refused to add another log to the fire, fearful of burning too much costly wood. They were hungry, too, for the price of food had risen and their income was threatened; sewing supplies were running low.

Jane Campbell faced an even greater worry—her eyesight. Lately, no matter how she held her work, whether farther away or closer, her eyes would begin to tear and she could not see.

She confided her fears to Mary Moore. "If my eyes get any worse, I won't be able to sew at all." Then she would have no money to buy extra food for the children.

"The girls and I will help you," the older woman volunteered. "Back home, imagine either of us worrying about food or firewood or sewing supplies."

"Yes, home." Jane caressed the word. She could almost hear Sam's cheerful voice calling out, 'I'm home. It's eleven o'clock; morning chores are done and I've earned a glass of bitters.' She pictured him sitting beside her while she twisted the flax on her spinning wheel. She heard the noisy laughter of their children playing.

"Mrs. Campbell, you're not listening."

"I'm sorry; I was just remembering. If only I knew about Willie and James. Not knowing is such torture."

Mary leaned close to Jane and clutched her arm to make sure of her attention. "Seeing my daughter romancing with the enemy is also torture."

"Yes, I can see how it might be." On the other hand, she thought Jaynie's romance with John Powell was the one bright spot in their otherwise dreary lives. Everyone welcomed his daily visits and looked forward to his recounting the latest news. She did wonder, however, how he could do his courting with so many hovering females around.

Jaynie was asking herself the same question. "I don't know what to do," she confessed to her sister. "Should I encourage him to propose? Or should I stop seeing him?"

Abigail giggled. "Don't be silly; he's fascinating and so handsome."

"Be serious. How can I leave my family, and friends, and home? To marry an enemy?"

"Well, I never thought about it like that." Abigail's face turned solemn.

"But you know, our home is gone and our friends may all be dead. Besides, doesn't the Bible say a girl leaves her family when she marries?"

"You're right, Jaynie. And when peace comes."

"Yes. John won't be our enemy."

* * *

Mary Moore drew Jaynie aside, putting an arm around her daughter's shoulder. "What's troubling you, dear? You've hardly said a word for days."

"I may as well tell you, Mother; I'm worrying about John, Captain Powell, I mean." She sighed. "I love him and he loves me. I know he'll ask me to marry him, and I want to accept but I don't want to hurt you."

"What!" Mary reared back. "How can you be so contrary even to think of marrying an enemy, especially one who helped destroy your own house? You've seen with your very eyes what he does: he burns and plunders our settlements, then looks the other way when the Indians murder our kinsfolk and friends." She shook her finger. "All your family are Rebels and proud of it. How can you humiliate us?"

"But Mother."

"And above all, how can you leave me?"

"I love him." Jaynie threw herself onto her bunk, burying her face in a blanket, weeping disconsolately.

The sewing circle stitched on silently.

In time Jane Campbell slipped over and sat down beside the girl.

197

"Don't cry, my dear. Tears won't solve anything."

"I'm so miserable. You couldn't help but hear what Mother said. I love my family. But I also love John and can't imagine life without him."

"I understand." She stroked Jaynie's hair. "You have to remember, however, John is a Loyalist, though a charming one. Can you accept his Loyal sentiments? Can you forgive him for helping destroy Cherry Valley? Can you forgive him for being the enemy?"

Jaynie sat up to listen.

"God willing, the war won't last forever," Jane continued. "Then John will be starting a new life and wanting a helpmeet to share in his future. Do you love him enough to be part of that future?"

"Oh yes, positively yes."

"Are you willing to cut all your ties and make entirely new allegiances?"

Jaynie hesitated, then nodded. "I think so."

"Still, before you commit yourself, search your soul to be sure."

"I wish my mother were as sympathetic as you."

"Don't be so hard on her. She's been through a great deal, as have we all. She's worried sick about young Mary and now she's afraid of losing you."

"She'd lose me no matter whom I married."

"Your John has a strong character, and he's certainly considerate of everyone here." She paused. "I think he'd make a good husband."

"Oh yes, he would! Yes, I must have him, no matter what." She jumped up from her bunk. "Now you've got to help me catch him. And persuade Mother, too."

"Catching him will be no problem, but persuading your mother, that's another story." Jane Campbell shook her head. "Well, all right, I'll do my best."

The very next morning Jane broached the subject to Mary Moore. "My friend, you have to realize Jaynie's made up her mind. She's set her heart upon marrying John Powell."

"She's being headstrong and defiant."

"Call it whatever you wish. In my opinion, John is a fine man, worthy of your daughter, and unless you accept the situation graciously, you'll lose her now, before we ever return home. Think about it."

The two women sewed on in silence.

"Mrs. Campbell, do I really have a choice?"

"No."

From then on, after the captain brought the daily news, he and Jaynie were allowed to drift toward the rear of the barrack, behind the backs of the sewing circle. Ears, however, strained to hear snatches of the couple's conversation.

"Colonel Bolton had the troops drilling this morning," John announced in a loud voice. "They had to clear off more than a foot of snow." He took Jaynie's fingers, kissed them and held them against his cheeks.

Jaynie, following his lead, also spoke for the benefit of the listening ears. "I noticed the lake is starting to freeze." She tittered and gave an appropriate shiver before snuggling into his arms. "Do you like ice fishing?"

"Yes, but only if I have the right companion." They kissed long and passionately.

Each night the Moore girls whispered to one another across their bunks, Jaynie always asking, "When will he propose?"

"Maybe tomorrow."

"Oh Abigail, why is being in love such divine misery?"

John Powell was equally miserable. "Lottridge, how'll I ever ask her to marry me with females eavesdropping on our every syllable?"

"Why don't you take her for a stroll?"

"You've lost your senses. Can't you just see me dropping onto my knees in all this snow?" They both laughed. "No, I need some fascinating news that will occupy those gossipy women."

The opportunity arrived, but not as he would have wished.

"Scurvy has broken out among the Indians and also among the Rangers at Butlersbury," the captain announced. "Alas, our cranberry supply is used up and the reserves of cider vinegar are perilously low."

"What else can the doctor use to combat the disease?"

"He doesn't seem to know."

At last the sewing circle was abuzz with an all-consuming conversation, and the lovers could retire in privacy.

Glancing around to make sure everyone was indeed occupied, John quickly knelt and took Jaynie's hands. "I love you. Will you marry me?"

"Yes! When?"

His ordeal over, he heaved a sigh of relief, clambered to his feet and drew Jaynie tightly to him. He smothered her with kisses, relaxing his embrace only long enough to whisper, "As soon as possible."

199

46

May I?

John Powell fingered his cap nervously as he entered Colonel Bolton's sickroom where Colonel Guy Johnson was already waiting. He swallowed hard and took a deep breath. "Sirs, I wish to marry one of the prisoners here, Miss Jaynie Moore of Cherry Valley. As soon as possible."

Johnson coughed discretely into a ruffled cuff. "I understand what you mean, but duty forces me to cite General Haldimand. Our Commander-in-Chief disapproves of marriage in the military; a soldier's first obligations must be to the war effort and to his country."

"I've always served with spirit and zeal, sir."

"True, but you should realize how distracting a wife can be, and especially an enemy wife."

"Sir, Miss Moore may be an enemy, but she is deeply concerned about the welfare of our Indian allies."

"Oh?" Johnson pursed his lips in surprise, then sputtered, "Even so, Captain, you must admit such a marriage would be impolitic."

"Impolitic?" Bolton interrupted from the middle of a sea of blankets. "I wonder. As I consider the matter, the liaison would actually improve morale here at the fort."

"How so, sir?"

"Since your young lady comes from a notorious Rebel family, isn't she tacitly acknowledging the rightfulness of His Majesty's cause?"

The captain smiled enigmatically.

"In short, Powell, as commandant of Niagara, my answer is 'Yes.' Of course, I can't speak for your colonel here."

Johnson positioned a hand upon his sword and drew himself up to full height. "Taking into consideration Colonel Bolton's remarks and my own thoughts, I do believe that I, too, am inclined to view the marriage in a favorable light. As Superintendent of the Indian Department, I possess final authority to grant or deny permission, that is, without consulting His Excellency General Haldimand. Accordingly, it is my determination to grant the petition."

"Thank you, sirs." Powell beamed with relief. "And as for the date. . . ."

Bolton feebly raised a hand. "Not so fast, Captain. You have one more hurdle, publishing the banns in Chapel for the next three Sundays. If no one objects, you and Miss Moore are free to marry any time thereafter."

"Until then," Johnson added, "you'll have to wait patiently, or is it impatiently?"

All three men laughed.

The sewing circle did not wait for even the first Sunday to pass before they began to work on two simple outfits for the bride's trousseau. And the prospect of a wedding did lift morale at the fort; everyone delighted to see love blooming in the midst of hatred and death.

47

A Celebration

January 1, 1780.

"Happy Birthday, Mama." Elly gave Jane a big hug and kiss.

Samuel and Matthew threw their arms around her. "You're our special mama."

"Thank you, my sweethearts. Perhaps this time next year our whole family will be together again." Smiling, she thought, "At least I can dream."

Early that afternoon John Powell and several other officers arrived. "Surprise. Surprise for Mrs. Campbell. Happy Birthday." They laid a small object in her lap.

"Spectacles." Trembling, Jane put them on, picked up some sewing and beamed. "I see perfectly—every stitch. Why, it's miraculous!"

"Not exactly." Powell smiled sheepishly. "A soldier in the Corps of Artificers made them for us." He strode out the door, only to return with an armful of dark brown fur which he deposited at Jaynie's feet. "And these are for you, my love."

"Beaver pelts. How wonderful." She knelt down to admire them. "Oh John, there are enough here to line a cloak and hood and even make a matching muff."

"I thought you'd like them." Flushed with embarrassment, he turned to the gaping women. "And now I have a surprise for all of you here, an invitation to the Stone House. This year's reception is in honor of Miss Jaynie Moore of Cherry Valley." He bowed in her direction, offered his arm and escorted her toward the door. "Come along, everyone."

John Powell shepherded the group into the Great Hall at headquarters. Colonel Bolton was already there, wrapped in a bearskin and valiantly receiving his guests.

"May I present my betrothed."

"My best wishes, Miss Moore. We're all looking forward to your wedding."

"Oh yes, thank you, sir."

"Her mother. And her sister Abigail."

"You have two beautiful daughters, Madam."

"No, three, but. . . ."

"Ah, Mrs. Campbell," Bolton pointedly interrupted.

"Good afternoon, Colonel." Jane was somewhat startled to be remembered; little did she realize how many of his letters had discussed her exchange. "You're most kind to include us all in these festivities." As she walked on toward the punch table, Mary Moore grabbed her arm. "Look. There's Colonel Butler. Who's the squaw he's with?"

"Isn't that Lyn Montour, Queen Catherine's daughter?"

"No wonder she's familiar. That spawn of a she-dog," Mary hissed. "If his son Walter does marry her, he'll be getting exactly what he deserves."

"He deserves worse than that." Jane drew her shawl closer, chilled from the very reminder of Walter and the long march from Cherry Valley. "Do you realize we haven't laid eyes on him since we've been here?"

Abigail chimed in, "I heard he's on an expedition into Ohio country." She lowered her voice. "To try and keep the Indians there from deserting the British."

Musicians struck up a Highland fling, interrupting their conversation. No sooner had Powell and Jaynie opened the dancing than Colonel Guy Johnson, Joseph Brant and his wife walked directly across the floor, cutting a pathway to the commandant. They proceeded slowly, as if inviting the onlookers to admire them.

Guy Johnson was wearing a scarlet British uniform complete with gold lace, ruffles, silk sash, cocked hat and sword. Abigail stifled a giggle. "Does he really think all that finery will hide the fact he's a puffy little toad?"

"Humph," her mother snorted. "Seeing him you'd never think anybody here was on short rations."

Brant's wife was dazzling in her Indian costume of fine blue wool, its gold lace and silver ornaments glittering in the candlelight.

"Well, as I live and breathe," Jane exclaimed, "that's Catherine Croghan." She recognized the daughter of George Croghan and his Mohawk wife; he had been an Indian agent on Lake Otsego.

"Look," Abigail squealed, "look at Joseph Brant."

"Daughter, he might have gotten rid of the blood and scalps, but he's still a savage as far as I'm concerned."

Captain Brant had donned a short, green, British army jacket with silver epaulets and had hung at his side a cutlass sheathed in a silver scabbard. He also wore a breech-cloth and elaborately beaded leggings and moccasins. In contrast to Colonel Johnson, his uniform served to emphasize his spare figure; he looked every inch the warrior-soldier.

After a proper interval, Colonel Bolton retired into his private quarters with Colonel Johnson, Joseph Brant and his wife. The music and dancing resumed, the remaining officers rapidly becoming drunk and amorous.

John Powell offered his arms to Mary Moore and Jaynie. "Perhaps we should be leaving."

"Indeed, yes." Mary looked down her thin nose at the men kissing, ogling and carrying on with every female in sight. "First thing you know they'll be after my Abigail."

"Mother, I'm quite old enough to take care of myself." She flounced over to Jane Campbell.

"Once upon a time that's what those women also said," her mother called back. "Now see what they've come to."

Jane whispered in Abigail's ear. "Yes, look at them; some of those poor creatures are so starved they'll do anything for food."

48

Double Wedding

In the days that followed, more fierce, biting snows and winds pommeled the fort. Relentless sub-zero temperatures changed the Niagara River into solid ice and Lake Ontario froze as far as anyone could see.

Despite daily snow storms and drifts as high as eight feet, Colonel Bolton still insisted upon constant parading. "My men need exercise to keep in fighting trim," he would remark as he gave orders to practice tramping with snowshoes or to shovel clear a patch large enough for marching. "Let them drill until their eyelids freeze and icicles grow from their beards. Only then may they stop."

By sheer force of will the sewing circle worked, ignoring their benumbed fingers; even girls as young as Elly were enlisted to do simple stitching. Everyone was determined to finish the bride's trousseau by the last reading of the banns in the chapel.

"Thank heavens for these wonderful spectacles," Jane Campbell thought as she wiped them clean. "Otherwise I'd never be able to finish my share of the sewing."

By the third Sunday the trousseau was completed and Jaynie modeled her wedding dress: a ruffled blue shift with matching jacket, a quilted petticoat skirt, a white neckerchief and small white cap. "It's beautiful. And how perfectly it shows off the silver belt buckle John gave me." She twirled around. "I love them, and all of you!"

* * *

206

Mary Moore sat beside Jane Campbell in the chapel as Jaynie and John walked down the aisle to the altar. "Doesn't my little girl look radiant."

"Oh yes. And doesn't he look handsome in his captain's uniform. And so proud to have 'captured' her."

"I hope they'll be happy." Mary daubed tears from her cheeks.

"I know they will. They're so right for each other." Jane thought of Sam, of their wedding; her eyes misted over.

At the altar, Colonel John Butler, attired in his green Ranger uniform, stepped forward; in his capacity as King's Commissioner of the Peace for Tryon County, he would perform the ceremony. "Dearly beloved, we are gathered together here in the sight of God. . . .

"I pronounce that they are man and wife. Amen."

"Colonel Butler." A majestic, blue-blanketed figure strode down the aisle: Chief Joseph Brant. "Colonel Butler, wait." The warrior raised his hand to silence the gasps of astonishment. "I have been greatly moved by God's words. You must marry me and my wife in this same ceremony."

"But, but you two are married already."

"Indian weddings are only informal arrangements, and I want a sacrament 'instituted of God'." Brant marched back to his pew, oblivious of everyone's murmurings, and escorted Catherine Croghan to the altar.

Jane leaned over to Mary Moore. "Such hypocrisy. And in God's own house."

"How dare that savage spoil my dear child's beautiful wedding!"

Stunned, John and Jaynie Powell stepped back as Colonel Butler began again. "Dearly beloved . . . ."

The wedding reception took place in the Stone House, where Colonels Bolton and Johnson had provided precious cake and rum.

John Powell nuzzled his bride's ear. "There go Brant and his wife slipping off. They must be bored, leaving before we even begin the dancing. I hope *you're* having a good time."

"Oh darling," she laughed, "of course I am. I love you."

Duty-dancing completed, John brought out the beaver-lined cloak and lovingly enveloped Jaynie in it.

"Mmmm. How delicious." She drew it around, cuddling against her husband.

"You're delicious, too, my dearest."

As John and Jaynie began bidding family and friends good-bye, Mary

Moore pulled them aside. "Don't you think you should stay longer with your guests?"

Jane Campbell, overhearing the question, intervened. "Why, that's the silliest thing I ever heard. Surely you remember your own wedding day."

"Thank you, Mrs. Campbell." John winked, took his bride by the hand and led her over to Colonels Johnson, Bolton and Butler. "Sirs, we are most appreciative."

"Well, Captain, your wait is finally over." Johnson pinched Jaynie's cheek. "Now you're going to learn just how distracting a wife can be."

"Yes, sir. I look forward to that lesson."

The newly-weds left the Stone House and escaped across the frozen Niagara River to Butlersbury. As John carried his bride into their tiny log cabin, she snuggled against him. Ever so slowly he set Jaynie down, pressing her against his body.

The following day they awoke to swirling whiteness outside. "Darling, Mrs. Powell, I do believe we are snowbound."

She nestled closer to him. "I don't mind; you'll keep me warm."

"Yes!" He covered her with kisses.

49

A Mission for Peace

Walls of snow and ice engulfed Butlersbury and Niagara. Freezing storms, high winds and blizzards, rather than the King and his generals, governed the rhythm of life at the fort. Despite fierce gales blowing off Lake Ontario, soldiers still attempted to perform their duties; sentries, although buffeted, managed to cover their rounds, often however, reduced to crawling their beats. On rare days when the winds ceased, thick mists enveloped the fort; the sun was too faint to burn them away.

Colonel Bolton hardly left his sickbed. He scribbled only the most urgent messages, and then huddled beside a fire, blazing and yet so inadequate that the ink froze on his pen.

In Barrack A Jane Campbell and her friends worked listlessly, tortured by sickness and the cold. One young girl had just died of scurvy and several other children suffered from it.

As Jane helped make the dead child's cap and shroud, she glanced anxiously toward Elly, Matthew and Samuel. Even crowded together under all the covers they could find, their thin bodies trembled and shook.

Throughout the fort sickness and death held sway.

On the other side of the walls only the Great Spirit knew the agonies of his Indian children and their intense desire for revenge.

In early February the winds and storms abated. The snow-covered land lay still, its silence shattered by the snapping of an ice-coated tree or by the roar of snow sliding down a roof; snowshoe weather had arrived. To the sounds of war whoops and farewell salvos from the fort's cannon, the Indians departed for the frontier. They were hunting captives and scalps, food and plunder, to avenge their months of suffering. From now on their warring season would last the year round.

"I've lost count of how many raiding parties have already left." Jane peered over the rim of her spectacles. "You know, Mrs. Moore, we're not really out of danger ourselves."

"Why what do you mean?"

"You heard John Powell say the Indians are angry because the family of their good friend Colonel Butler has not yet been exchanged. They could even be angry enough to force the British to give us back."

"I'd sooner die than live with the Senecas again!"

Meanwhile four "Rebel" Indians arrived at the fort from Albany: Chiefs Skenandon, Little Abraham and two others. They had been closely escorted the final miles by Captain Powell, who went out to meet them in order to bring the group directly to Colonel Guy Johnson. Before allowing them to speak with their fellow Iroquois, the colonel and his officers in the Indian Department wanted to learn the purpose of their trip to Niagara.

"O Sago, White Brethren of Niagara." Skenandon folded his arms across his chest. "We are delivering up a letter from our great chief, General Schuyler, to Colonel Guy Johnson."

"Hineaweh." Johnson quickly skimmed the message, noting the key sentence: *"Mrs. Butler will be permitted to proceed to Canada with her family whenever proper assurances are given that Mrs. Campbell and hers* [with Mrs. Moore and daughters] *will have the like indulgence."*

"Further attend," the chief continued. "We are also pleased to hand over a packet of letters for your Loyalist families. One, however, is for Mrs. Colonel Samuel Campbell, friend of our General Schuyler."

"We will distribute them for you." Johnson studied Skenandon's face, waiting to hear the real reason for the chief's mission.

"Brother of Niagara, now listen with a sympathetic ear: We bring a proposal for peace from the great Schuyler to our Iroquois brethren living under your wing. We wish to confer with them."

"Oh Great Chiefs, harken: Your white brethren here assembled are also anxious for peace," Johnson replied coldly, trying to hide his growing suspicions. "Lay down your proposal to us first." He gestured around the room toward Captain Powell and his other officers. "Afterwards we **will** summon your Iroquois family."

"White Brethren, we will do as you wish." Drawing his red and blue-striped blanket around, Skenandon continued, "Listen with a peaceful ear:

211

General Schuyler says, 'Loyal Indians, return to your former lands, settle upon them to live in peace and harmony among yourselves and all white men, both British and Yankee'."

Johnson leaped up, bursting with anger. "Emissaries of General Schuyler, enough. We ourselves will deliver that message to your Iroquois family. In the meantime you will be detained in private quarters. Naho!"

As soon as the four Indians had been removed from the room, Johnson turned to Powell and the other officers. "That Schuyler is a wily one; thought he'd neutralize our Indian allies by proposing peace."

"Sir," Powell pointed out, "he might yet succeed unless we keep Skenandon and his group separated from them."

"You're right, Captain. For appearances' sake, I'll allow them to confer a few times with Old Smoke and other 'Loyal Chiefs,' but only in our presence. We must prevent them from sowing their evil seed among our allies."

After several days of such fruitless conferences, the envoys wished to leave, but instead were thrust into the "black hole," the windowless dungeon of the Stone House. Had they returned to Albany, Johnson feared, they might have proved useful spies to General Schuyler. Little Abraham was to die in chains. Skenandon and his two surviving companions would not go home until after the war.

Colonel Johnson and the Indian Department had thwarted Schuyler's "peace efforts." The officers, however, did decide to turn their attention to the Butler-Campbell exchange. Therefore, Captain Powell would return to Mary Moore's Indian family as soon as possible and attempt to secure his sister-in-law's release; and the entire corps would be sent out to try and find James Campbell.

50

For Humanity's Sake

Jane Campbell looked at John Powell in amazement. "You mean General Schuyler has actually written to Colonel Johnson about us? And James and Mary might yet. . . ."

"Have you forgotten Buffalo Creek?" Mary Moore interrupted. "He found my daughter, but didn't bring her back. So don't get your hopes up."

"Madam, you're much too pessimistic." The captain could barely conceal his annoyance with his mother-in-law as he brought out Skenandon's packet and began distributing letters. To his great relief the women were too overjoyed to ask how they had been delivered.

Jane trembled as she unfolded Sam's letter. She scarcely noted that it was worn from having gone through many hands. She could almost hear his voice:

Dearest Wife,

I hope my few lines may find you and our children as well in health as are William and I. . . .

"Children, Willie's alive! He and Papa are all right." Elly and the boys clustered around, straining to look at the writing.

We send you all our love.

I hear word of you through our friends in Albany, who receive letters on your behalf from Canada. We thank Almighty God to learn you are yet amongst the living and trust that with His aid you will in short be restored to us.

By this post I have forwarded a warrant for monies to be issued as necessary in your behalf. I am in hopes it will help relieve your disagreeable circumstances.

Until our joyful reunion, I remain, dear wife,

> Your ever loving husband until death,
> Samuel Campbell

Underneath was another precious message:

P.S. Mama, I love you. Come home soon. We miss you awful much.

> Your son,
> Willie

*   *   *

In Quebec on that same day, February 12, 1780, General Haldimand was writing to Colonel Butler at Niagara:

A flag [of safe conduct] shall be sent, in the course of a few days, requiring that Mrs. Butler and family be sent into [Canada, via Lake Champlain and Fort St. John], in exchange for Mrs. Campbell's [and Mrs. Moore's] family rescued from the Indians for that purpose. Colonel Bolton shall be informed of the result.

The very next day that flag did leave Fort St. John to pick up Mrs. Butler in Albany. The commandant, Brigadier General Henry Watson Powell [no relation to John], sent an accompanying letter to the American commander there, Colonel Goosen Van Schaick. The colonel had been authorized by General Schuyler to *"negotiate the business* [of the exchange]."

Watson Powell specified the rules and procedures:

[As soon as possible Mrs. Butler and her family must be given] safe conduct to my advance post upon Lake Champlain in order that they cross the Lake before the ice breaks up. On their arrival in this province the utmost dispatch shall be used [to return Mrs. Campbell, Mrs. Moore and their families].

The general gave a second reason for hastening the proceedings:

humanity . . . the Indians being already much displeased that the exchange has not taken place. . . . If it should be [further] delayed, they will expect to have their prisoners restored to them. . . . Altho their lives would be in perfect security. . . , [he did not hesitate to threaten] that event . . . must necessarily subject them to many painful circumstances.

Colonel Van Schaick replied the same day that Watson Powell's letter arrived, February 23.

[I, too, am motivated by] humanity. [Mrs. Butler and her party] will be immediately advised that they have permission to proceed to Canada whenever they please.

At long last Albany and Quebec decided to move their pawns. But they reckoned without the Indians, who still held two captives and who could still reclaim all the others.

51

Carnival

While the inhabitants of Fort Niagara were barely sustaining life, Montrealers were reveling in Carnival season.

Despite twenty years of English rule, the city was still more French than English. The *Habitants* were indifferent supporters of King George, ofttimes openly aiding their American friends. The merchants were concerned more that the war not disturb their lucrative fur trade and their wives, more that French dressmaking supplies not be interrupted. In the main only the British and their Loyalist allies flocking to Canada cared about the war.

Captains Walter Butler and John McDonell, newly arrived in Montreal from their Ohio expedition, threw themselves into the season's festivities; they were anxious to forget the war and eager to enjoy the parties.

"We do very little else but feasting and dancing. It has nearly turned my head," Walter wrote on February 21, 1780. *"I find it as hard as scouting. In order to change the scene, McDonell and me intend to make a tour of the mountain every other day on snowshoes."*

He did not, however, reckon on the young wife of an older merchant called down to Quebec on business. Butler and she met at a Carnival ball.

McDonell and Walter had scarcely entered the ballroom when they noticed Madame X. She was wearing an emerald green satin dress, and her auburn hair, piled high on her head, was crowned with matching green ribbons. Entranced, the two officers watched her graceful movements as she danced first with one admirer and then another.

"Etiquette be damned," Walter announced. He adjusted his uniform jacket, smoothed his black hair, and with hand on sword, glided off to present himself to her.

"*Capitaine*, I am *enchantée* to meet such a *distingué* soldier." Her eyes seemed to tease. "I 'ave perhaps 'eard of your *grands exploits?*"

"Perhaps, but let us forget the war."

She smiled and asked, "For 'ow long are you 'ere in our city?"

"Alas, for not long enough." His eyes wandered downward. "What a beautiful necklace you are wearing. Is it French?"

"*Mais oui.* You are very clever to be so observing."

"On the contrary." He smiled, thinking, "My dear Madame, how can I help from noticing it and the bosom it covers?"

The next day as he was leaving headquarters, Madame X happened by in her sleigh. "May I offer to take *monsieur le capitaine* 'ome?"

The home was hers.

"My dear Walter, you 'ave no *idée* the loneliness I feel. My life is so cold, so *misérable.*"

"Let me comfort you." He put his arm around her shoulders. "You are too precious."

"*O merci.*" She nestled close. "I can be no more *misérable,* for you will be my *grand comfort. Oui?*"

"*Oui!*"

They embraced tentatively, then furiously, oblivious of family, friends, duties, loyalties, everyone, everything.

52

Captain Alexander Harper

At Niagara the brutal winter continued until the middle of March, when the first hints of spring brought relief from the cold but not from hunger. Indian hunting parties seldom returned with fresh game; more often they carried back the frozen carcasses of starved deer. Soldiers, despite the dangers of shifting ice, tried to fish.

The sewing circle could only wait, their patience exhausted. Sam's warrant for money, however, was some consolation to Jane and Mrs. Moore; at least they could now supplement their meager food rations and even sew clothes for themselves.

"How 'll I ever pay back Colonel Campbell?"

"For heaven's sake, don't concern yourself about that." Jane could scarcely hide her irritation. "Why don't you fret about how we're going to get home."

Niagara awoke to yet another snowstorm. Ferocious winds raised up huge blocks of ice in the lake, shoving one on top of the other and releasing waters to pound against the shore and walls of the fort. Then torrential rains melted the snow and ice and turned bare patches on the parade grounds into larger and larger pools of water until they formed a small lake. Soon the entire fort was flooded.

Barrack A did not need to be evacuated, but other parts of the fort were not so fortunate. In addition, many precious provisions were destroyed and part of the fruit orchard was washed away by Lake Ontario.

Mid-April 1780.

At last the flood waters receded, leaving a sea of mud and slime. Once John Powell and other officers were finally able to make their rounds among the Indians, they discovered hundreds of corpses, mostly old people and small children. Their putrifying bodies lay scattered in the mire or tossed into hovels and caves; some dangled in high tree branches, protected from ravenous bears and wolves.

When Jaynie Powell stopped by to visit her family, Mary Moore immediately confronted her. "Your husband's got to get rid of that smell of dead Indians; it's nauseating."

"John's men are working full time to collect the remains and bury them, Mother."

Unspoken was the worry: did James and young Mary survive the winter?

* * *

John Powell scraped the mud off his boots, then greeted the waiting Jaynie with a kiss.

"I can tell something's wrong."

"Yes." He took Jaynie by the shoulders. "Joseph Brant has just sent me a special message by runner: his war party is bringing in a number of prisoners from Schoharie, and in particular, one militia captain Alexander Harper."

"Uncle Alexander, oh no! They'll make him run the gantlet."

"Yes, but perhaps there's hope. Joseph also said, 'Prepare for their reception accordingly.' "

"Meaning?" Jaynie looked quizzical.

"I'm to do whatever I can to save your uncle and the others."

"What have you in mind?"

"I'm still puzzling, for they've got to run the gantlet. At the Seneca's village of Neahgah and also at their encampment next to the fort. Otherwise the Indians might turn on us, you know."

She thought for a moment. "What about providing a frolic?"

"Darling, you're brilliant." He drew Jaynie close. "And adorable."

* * *

When Brant's war party reached Neahgah, Captain Harper and the other painted captives stared in astonishment, for where were the village's warriors? The Indians exploded in anger: "Why do British soldiers greet us instead of braves? A feeble gantlet of old men, boys and squaws cannot satisfy our thirst for prisoners' blood."

Comprehending, the chief tried to calm his men. "Let this trial be a prelude to the punishment our captives will soon receive at the hands of brothers up the way."

"We will nurse our fury. So be it."

Harper and his fellow prisoners managed to dodge the gantlet's sticks and knives, merely suffering minor injuries. Without a moment's pause the enraged war party drove them onward to the Seneca encampment just outside the fort. Again only old men, boys and squaws met them. This time, however, troops were drilling nearby, forcing the gantlet line to point toward the sally port.

A warrior grabbed Harper and with his tomahawk prodded him to the starting point. "You first. Joggo."

Harper sprang forward, rushing through the flailing weapons, almost untouched until an old Indian stepped out to trip him. He struck the man with his fist, knocked him down, leaped over the body and raced toward the sally port. In yowling fury all the Indians charged in hot pursuit. The door opened, then slammed shut.

Harper was safe inside, leaving his enemies pounding at the gates.

"Captain Harper, welcome to Fort Niagara." John Powell extended a helping hand to the breathless officer.

"The others?" He dropped to the ground, panting.

"Don't worry. My soldiers will rescue them."

"Uncle Alexander." Jaynie threw her arms around him, then drew back and stared at her mother's younger brother. He was bruised and ragged from his ten-day ordeal; she could hardly recognize him through all his war paint.

"Great Scot!"

"The man who saved you is my husband." She gestured toward John. "Captain John Powell of the Indian Department."

"Well, I'll be damned." Harper clambered to his feet and stared him up and down. "A Loyalist. But I'm mighty thankful to you."

"Mother and Abigail are here, too," Jaynie hastened to say. "They're longing to see you."

"How in hell did you know I was coming?"

John spoke up. "Your old schoolmate Joseph Brant sent me word. That gave us time to lure away the warriors with a frolic up the lake a bit."

"So that's where the warriors were. Nothing like the power of rum. Let's drink a toast to old Joseph."

Captain Alexander Harper was soon transferred to Chambly Prison near Montreal, but later was confined in Quebec and Halifax. He returned to the United States only after the peace of 1783.

53

Hope

Quebec, April 16, 1780

Some days ago, [General Haldimand notified Colonel Bolton] a flag arrived in this province from Albany, conducting Mrs. Butler and [her party] . . . . I have given directions that the best care, circumstances will admit of, be taken of them, but the situation of provisions renders it impossible to permit them . . . to proceed to Niagara [at this time].

Reminded of the Indians' impatience concerning the slowness of the exchange, he cautioned Bolton:

As soon as the navigation [on Lake Ontario] will permit, you will send a flag with such officer and party as may be necessary, to give safe conduct to Mrs. Campbell's and [Mrs. Moore's] families captivated by the Indians. If it should be found more convenient on account of the Indians, . . . send them by way of Lake Champlain. You will lose no time in forwarding them to Montreal.

When John Butler heard the news in early May, he immediately wrote General Haldimand:

I am exceedingly obliged to Your Excellency for your attention to procure the liberty of my family. . . .

Since he had not seen his wife and children in five years, he wished to meet them in Montreal.

I hope Your Excellency will indulge me with permission to go down for about a fortnight. [Of course,] I would not make this request if I thought it could in any way materially interfere with the good of His Majesty's service.

John Powell brought the news right away.

"Oh no." Jane pulled off her spectacles in dismay. "But James isn't here yet. I can't possibly leave without him."

"And as for me, Captain," his mother-in-law declared, "until you bring back my Mary, I'm not budging from Niagara. Do you understand me?"

John laughed. "I'm returning to Buffalo Creek this very day—with plenty of food, grain and hoes as well as trinkets for her family."

"Do you think they'll work this time?" Mary Moore demanded, a note of hope entering her voice despite herself.

"They ought to, but I only guarantee they'll be mighty powerful persuaders."

"Captain," Jane asked hesitantly, "what of my James? You haven't said one word about him."

"We're all still searching for your boy, Mrs. Campbell. I promise I'll look again for him in Buffalo Creek; that's the best I can do." He heaved a deep sigh. "Please, ladies, please be patient."

"Don't tell us that," Mary snapped. "We've been patient long enough."

John Powell escaped out the door and the two mothers forced themselves back to their needlework.

Ten days later Powell returned.

"You're alone." Mary's voice started to crack. "Where's my girl?"

"Please, no tears." John sat down beside her. "I've good news for you. Although I didn't see young Mary myself, she's all right. Her family said they needed her to help with spring planting, but as soon as it's finished, they've agreed to bring her to the fort themselves. I believe them."

Elly took his hand and looked at him searchingly. "You didn't mention my brother."

"Dear child, I wish I could say I know where he is, but I can't." He walked over to Jane. "Since your boy was last known to be with the Mohawks, perhaps he is in *Caughnawaga*."

"Where?"

"Caughnawaga. That's a Mohawk town directly across the St. Lawrence from Montreal. Mrs. Campbell, I think you have more chance of finding him there than here at Niagara."

"I pray you're right."

* * *

As soon as Colonel Bolton received John Powell's report, he replied to General Haldimand's letter.

May 16th, 1780.

Sir,

. . . I should have sent down Mrs. Moore's and Mrs. Campbell's families by this opportunity had there not been a daughter of Mrs. Moore's still with the Indians. . . . Notwithstanding [our repeated efforts] to get her in . . . , they have still detained her. However I have hopes she will be delivered up in a few days.

. . . I intend to send Mrs. Campbell's and the other families by way of Montreal as it would be improper to suffer them at this time to pass thro' the Indian Country.

Several days later Mary's family delivered their beloved child to the fort as promised, and Captain Powell rewarded their sacrifice with more gifts of food, trinkets, blankets and kettles. Thus laden down, they stoically bade farewell and retreated.

John Powell took young Mary's arm and guided her to where her family was waiting.

Mary Moore rushed to embrace her daughter, only to stop short, staring dumbfounded. In front of her stood a filthy, haggard squaw. That's not, that can't be, she thought. My child is lovely, bonny and bright-eyed—always smiling. She stands tall and straight. How can that shrunken, miserable, stooped-over creature be . . . ?

"Mother."

The voice was Mary's.

Mid-June 1780.

A sailing vessel left Niagara, carrying Colonel Butler for the long-awaited reunion with his wife and family in Montreal.

Shortly thereafter, John Powell appeared in the doorway of Barrack A: "Mrs. Campbell, Mrs. Moore, I've the pleasure of escorting you to Colonel Bolton at headquarters."

PART IV
MONTREAL AND
CROWN POINT

54

Seneca

Mid-June 1780.

Jane looked around the commandant's office and swallowed hard, her mouth dry from nervousness.

"Mrs. Campbell, Mrs. Moore, I've good news. His Excellency, General Haldimand has ordered me to sign over your passport at once." Mason Bolton drew a lap robe closer around his frail body, offering no explanation as to why they had been so long delayed. "You and your families should prepare to depart for Montreal."

"When?" Jane burst out, too excited to wait another moment.

"Well, if the winds are favorable, the vessel could set sail for Carleton Island as early as tomorrow morning. Once there, you'll transfer to any trading batteau for the trip down the St. Lawrence."

Mary Moore looked questioningly at Bolton. "You didn't mention food."

"You're responsible for most of that."

"But, Colonel, we can't possibly carry enough for such a long journey. It could take us a good two weeks."

"Quite correct, Madam. I suggest you purchase a few supplies from traders here at Niagara and after that replenish them at posts along the way." He pushed a sheet of paper toward Jane and Mary Moore. "This passport allows you and your families to proceed to Montreal, at which point His Excellency will order a new permit issued for Albany."

As Jane reached for the paper, she asked, "Sir, have you news of my son, James, or my father, Matthew Cannon?"

"Cannon, yes; he's among a group of older men being released from prison in Quebec [City]; he will be transferred to Montreal and join you there." A hesitant smile crossed Bolton's face. "As for James Campbell, the Rangers have found a young white boy living with the Mohawks in Caughnawaga and have reason to believe the lad might be your son." He emphasized the word "might." "Last I heard, they were trying to persuade the Indians to free him so they could take him across the river to Montreal."

"Oh, that's wonderful news!"

"I wish I were sailing with you." Bolton gazed out at the lake, as if dreaming, then turned official once more. "My orderly will inform you about the hour of departure."

Jane stood up to leave. "Before Mrs. Moore and I go, we should like to thank you for your protection this past year, especially considering the difficult circumstances."

"Yes," Mary echoed. "I can't say that I enjoyed our stay here, but I guess you did your best, Colonel."

"As His Majesty's commandant here, I could not do otherwise. And now, good-bye." Colonel Bolton would be granted his wish for a transfer some four months later, but on the way to Carleton Island, his sailing vessel sank in a violent storm. All hands on board drowned.

Jaynie and John Powell were waiting with Abigail and Mary outside the commandant's door.

"Girls, we're finally going home." Mary Moore's voice broke. She threw her arms around her oldest daughter, bursting into tears. "I'll never see you again."

"Oh, Mother. Abigail. Mary." Jaynie choked.

Mother and daughter clung to one another.

Back at the barrack, Jane Campbell's children danced around gleefully. "We're going home. We're going home."

Matthew stopped still. "But what about James? What if he comes here, and we're all gone?"

Jane leaned over and squeezed him tightly. "Colonel Bolton told me they might have found James. And he said Grampy will be meeting us in Montreal." She drew the children around her, hugging them. "Then we'll all be going back to Papa and Willie."

By the next morning the two families had packed their few belongings, purchased some provisions, said their good-byes and were ready to sail. But no word came either that day, or the next, or the next.

End of June.

"Mrs. Campbell, Mrs. Moore," an orderly called out from the entrance of Barrack A. "Colonel Bolton presents his compliments. Winds now being favorable, Captain Bouchette will sail within the hour."

The two women scurried about, making sure they were leaving nothing behind.

"Mama," Elly cautioned as she picked up her bundle, "don't forget the apple and pear seeds we're going to plant when we get home."

"Packed long ago."

John and Jaynie Powell appeared, hand in hand. "You've a good day for sailing," he said trying to divert the family's thoughts from their imminent separation. "Winds are finally due west."

Without a word Mary Moore took their arms and walked outside, followed by young Mary and Abigail, then Jane Campbell and the children. Their friends stood in the doorway, waving and calling out, "God be with you. Fare-ye-well."

The silent procession crossed the compound, halting at the portals of the blockhouse. They all held their breath, waiting to see if the drawbridge would indeed crank open. At last it dropped into place and they passed over.

At the wharf their vessel was lying in readiness. "Why look at her name." Powell pointed to the stern. "You're sailing on the Seneca."

"Seneca."

Everyone laughed.

55

White Waters

"We're on our way, children," Jane's voice sang out, "and we're not dreaming. Oh, look, over there." She pointed toward the far distance. Hovering hundreds of feet in the air was the thick, smoky spray of Niagara's Great Falls. "You'll not see that cloud again. Wave good-bye."

The children obeyed laughingly. "And how 'bout the fort, too?"

"All right." They waved again.

The Seneca sailed around the northern rim of Lake Ontario, passing an unbroken wilderness of trees and rocks. Overhead, flocks of swan, gull and wild duck constantly soared and flew off as the vessel cut through the water toward Carleton Island, 160 miles to the east.

Five days after leaving Fort Niagara the ship reached the beginning of the St. Lawrence River and soon the busy harbor of Carleton Island. Boats of all descriptions dotted the waterfront: merchant and naval vessels, canoes, flat-bottomed batteaux.

A buck-toothed soldier meeting the families had disappointing news. "And so, folks, you'll have to wait here at the fort till we've enough people 'n goods to send down to Montreal in a brigade o' boats."

"Why?" Mary Moore demanded.

"There's safety in numbers—what with all that rough water ahead." As if to placate everyone, he added, "Tell you the truth, this here's a good place to get more victuals."

After some days Jane and her group were assigned to a brigade departing for the 200–mile journey. The French-Canadian crew carefully seated each of them at certain intervals along the batteau's hard, wooden seats. Then they stuffed sacks and heavy bales of traders' furs around them for balance.

The first day the procession lazed along, alternately rowing and sailing through the Thousand Islands until it reached Fort Oswegatchie [now Ogdensburg, New York]. There, the leader told his passengers to prepare enough food for the next several days. "Tomorrow we begin shooting the rapids, and from then on camp sites may not be suitable for cooking."

Shortly after dawn the boats arrived at rapids known as "The Gallop." "Hang on tightly," helmsmen warned their charges. Suddenly the batteaux were pitching and tossing on heaving swells, rushing madly through a torrent of water. Jane and the children hung on for dear life as their boat surged and swerved, shot downward and popped straight up.

"Mama, isn't this fun." Matthew called out.

Jane smiled grimly, too breathless from the pounding boat to answer.

For the next two days the brigade fought the rapids. Pilots and helmsmen defied gravity, somehow remaining upright, seemingly suspended perpendicular to the raging foam. They barely emerged from one stretch of white water before the next assault began.

The group reached Lachine, the last stop before Montreal, on the morning of the fourth day. A special pilot joined them for the final rapids, the Sault de St. Louis. One after another, batteaux shot into the shallow, frothing waters. They twisted and turned along the crooked channel, zigzagging between stones and boulders. At times they flew directly toward a massive rock; Jane and her children would brace for the impact, only to have the boat wrench around and shoot onward.

Toward noon the brigade of batteaux passed through the last of the rapids, glided safely into the busy harbor of Montreal, threaded among a maze of ocean-going sailing vessels and drew up at the assigned beach. The walled city with its jutting church spires and windmills was just beyond.

Anticipating their arrival, authorities had stationed a Ranger there to meet them. "Are you Mrs. Campbell and Mrs. Moore?"

"Yes." Jane slowly unfolded her cramped body and climbed out onto shore. "And by the grace of God we're all in one piece."

"As soon as you've collected the children, swing up your bundles and follow me." The stern-faced soldier guided them through a nearby gate and along the narrow streets lined with stone houses.

The Ranger did not stop until they reached an imposing building on a hill overlooking Montreal. "Headquarters," he announced. [The château de Ramezay]

Hardly was the group inside before a motherly, grey-haired woman appeared: Catalina Butler. She radiated warmth, despite the strained look that five years of captivity in Albany had left on her face. "The colonel and I rejoice at your release."

"Thank you. Mrs. Moore and I rejoice for you as well," Jane heard herself saying. She realized she no longer harbored any emnity toward Walter Butler's mother; they both had been pawns in a war not of their choosing.

Catalina, as if sensing Jane's thoughts, smiled. "Come with me. I believe I have happy news for you."

56

The Test

"Mrs. Campbell," said Catalina Butler, "may I present Lieutenant Wemp. He's the Ranger who may have found your son."

"Where is he?" Jane's voice rose with excitement. "Where'd you find him?"

"Well, ma'am," the blond, back-woodsman drawled, "we knew for a long time there was a white boy of about eight living at Caughnawaga. But since he was adopted by the Williams family, we had a hard time getting him released."

"Why who are they?"

"Probably the most powerful Indian family in Caughnawaga. Their grand-folks were captured by the Mohawks in the Deerfield, Massachusetts raid [of 1704]." Wemp shook his head. "Old Man Williams was pretty mulish and beat us a hard bargain. So the boy ended up costing us a goodly sum."

"Oh?"

"Well, when me 'n some other Rangers went over to get the child, Williams led us to a group of Indians boiling down maple syrup. He pointed to a boy making little birch bark baskets—you know what I mean, mococks—and said, 'There's my son.'

"So we march up 'n tell the lad to come with us, but he replies in Mohawk, 'No, can't you see I'm busy?' He goes back to his mococks.

"So we say, 'Montreal is a big city, full of horses 'n carriages 'n soldiers. Wouldn't you like to see it?'

"The lad pretends to ignore us.

233

"But then we tell him, 'Soldiering is much more exciting than maple sugaring. We Rangers go out on long, dangerous journeys, and when we're at the barracks, we practice shooting.'

"The boy turns round and looks up at us with his big blue eyes. By the way, the Williams family named him 'Big Eyes'."

Jane gasped. "James' eyes are big, too."

"Suddenly the lad asks, still in Mohawk, 'Do you always wear those green uniforms? Can I have one, too?'

" 'Of course, boy, but you'll have to come back and live with us Rangers in Montreal.'

" 'All right, I'll go. When do I get my uniform?' "

"Oh, that must be my James. We'd promised him a uniform for his birthday, but," Jane paused, glancing at Catalina Butler, "that was the very day we were captured."

Wemp ignored her reference to Cherry Valley. "And so we take the young fella back to our barrack and now, since we give him the green uniform, he won't wear nothing else. Stubborn little cuss."

Jane smiled. Then she touched the lieutenant's arm, almost whispering, "Does he remember me?"

"Well, to be honest, Ma'am, Big Eyes doesn't remember who he is, where he comes from, or even any English, though I have heard him mutter 'Mama' and 'Papa.' Otherwise he speaks only Mohawk."

Jane turned to Catalina Butler. "I have to see him. When?"

"Tomorrow." Her eyes lit up. "I've arranged for, well, call it a test."

*   *   *

Jane scarcely noted the route over which she and her little group were led, for her thoughts were of James and the next day. She knew Big Eyes had to be her son. But what if he were not?

Their escort took them to a complex of stone buildings not far from the western gate of Montreal: the French Monastery of the Récollets."You'll be staying here." The British shared the church for services and used part of the monastery to billet war prisoners.

Jane settled herself and the children into the stark cells they would now call home. Sleep that night, however, eluded her; she was plagued with doubts about James. What if he were so changed, so Indian, that she was not sure? Yet how could she not recognize her own son? But then, it had been almost two years. What if he refused to accept her as his mother?

Somehow the long night passed.

The next morning Catalina Butler greeted Jane at headquarters, took her hand, squeezed it and smiled in sympathy. She led the way into the main reception room where a number of officers' wives and other women of Montreal's English community had already gathered. "Ladies, please be seated and wait quietly; Mrs. Campbell, you sit there, opposite the door.

"When the child arrives, keep on with your sewing, but make no distracting movements or in any way call attention to yourselves. Mr. Wemp," she explained, "has told the boy to come in and sit down beside any woman he chooses." Without further ado, Catalina left to fetch the child.

Jane glanced around the room at the other women and her heart sank. They were all wearing caps and looked more or less alike; she knew James would never be able to single her out.

235

The door opened and standing in the entrance was a young boy dressed in a green Ranger uniform: James!

No one moved; all needles froze in position.

Jane drew in her breath to keep from screaming out, "James, I'm over here." Her heart pounded wildly as she watched and waited.

The child stood gravely still with only his eyes darting from one woman to the next, searching for a familiar face. Suddenly he bolted.

"Mama, Mama." He ran straight to Jane, flung his arms around her, hugged and kissed her. Then he hugged and kissed her again and again, all the while babbling in Mohawk.

"Oh, James, my son. James!"

57

Cap'n Cannon

"Why are we still here?" Mary Moore grumbled. "Your James has been back with you for three weeks now, and Colonel Butler has already left for Niagara with his wife and family."

"My friend, you know full well we can't get our passport without my father."

"Why not try? Who knows how long before he'll arrive."

Without replying Jane stomped out of the room and joined her children in the courtyard, watching them play. James, except for a certain hesitancy of speech, appeared outwardly like any other white boy of his age. At night, however, Jane was often awakened by him calling out in his sleep in Mohawk. She knew he was still not comfortable as her child, torn between her and his Indian family, the way Matthew had been.

No sooner had Jane, Mary Moore and the children reconciled themselves to a long stay in the monastery than a British soldier appeared. "I am commanded to transfer you to the main prisoner depot. Pack quickly and come with me." He led them to a large, grey stone building outside the city walls near the St. Lawrence; it housed some 200 other prisoners all waiting to be exchanged. "You will remain here until further notice."

Early August 1780.

A grizzled old man stood in the doorway of the Campbell family's cubicle. Unbelieving, Jane stared at Captain Cannon; he had aged so

237

greatly from close confinement in Quebec's prison. "Father!" She ran and threw her arms around him.

"I'm here at last." Cap'n held her tightly.

Despite his appearance, he was the same Grampy, and the children were enthralled to have him back, recounting his adventures since they had been separated. ". . . And then Captain Montour not only demanded but got $10 ransom for me. Imagine me worth $2 more than most anyone else. All 'cause Tom an' me had the guts to shoot at those Injun divils."

In a quiet moment Jane drew her father aside, removed her mother's wedding ring and handed it to him. "I did keep this for you."

Cap'n put the ring on his little finger. "Grammy's gone to her heavenly reward." He gave a throat-clearing "harumph," then said, "Daughter, now that I'm here, let's see about our passport to Albany. Or we could face something really disagreeable."

Jane nodded. She knew what he meant: the Indians could reclaim them.

"We'll fire off a petition."

Jane, Cannon and Mary Moore sent their petition requesting the passport to the British commander in Montreal, Brigadier General Allan MacLean; they waited for two long weeks, but none arrived. Again they petitioned.

"Maybe if we bother 'em enough," Cap'n growled, "they'll say 'Yes' just to get rid of us."

Finally a British officer brought General MacLean's reply:

[I regret my inability to grant the desired passports. Only His Excellency General Haldimand is empowered to sign the documents and he will do so in due course. The Campbell and Moore families will have to await his pleasure.]

"That damnable Haldimand, that son o' the divil," Cap'n cursed. "What else could we expect? His heart's as hard as a two-fold Satan."

Eleanor Cannon's wedding ring. *Sketched from a photograph of the ring which is in the Cherry Valley Historical Association.*

58

Invasion from the North

In truth, the prisoners were presenting a vexing problem to British officialdom.

Quebec, 31st August, 1780.

Sir:

[They cannot be sent back at this time, Haldimand's secretary confided to MacLean, because they are in a position to betray our forthcoming attack on the colonies.]

A number of parties [are] now collecting [for an invasion of New York via Lake Champlain. Obviously,] the people returning to their homes . . . cannot be strangers to it. [Particularly dangerous are] the Moores . . . the most inveterate Rebels, and implacable enemies to Loyalists perhaps in the Continent.

Haldimand was also concerned about sending off Captain Cannon and several other elderly men he planned to include among the returning prisoners.

Tho' not able personally to do mischief, they may, by advice and persuasion, give more trouble than active young fellows. Besides that, their long residence here enables them to give better intelligence and make more perfect remarks on what has passed than any scout the enemy can send for that purpose. The General therefore thinking it unsafe to trust them at present does not choose to comply with their request. . . .

[Be assured, however,] care will be taken to send [the people] before the severe season comes on. In the meantime you must amuse them as well as you can.

Jane, her father and Mary Moore were certainly not amused. With each passing day their suspicions grew: the British had decided not to honor their agreement.

September 17.

Haldimand sent specific instructions concerning the approaching invasion to Brigadier General Henry Watson Powell at Fort St. John:

[Major Christopher Carleton will command the war party of some 1,000 British and Tory soldiers and Indians, while naval Captain William Chambers is to take charge of the vessels transporting troops and provisions.

[The army will penetrate enemy territory by way of Lakes Champlain and George. Their orders: destroy all newly harvested grain and other supplies along the northern frontier. One detachment is to push forward to the Mohawk River and there join forces with Sir John Johnson; he will command a second expedition to carry out similar destructive raids along the Mohawk frontier.

[All men and supplies must be assembled and ready to embark from Fort St. John and the Isle aux Noix by the 27th or 28th of September. That will enable them to arrive at their destination on or before the 8th of October.

[The entire enterprise hangs in great measure upon two things: absolute secrecy] and dispatch. . . . I depend upon your prudence for the former, and your zeal and activity for the latter.

To Haldimand's great annoyance, his plans of necessity involved the Campbell and Moore families. Unless sent south to Crown Point at once, they would be caught up in the invasion.

[Therefore, he concluded in his letter to Powell, I am ordering Brigadier General MacLean to send them to St. John's immediately.] Lieutenant [Jacob] Maurer will conduct them [as far as the fort, and] you will please dispatch the flag of truce without loss of time.

September 21.

Abigail wove her way through the families' bundles littering the floor of the prison's waiting room to perch herself atop a cooking pot.

Little by little the room filled up with fellow passengers:

five of Cap'n's cellmates from Quebec prison:

- Peter Sitz, captured by Brant when Lt. Wormuth was ambushed,
- Cherry Valley prisoners William Henderson and John Scott,
- George Wints and George Weaver from the Mohawk;

also:

- Peter Hanson,
- a Mr. Williams from Detroit,
- thirteen-year-old Mary Crawford, and her sister, twelve-year-old Betsy Lewis.

A stolid officer strode into the room, Lt. Jacob Maurer. "I am your escort to Fort St. John. Collect your belongings and follow me."

As the group of eighteen walked to the riverside, Lt. Maurer asked Jane if she would watch over Betsy and Mary. He explained that the two sisters had been in boarding school in Montreal for several years and were now being exchanged for an uncle and returning to their father Robert Lewis in Albany.

A batteau was waiting to ferry them across the St. Lawrence to La Prairie, where they encamped for the night.

The next morning the group was piled into wagons for the half-day trip to Fort St. John and the Richelieu River. As they joggled along, Cap'n and his friends signaled one another, noting the large numbers of troops heading in the same direction.

Immediately upon their arrival, Maurer herded the prisoners on board a waiting vessel. "You'll be sailing right away."

As his grandchildren gathered round, Cap'n pointed to a white flag flying at the mast. "That's our flag o' truce telling people we're unarmed and carrying a boatload of prisoners."

"Grampy, look yonder." James pulled at his sleeve. "Indians and soldiers."

"I don't like the looks of 'em, m'lad. When hundreds o' troops get together, there's trouble a-brewing."

Lt. Maurer welcomed on board a tall, thin man richly dressed in green velvet, his wavy hair powdered and drawn back into a short queue. "Ah, Stevenson," Jane and her family overheard the officer say, "I was wondering where you were. I thought perhaps you'd changed your mind about sailing."

"No. I have too many—affairs—to clear up in Albany."

"Doubtless." Maurer turned to the others. "And this is Mr. John Stevenson. He will accompany you home to Albany."

"Home?" Cap'n hissed into Jane's ear. "With those fancy clothes he's got to be a Loyalist coming back to spy."

"Within two weeks," Maurer continued, "you should all be back in the bosom of your families." He turned to go. "And now, good sailing and Godspeed."

But God did not speed.

59

Lake Champlain

Up the Richelieu River and into Lake Champlain they sailed, fall foliage in all its splendor welcoming them from both sides of the lake. Reds and golds, greens and yellows greeted them from the Adirondacks in the west and the Green Mountains of Vermont in the east. And Jane knew each day brought them closer to home.

At Crown Point, as soon as the vessel tied up to the wharf, Stevenson stationed himself close to the gangplank. He paced back and forth, his cloak flapping in the cool breeze until the sailing captain joined him.

"Let's be off," said the officer, a squat, bow-legged man of about forty. "If the exchange papers are in order, we shouldn't take too long."

"Good. Time is of the essence."

The two men quickly disembarked, strode past the ruins of a small French fort situated on the point itself and headed inland, up a slight hill to King George's great unfinished fortress of Crown Point. Meanwhile, the passengers waited, at first hopeful, then anxious as the minutes turned into an hour.

"Jane," Cap'n asked, scanning the area once more for an American batteau flying its white flag of safe conduct, "can you see our cartel boat anywhere?"

"No." Squinting, she put a hand above her eyes to search again. "You don't suppose it's hidden in a cove, do you?"

"I doubt it."

They lapsed into worried silence.

At last the captain and Stevenson returned, the latter's face clouded with anger. The officer cleared his throat nervously before announcing: "I'm afraid I have disagreeable news. The Rebel flag intended to transport you south left yesterday."

"Oh, no," Jane groaned.

"What do we do now?" Cannon asked. "Swim back?"

"I'll thank you not to comment," the captain said. "You and all the prisoners of war have no choice; I've been ordered to take you back north and deliver you to Pointe au Fer."

"An' just how long will we have to stay there?"

"Until you receive fresh orders."

The return took several days. As the vessel drew into the small bay at Pointe au Fer, Jane and the other passengers studied the "White House," a large fortified stone building with brick barracks, all surrounded by a high wooden fence, a palisade.

"Captain, I'll return with you to Fort St. John," Stevenson declared. He had heard the White House fireplaces were in such disrepair that they were virtually unusable. "My comfort is worth an extra day's sailing."

"So you're deserting us, eh," Cannon sneered.

He laughed. "Never fear, I'll be back. Meanwhile, General Powell will certainly hear from me about our unfortunate delay."

"Mr. Stevenson," Jane asked, "would you also tell him the children need warm clothing? In fact we all do."

He made a deep bow. "My pleasure, Madam."

September 30.

As the vessel carrying Stevenson disappeared into the distance, eight warships, countless batteaux and canoes hove into view: Major Carleton's invasion force.

"My God, Jane." Cap'n's eyes opened wide with sudden comprehension: the troops they had seen massing near Fort St. John were now an army on the attack. "Damn it, we're in for a hell of a long wait."

The weather grew sharply colder. The children, no longer able to play outside within the palisade's confines, joined the others in their heatless barrack. Just when the prisoners concluded they and their needs had been forgotten, a boat from St. John dropped off warm clothing made from red Indian blankets.

"At least Stevenson kept his promise to us," Cap'n muttered loudly as he put on an ill-fitting jacket. "An' that's more than the British are doing."

"Does anyone really care if we ever get home?" Mary Moore whined.

"Aw hell," Cap'n exploded. "Stop complaining, woman. Let me tell you, a Quebec prison is far worse than life here or even in an Indian village."

James, in his new red cloak, folded his arms across his chest. "Me Big Eyes." He let out an ear-splitting whoop.

Mid-October 1780.

Returning British spies arrived at Pointe au Fer, pleased to report:

> Our invading forces took the country completely by surprise, even capturing Forts Ann and George north of Saratoga. In addition, a secondary Indian raiding party is now pushing into Vermont to divert the enemy.

As October crept onward, the days became raw and cold, the nights freezing, the lake black and menacing. "Snow's in the air," Cap'n announced. "See that rim of ice along the shore? Every morning it gets wider; in another three weeks Lake Champlain won't be passable."

October 20. Twilight.

A long drum roll sounded from a batteau entering the bay at Pointe au Fer. Stevenson and an equally tall, thin officer stepped ashore and strode up to the palisade to meet the commandant waiting at the gate.

"Ensign Robert Battersby, 29th Regiment at Fort St. John, sir, with orders from Brigadier General Powell," the young officer reported in a high, penetrating voice. "At the command of His Excellency General Haldimand, the prisoners now detained at Pointe au Fer are to proceed to Crown Point with all deliberate speed."

The next morning, as the group waited just inside the wooden fence to depart, whoops and halloos erupted from mid-lake. The Indians were returning. Jane turned to meet her father's troubled gaze. Stevenson, uneasy, marched over to confer with the commandant.

Dismal, blood-curdling signals echoed and re-echoed with their message: Brave warriors are bringing home fifty prisoners, scalps and much booty.

Musket shots—three running volleys—roared across the lake, then as if in chorus, warriors exploded with three yells. Silence.

The fort's cannon boomed in salute.

As the commandant hurried through the gate, he called back to Stevenson, "Stay behind. I'll meet those Injuns on shore and keep 'em there."

Jane and her companions stationed themselves along the palisade, peering out between the cracks.

"You have 'milk'?" the Indian leader shouted.

"No. Get rum at Fort St. John."

That Indian leader, the group learned, was none other than "Savage Johnson," one of Sir William's countless Mohawk sons.

"Caughnawaga." James pointed to several canoes filled with painted warriors, their prisoners and the inevitable scalps flapping like banners in the breeze. He darted for the gate, yelling: *"Hoc-no'-seh,* hocnoseh!" [Uncle]

His mother started after him, flailing her arms for help. A soldier caught the boy, picked him up and brought him back, kicking.

Not long afterward the Indians paddled off toward the north.

At dawn the following day Stevenson and the shivering prisoners climbed into their waiting batteau and Battersby gave the signal: push off for Crown Point.

60

Free at Last?

October 24, 1780.

Bristling activity greeted Jane and her group as they disembarked at Crown Point. Soldiers, sailors and painted Indians thronged the wharf area, milling around restlessly. Boats, too, were everywhere, sailing vessels tied up or at anchor, batteaux and canoes darting about or hauled up on shore. But only one boat interested the passengers: their cartel batteau waving a white flag.

"There it is. There it is!" Cap'n gave Jane a squeeze as the others cheered with relief and joy.

Ensign Battersby signaled for quiet. He was leaving Mr. Stevenson in charge while he handled the exchange formalities. "I caution you to be circumspect in behavior; remember you're still prisoners until officially released."

Time passed.

Cap'n marched up to Stevenson. "Where's Battersby? He's been gone a good hour."

"Patience, my good man. Papers have to be verified and our vessel properly identified; otherwise local militia might attack us." Stevenson fumbled nervously for his gold pocket watch.

Cannon suspected Stevenson's nervousness was really fear; with his fancy green cloak, militiamen could easily take him for a Tory.

Before long, Ensign Battersby returned with two officers: Captain William Chambers, in a blue naval uniform, and Major Christopher Carleton, in a red British jacket with Indian leggings and moccasins. The young officer introduced them, then departed to bring round the cartel boat.

Carleton stepped forward to address the group, his dangling silver earrings reflecting the afternoon sun. "His Excellency General Haldimand regrets your prolonged detention at Pointe au Fer—as do we all." The major flourished two papers for everyone to see. "Here's the official letter permitting your exchange, dated September 22. And this is my covering note explaining the delay. The originals have already been dispatched to Rebel Colonel Goosen Van Schaick.

> Unfortunately you have been caught up in a current of unforeseen events. (Carleton was paraphrasing from his note to Van Schaick.)

> [You] could not . . . have [had] the protection of a flag and without it, [who knows what] misfortune might have befallen [you] while the Indians remained [south of Crown Point].

He paused to observe his listeners' reaction.

Jane certainly needed no further apology or muddling explanation; painted warriors were swarming everywhere, and the whoops and halloos of Savage Johnson's returning party still resounded in her ears.

Carleton breathed a sigh of relief. His audience had heard only one word, "Indians," and asked no questions.

He could not reveal the truth:

> Powell and Haldimand knew that Jane and her companions, having seen enough to betray the invasion, would have sounded the alarm had they been allowed to proceed. Furthermore, the Rebels would have considered it *a breach of faith to attack one of their posts immediately after a flag had been sent into it;* they would have suspected that the British soldiers accompanying the returning prisoners had been sent in as spies for the invasion forces.

Battersby's cartel boat drew up alongside the prisoners' batteau and Captain Chambers handed the pass of safe conduct to the pilot. "Soon as the luggage is shifted, you're free to push off."

"Free, we're free at last!"

Chambers and Carleton shook hands with Stevenson, saluted farewell to the others, then departed, winding their way through the maze of boats and people toward a schooner docked nearby, the Maria.

As Jane and her family were collecting their possessions, James suddenly called out, "Mama, look." He pointed toward the Vermont shore: a bonfire was bursting into flames. Within instants musket shots erupted from the forest behind.

248

"Children, drop everything. We're being fired at!"

Shortly thereafter, two boatloads of Carleton's soldiers set off for the far shore. As they drew near, four men darted from the woods and splashed into the water, waving their arms wildly and shouting for help. While one of the boats moved alongside the frantic men, the other stood by, its soldiers poised to shoot.

"We're not being attacked after all." With relief, Jane realized those men were only Loyalists come to join the British.

No sooner had the Tories been pulled on board than gunfire from pursuing Rebels burst forth from the trees, bullets pelting the water around the retreating craft.

Back at Crown Point, the Indians broke into frenzied war whoops, eager to pursue the attackers. Soldiers surged into their batteaux, chafing at the oars while they waited for the signal to push off.

"Stay put," Battersby shouted to the cartel boat pilot. "Wait for further orders; I'll be back." As he rushed away, Stevenson grabbed his belongings and bolted after him.

"My God, what's next?" Cap'n shook his head.

Jane and her father watched as Battersby and Stevenson threaded their way toward the Maria, clambered on board and confronted Chambers and Carleton. After much gesturing toward the Indians and the waiting soldiers, then toward the darkening sky, the ensign departed, alone.

Returning to the cartel boat, he cautioned the pilot, "Major Carleton releases you with this warning: proceed south as rapidly as possible." The warriors were angry because he had commanded them not to pursue the Rebels. If they were to disobey his orders, the returning flag could be caught in an exchange of gunfire.

"Mr. Stevenson isn't going with us, eh?" Cap'n inquired.

"No." Battersby hesitated. "He, uh, decided to return to Canada."

The young officer turned back to the batteau pilot. "You may now depart, but make haste. Remember the angry Indians."

Crown Point soon disappeared into the evening darkness. All night long the crew rowed, battling rough, angry waters, not daring to stop for rest. Jane and the other passengers sat motionless, their Indian blanket coats and cloaks barely protecting them against the freezing wind. She peered into the night, seeing only blackness, and hardly believing they were free and going home.

Dawn.

The wind had calmed. Jane looked around at the sparkling water and the mountains reflecting the first rays of the sun. Her spirits soared and she smiled across at her father.

The children were also in high good spirits. "Let's pretend we're squaws and braves." Betsy Lewis cast her red cloak Indian style across one shoulder.

Shots rang out from the Vermont shore; bullets splashed around the batteau.

"Head out of musket range," the pilot shouted.

The oarsmen rowed furiously toward the New York side, but rifle shots soon peppered the water around the boat.

"Turn back; we'll have to surrender."

"Oh, dear God, no!" Jane put her arms out, trying to shield the children. "Captured again, just when we're so near home and safety."

61

Ethan Allen

As the batteau drew ashore, armed men rushed forward, stopped short, studied their prey, then lowered their guns. The hulking leader spit out a cud of tobacco. "Who are you? An' what in hell are you doing here?"

"We're exchanged war prisoners returning to Albany," Cap'n explained. "And who are you?"

"A scouting party of Ethan Allen's Green Mountain Boys. We saw your red blankets and thought you was a boatload of Injuns 'n Tories. All Vermont's up in arms, afeared of invasion. A raiding party just left."

"Didn't you see our white flag?"

"Sure, but m' Boys disbelieved it." The leader hung his head in a wordless apology. "You know, if mine did, others will too. Better you quit the boat 'n follow us."

Everyone shouldered possessions and followed the Vermonters into the deep forest. The group tramped southward, single file, snaking their way through dense underbrush, around evergreens and jutting branches of bare trees.

Two days later Ethan Allen's Boys deposited Jane and the others at a frontier fort four miles from Castleton and their leader's blockhouse. They were welcomed by the commandant himself: "Colonel Samuel Herrick of the Vermont militia at your service." The green-uniformed officer clicked his heels and saluted. "Lucky for you Ethan's scouts saved you from harm's way. At this very moment enemy forces are ravaging the state of New York and they're bound to strike us next. But my garrison is

300 strong—with each man ready to lay down his life for liberty."

Cap'n picked up his sack. "Then we'd better flee before the enemy arrives."

"No!" The Colonel could not spare even one private to conduct them farther. "You'll have to wait right here in this haven of safety." Ethan, he explained, had 1,000 men, Boys and militia, on the alert, ready to back them up, and poised to charge forward. "All you need is patience and faith in Ethan Allen."

They waited that night and all the next day. Nothing happened.

October 28, 1780. 7 P.M.

The sound of a fife and drum, and then the sentry's call broke the evening silence: "Flag of truce approaching."

An alarm bell clanged.

Colonel Herrick dashed into the center of the compound, shouting: "Rally round. The damnable enemy has come to demand our surrender." He whipped out his sword, slicing through the air as he raised it on high. "But we'll never surrender this fort—or even this dot of ground." He stabbed the earth with all his strength; the sword snapped in two.

Unperturbed, he flung aside the hilt. "Destroyed. And that's exactly what we'll do to our enemy."

"Halt. Who goes there?" the sentry challenged.

Herrick marched off to the gate, followed at a respectful three paces by several soldiers. Jane, Cap'n, everyone was left back, straining to hear.

"Colonel Justus Sherwood of His Majesty's Loyal forces with fifer, drummer and two privates."

"On what business?" asked the sentry.

"Colonel Sherwood begs leave to confer with Ethan Allen."

"Let them in." Herrick turned to his soldiers. "Blindfold the officer and lead him to my quarters. Keep the others in close confinement." He stalked away.

Within minutes an express rider galloped out of the compound, heading for Castleton and Ethan Allen, and leaving the blockhouse consumed with curiosity: what does that Loyalist want with our Ethan?

After spending the next morning snooping and prying, Cap'n reported back to Jane and their companions in the crowded common room. "Damned if I know what's going on, but Allen met Sherwood for breakfast in a farmhouse not far from here. Then he summoned his council of field officers."

In mid-afternoon the council arrived at the compound, headed by a strapping, bull-like man with a ruddy face: Ethan Allen. He waved to the assembled throng before striding off to confer with Herrick.

As the crowd dispersed, one rumor kept swirling around the fort: the British were offering a truce, promising not to invade; in return, Vermont would go back under the King's protection with Ethan made head of a new Province.

Once again in the common room Cap'n pondered the situation. "The Province of Vermont?" He stroked his chin, puzzled. "Jane, I wonder." The Vermonters, he had learned, were furious with New York because it refused to allow them to break away and become a separate state. Yet at the same time the Yorkers did not protect them against Indians or Tories or land grabbers and their ilk. "Some say since they're not getting satisfaction from New York, why not ask the British to defend them?"

"Vermonters might say that, Father." Jane stood up, almost spitting out her words. "But if they want freedom, they'll certainly not get that under King George."

"Positively correct, Madam," a voice boomed out. Ethan Allen stepped into the room, followed by Colonel Herrick. "Vermont does indeed want liberty and freedom from tyranny." He bowed. "Welcome to peaceful Vermont. The voice of reason has just overcome the threat of invasion; I am overjoyed to announce I have concluded with General Haldimand's emissary a truce and cessation of hostilities." He paused, allowing time for everyone in the room to give three huzzahs. "And now, my New York neighbors, you may resume your trip to Albany."

The children squealed with joy. Their elders clapped and shouted.

Allen raised his hand for silence. "You will proceed under my personal protection, and I will so notify the New York authorities." A sly smile crossed his face. "Colonel Herrick, round up 100 of my Boys to escort our new friends. Mount them on horseback so they can ride into Albany with all the panoply due them. Let those Yorkers see that Vermont has more than enough strength to protect both itself and its guests. We'll show Governor Clinton and his smug henchmen a thing or two."

Allen turned to Jane and made a sweeping bow. "*Never again will you fall into the hands of the enemy.*"

October 30. Dawn.

The long journey to Bennington and Albany began, but hardly were they under way than a tedious snowstorm slowed their progress almost to a halt.

November 7.

Reaching Albany in late afternoon, the returning prisoners and their escort of Green Mountain Boys drew wondering crowds:
- If Allen can spare so many men, his army must be enormous.
- We could be wrong about Ethan. Maybe he is a powerful soldier after all and not just some pompous philosopher.

As Jane smiled and nodded at the waving onlookers, all her weariness vanished. She was safely home; she was about to be reunited with Sam and Willie.

At City Hall, Mayor Abraham Yates and his aides greeted the arriving procession. "Thank you, Boys, and our compliments to your leader." The grey-haired mayor was icily polite, for he sensed the reason behind Ethan Allen's parade of power.

Seeing Jane, Yates hastened to take her hand and help her dismount. "Welcome home, Mrs. Campbell. It's good to have you back."

"Thank you." She swallowed hard to dispel the lump in her throat. "I never thought the day would come. To see my husband and son again."

"Colonel Campbell is at Stanwix, and I've heard your son is with family in Niskayuna," Yates hurriedly said as he led Jane and the others inside. "First thing tomorrow morning I'll dispatch an express rider to the fort; you should have your husband and son back in about four days."

"Oh, I hope so." Tears of joy and disappointment welled up in her eyes.

The mayor turned to the assembled prisoners. "Until interrogated— and cleared—you will all be billeted in Albany." The Commission for the Detection and Defeating of Conspiracies in the State of New York hoped to learn valuable information and certainly had to assure itself that no one was in reality a damnable spy.

The next day, November 8.

Three interrogators quizzed Jane: did she know certain people in Canada and New York, and had she heard anything about their possibly traitorous activities?

"I really can't say," she replied. "I spent all my time sewing." Suddenly she realized they were the very words she had used at Niagara; this time, however, she was telling the truth.

62

November 11, 1780

Sam Campbell had ridden hard for two days. He stopped in Niskayuna only long enough to change horses and pick up Willie before continuing onward to Albany.

Dismounting at the house where Jane was staying, father and son waited impatiently for the door to be opened. Once inside the front hall, sounds of children laughing and chattering greeted them. The two hesitated, then entered the common room.

Silence.

Sam opened his mouth to speak; no words came out.

Jane turned around.

Husband and wife stared into each other's eyes and slowly moved together. Their hands touched. They embraced, silently and long. Unashamedly they wept.

It was November 11, 1780; their nightmare had lasted exactly two years.

PART V
THE FULL CIRCLE

63

A New Life

Sam Campbell could not take his family back to Cherry Valley in November of 1780, for the entire frontier was still aflame. The Indian war parties which Jane and the children had seen leaving Fort Niagara the previous winter had increased in size and frequency as the months passed. Uprooted Tories, more embittered than ever, had also joined the raids with renewed zeal.

While Jane, her children and Captain Cannon were languishing in Montreal, the enemy marauders were ranging the Mohawk frontier, bringing more death and destruction. The few Rebel families still remaining in the river valley had withdrawn to the protection of little forts dotting the area, where they lived in a constant state of alarm and fear of attack.

By the time Jane and Sam were reunited, New York's frontier had so contracted that Governor George Clinton wrote, *"Schenectady may now be said to become the limits of our western frontier."*

December 14, 1780.

Jane and Sam had barely settled into their new farmhouse on the Hudson River four miles north of Albany when they were invited to the wedding of Elizabeth Schuyler and Colonel Alexander Hamilton.

General Schuyler's brick mansion was positioned on a bluff of land one half mile south of Albany proper. As Jane waited with Sam in the English drawing room for the ceremony to begin, she remembered her own simple wedding in January 1768 and slipped her arm into his. Her thoughts wandered back to the little chapel at Fort Niagara: "Is it really not even a year since Jaynie Powell and Catherine Brant were married? It seems more like an eternity." She smiled up at Sam.

After the ceremony they greeted the newly-weds. "Betsy, I do hope you and your husband will be as happy as Colonel Campbell and I."

"Thank you." The bride glanced adoringly at Alexander Hamilton, her black eyes sparkling. "How pleased we both are that you're back."

The colonel, resplendent in his blue wool and buff uniform, bowed. "May I also say, 'Welcome home'. "

"Yes, indeed, welcome home," General Schuyler chimed in. "I'm so glad not to be writing any more letters about your exchange." His thin face crinkled into a smile.

"I'm glad, too—and infinitely grateful."

The wedding party and guests tried to be lighthearted and gay, but the men's conversations inevitably drifted back to one topic, the war:

– "How long can we hold out against the enemy?" they asked one another. "Our soldiers are cold and hungry, without shoes and blankets, many without arms."

– "Come good weather, Schenectady and Albany are sure to be attacked."

"Albany," Sam exploded. "Don't talk defeat until we're staring it in the face."

During the reception the women guests singled out Jane, eager to learn about her Indian captivity; her spectacular return was still the talk of the town.

As they started home, Jane draped the blankets around them and snuggled close. Sam gave her a quick kiss, then snapped the horses' reins to make them go faster.

Snow began to fall as they followed the road along the Hudson. By the time they reached home a thick whiteness swirled over the ground, blowing into drifts.

"How warm and cozy our bed feels." Jane nestled against Sam.

He pulled her to him. "I'm so thankful to have you back. After the Indians took you away, I almost died of grief and worry. Life had no meaning except to find you and the children, and bring you home again." He buried his head in her hair, murmuring, "Oh Jane, dearest Jane, I love you more than life itelf."

Tenderly she stroked his head, then whispered, "Your love kept me alive."

Sam caressed her lips, then covered her with kisses.

64

Robert Campbell

Sam and Jane spent the winter of 1780–1781 settling into their new house and farm. Their family—Cap'n, five children, Lain and several other slaves—was cheerful and content, happy to be together again.

Jane often smiled to herself as she sewed, enjoying the sight of her children gathered in the common room around a roaring fire. Other times she would gaze out the window at the snow falling upon the frozen river, reminded of Fort Niagara; there winter was the lonely season.

But here in Albany it was the visiting season; the family sleighed down river into town for parties or people drove out to see them, curious to hear about their experiences.

Inevitably Jane was asked, "How could you live through it all?"

Her reply never varied: "God taught me *one can't always die when one longs for death.*"

Spring 1781.

Winter ended abruptly with the break-up of the frozen Hudson, signaled by long, thunderous booms far up river. The whole family ran to watch as the distant ice began breaking and bursting upwards. The rushing waters pitched forward, racing toward Albany and the sea; they heralded the coming of spring. And the return to full-scale war.

Sam kicked the mud off his boots and stomped into the house. "Cherry Valley 's been struck again." He had heard from Governor Clinton that thirty or forty people were captured and eight killed.

"Why, oh why did they ever return?" Jane shook her head in dismay.

Sam did bring home one piece of good news from Albany that spring: "On March 11th Congress ratified the Articles of Confederation." That meant the thirteen states were finally united into a real country.

Cap'n picked up his gun and patted it. "Now all we have to do is survive the war."

Otherwise Sam's news was unfailingly disastrous:

- "Fort Stanwix had to be evacuated; fire and spring rains damaged it beyond repair." Although the fort had become an isolated outpost now in Indian territory, it was still a symbol of defiance.
- "General Schuyler told me farmers in the Saratoga area are poised to abandon their lands, convinced we'll be invaded as soon as the weather clears." Even in Albany, Sam learned, families were packing their belongings, preparing to flee.

As the days passed, Jane tried to maintain a calm routine for her household despite the fears of Indians and Tories lurking in the woods, and the rumors of impending invasion. Sam, Cap'n and the slaves worked the fields and went hunting, but always close by. The older children trudged off to school each day, heeding their mother's warning not to stray from the road. At home Lain watched over young Samuel and took care of the house.

And Jane spent as much time as possible sewing; in September she was expecting a baby.

All summer long, as Jane made motherly preparations for the baby's arrival, war parties continued their reign of terror along the frontier.

The main invading army, however, had yet to descend.

"Sam, what do you think is keeping those varmints?" Cap'n sighted his musket out the window, pretending to shoot.

"Maybe they've decided that what's left isn't worth destroying."

Cannon put down his gun. "You mean you think they have something else in mind?"

"Yes, Schenectady and Albany." Then the British would finally control the Hudson and be able to cut off New England from the rest of the States. Sam shook his head. "It's only a matter of time."

* * *

264

One September morning, Jane awoke Sam at dawn; the baby was coming. "Go get Lain."

Within minutes the black mammy was at her side.

Sam gestured helplessly. "And what can I do?"

"Massa, yo' can fetch de boilin' water."

When Sam returned, he rushed to Jane's side. "Here, take my hand. Squeeze it as hard as you like." He kissed her forehead. "We'll fight this battle together, too."

Jane managed a smile, squeezing his hand hard, then harder and harder. . . .

"Yo' has a sweet lil' boy. Thank de good Lord!"

As Jane's arms enfolded her newborn babe, she looked up at Sam. "We won the battle, didn't we."

"Yes, my dearest. But are you all right?"

"Yes, just tired, that's all." Jane handed the baby to his father. "What do you think we should name him?"

Sam studied the tiny red face. "Robert." His voice cracked; he was overcome by the memory of his brother's death four years earlier at Oriskany.

Placing the child back in Jane's arms, Sam kissed her, walked over to the Bible and opened it to the pages listing the family births. He began writing:

Robert Campbell born
on 15th Sept. 1781.

65

Walter Butler

Invaders struck the Mohawk Valley: Major John Ross and a small army of British, Tories and Indians were pushing toward Schenectady and Albany; Captain Walter Butler was one of his officers. And rumor said a second force under Sir John Johnson would momentarily be invading from Crown Point, via Lake Champlain and the Hudson. Colonel Marinus Willett and his New York troops had the Herculian task of mounting the defense against both fronts.

The Campbell farm lay in direct line of the pincer attack.

"Colonel Willet's calling for volunteers," Cap'n announced as he took his musket down from the wall. "An' my trigger finger is itching for a good fight." He stroked the gun, hesitated, then replaced it. "Damn it, Sam, I'm too old to go off."

"But you're not too old to help me defend this house."

Each day Jane and her family expected to hear the worst. They heard nothing; heavy rains, then snow cut off communications. Finally information trickled in:

—On the morning of October 25, 1781 when Major Ross was within twelve miles of Schenectady, he suddenly retreated along the Mohawk River. Colonel Willett and his forces raced in pursuit. By late afternoon the two armies were locked in battle at Johnstown, but under cover of darkness the enemy escaped and started back toward Canada. In the meantime Willett regrouped, added reinforcements and renewed the chase.

Peggy Scott

—Sir John Johnson's army would not be attacking from Crown Point; the rumor had been a false alarm.

—On October 30 Walter Butler was killed!

"That scourge of the Mohawk, dead. Good riddance." Cap'n spit into the fire.

"Yes, Father, we can be thankful he's gone." Jane spoke quietly, pensively. "Captain Butler was a man of contradictions. Pitiless to his enemies. Compassionate to his men." She fell silent, remembering: With a wave of his hand he condemned us to a living hell with the Indians; he would gladly have let Mary Moore be scalped. Yet John Powell admired and respected him, and his soldiers were proud to serve under him.

Jane looked up at Sam. "Walter Butler was irresistable to women. To Lyn Montour and who knows how many others. How could they love him? A man with so much blood on his hands."

Sam put his arms around her. "Come now, my dear, that's all over."

"Yes, except the memories. You know, I can't help feeling sorry for Colonel and Mrs. Butler: they gave us back our son, but lost their own."

A few days later Sam brought the details of Walter's death:

Willett pursued Ross' men in a heavy snowstorm and finally caught up with them on October 30th at West Canada Creek. When Willett's advance party emerged from the forest, they discovered Butler's Rangers had already swum across; the captain, who was bringing up the rear on horseback, had just reached the opposite shore and was riding forward.

Apparently he thought himself out of shooting range, because he stopped, twisted round in the saddle and began making defiant gestures, in particular slapping his own backside. Anthony the Oneida took up the challenge, raised his rifle, aimed and fired: the bullet knocked Butler off his horse.

As soon as Butler fell, the Oneida threw down his rifle and blanket, leaped into the icy water and swam across. Reaching the opposite bank, he raised his tomahawk and with a great yell sprang like a tiger upon his enemy.

Butler pleaded for mercy, crying out, *"Quarter, quarter!"*

But Anthony shouted, *"Cherry Valley quarter! Cherry Valley quarter!"* and buried the ax in Butler's skull, then scalped him.

No subsequent event of the entire war caused more rejoicing in the Mohawk Valley than the news of Walter Butler's death.

66

General Charles Cornwallis

Sam burst into the house. "General Cornwallis has surrendered his entire army to George Washington. It all happened at Yorktown in Virginia, on October 19th."

"Oh, darling," Jane exclaimed, "surely that means the war will soon be over."

"The war's over!" The children danced around, shouting for joy.

But Sam held up his hands to quiet them. "Not so fast." King George and his government, he explained, would have to hear about the surrender and decide whether or not they wanted peace. If they did, then a peace treaty would have to be drawn up and sent back to Congress for adoption.

"Papa, when can we go home to Cherry Valley?"

"I wish I knew. The British may have laid down their arms, but the Indians and Tories are still on the warpath. We don't dare go back till Haldimand has called in all his raiding parties."

"If I know that so and so," Cap'n grumbled, "he'll keep 'em prowling the frontier till the last possible minute."

"I'm afraid so."

Jane's foot stopped rocking Robert's cradle. "The wait doesn't matter any more; now we can make plans to go home."

January 1, 1782.

"Happy Birthday, Mama." Elly gave Jane a kiss and presented her with an alphabet sampler.

"Why, thank you, my precious." She examined the needlework closely. "It's just beautiful and you've done every stitch perfectly."

Elly blushed with pleasure.

James pulled out his mother's spectacles from her sewing basket. "Here. Now you can really see it."

"But I don't need them any longer. My eyes are well now." Jane started to stuff them back into the basket.

"No." The boy took them from her hand. "Let's bury 'em in the ground, like the Indians and their war hatchet."

Elly snatched them. "Let's just put 'em away."

January 25.

Sam Campbell sat at his desk, going over his claim of losses with Jane and Cap'n. "Did we forget anything?"

State of New York Tryon County. An Account of the Damages which Samuel Campbell of Cherry Valley have Sustained by the Enemy on the Eleventh of November 1778.

	£.	S.	D.
To one Dwelling house burnt	150		
To two barns burnt	150		
To two horses taken away	30		
To two mears and one Coalt do [ditto]	20		
To one Cow taken away	5		
To one beef burnt	5		
To four fat hogs killed	12		
To one Negro boy carried off	50		
To one Waggon burnt	7		
To one Slay and Harness burnt	6		
To thirty Loads of hay do	30		
To wheat and peas and oats burnt in the Straw	50		
To Corn and Potatoes and flax burnt	10		
To one watch taken away	6		
To two Sadls and bridles carryed off	5	10	
To Cloathing and house all furniture burt or carryed off	200		
To Cash taken away	60		
	£. 795	10	0

Saml. Campbell (Col.)

270

Jane peered over his shoulder. "Seven hundred ninety-five pounds. Darling, do you really think New York will pay us that much money?"

"I should hope so. After all, we fortified our farm because the government especially asked us to stay. We could have fled."

Cap'n snapped off the end of his clay pipe. "We'd have sure saved ourselves a lot of agony."

"Father, don't say that; we sacrificed for our country!"

Sam's petition was eventually denied, the state's explanation being that New York's treasury would become bankrupt *"if all such worthy memorials were approved."*

* * *

Meanwhile, peace between Britain and the United States was coming closer to reality. In London on March 20, 1782, Lord North's government fell as a result of the Cornwallis defeat. When Lord Shelburne became Prime Minister, he and his cabinet saw no honor in continuing a war the Crown could not win, and consequently in April they dispatched delegates to Paris to negotiate a peace treaty with American representatives.

At the same time, Shelburne sent word to his generals in America to halt the fighting. Not until July, however, did Haldimand finally call in his raiding parties and even then, some Indians refused to obey.

With savages still skulking the length of the Mohawk frontier, Sam Campbell could not risk taking his family back to Cherry Valley.

* * *

On November 30, 1782 in Versailles, France, negotiators for Great Britain and the United States signed the Preliminary Articles of Peace. In late March 1783 a sailing vessel brought the news to American shores. And on April 11 in Philadelphia, Congress adopted the Articles.

April 19. Philadelphia.

> At noon, (Major General William Heath wrote in his *Memoirs,*) the proclamation of Congress for a cessation of hostilities was proclaimed at the door of the New Building, followed by three huzzas; after which a prayer was made by the Reverend Mr. Ganno, and an anthem (*Independence,* from [William] Billings) was performed by vocal and instrumental music.

The glorious news reached Albany: "*America is ours!* Peace has finally come!"

Jane ran to Sam's open arms, and he twirled her around. "Now, we can go home!"

67

Cherry Valley

Spring 1783. Peace.

Like the Israelites of old, Sam and Jane Campbell, their family and friends headed home from exile. Women and children piled into wagons for the journey to Cherry Valley, perching atop farm equipment, pieces of furniture and innumerable bundles. Men, older boys and slaves walked alongside, driving the cattle.

After four and a half years, Jane and Sam arrived home. But only wilderness greeted them. Brush and saplings grew where their former house and barns had stood; nothing remained except burned out, decaying ruins. Their once-cleared farmland was covered with underbrush and the forest was creeping in, its wild animals prowling at will.

Cherry Valley was desolation itself. Even its cherry trees had already lost their blossoms.

Jane shut her eyes tight. "I must not cry."

"Mama." Samuel tuggd at her skirt. "Mama, you mean this is home? It's terrible."

"Yes, it is now." She gave the boy a gentle hug. "But not for long."

"Son, your mother's right." Sam took an ax from the wagon. "Soon, with hard work, we'll bring this farm—and every farm in Cherry Valley—back to life again. Isn't that so, Jane?"

"Of course, darling. We haven't come back to give up now."

At first the exiles camped around the wagons while the men chopped down trees and shaped the logs for huts; the women cooked and cared for the young children. Within a few weeks log cabins dotted the settlement.

At last Jane and Sam could move their possessions inside a crude shelter built next to the ruins of the old house. First came the tall case clock Sam had purchased with warrants issued him for his war service. They placed it just opposite the entrance, to catch light from the open doorway and the oiled paper window.

Next came bundles of linen and clothing; two small objects dropped onto the dirt floor.

Matthew picked them up. "My pins! My Indian mother gave them to me when the soldiers took me away from her." He handed them to Jane. "Will you please put these on my shirt for me."

Suddenly Matthew threw his arms around Jane's waist. "I love you and I'm so glad you're my real mama!"

"Oh, son." She could say no more.

Lain and Willie had the honor of carrying in the Bible they had saved, and of placing the water-stained, leather-bound volume on the table in the middle of their hut.

At day's end Sam began family prayers by reading a passage from their Bible. Then everyone sang, "Praise God from whom all blessings flow." They were truly home.

The wilderness slowly retreated as Sam cut and burned off all the underbrush, then planted crops of corn, squash and beans. Soon neat rows of tiny green shoots appeared and the land began to look like a farm once again.

Jane called everyone together to plant the tiny fruit trees grown from the seeds she and Elly had brought from Niagara; the children had waited for this moment ever since they had first planted them outside the kitchen door of their Hudson River house. "Each of you, choose a spot for your own tree."

With great ceremony the family watched as one by one the children put their apple and pear seedlings into the ground. Lastly Jane led everybody halfway down the hillside. "This is where I want my tree to be."

As Sam finished digging, Jane moved to Elly's side. "Let me say a little prayer: May all our seedlings grow into strong trees bearing fruit for many years to come; and may those trees always remind us to be thankful for our safe deliverance. Amen."

The work never stopped, however. Sam and his helpers began expanding the shelter into a log house of several rooms while the younger children were given the task of exploring the ruins for anything salvageable.

"Buried treasure," Samuel shrieked out from amidst the debris. "Mama, everyone, come look." He held up two broken boards.

"Why they're from my old hope chest." Jane started rummaging among its shattered remains. She pulled out a mass of torn blue brocade and held it up to herself. "My beautiful wedding gown." Tears began to trickle down her cheeks.

"Well I'll be damned." Cap'n shook his head. "After all we've been through, you choose that rag to make a flap about."

Early July.

"Come see." Sam caught Jane by the arm and drew her to the doorway of their house. "Look at all the corn. And just think, three months ago underbrush was choking those same fields."

"If I live to be a hundred, I'll always cherish this view. Our own fields and the forest and the rolling countryside. Oh, sweetheart, during those two years away from you, I used to shut my eyes and see all this. It helped keep me alive."

Their tranquility was interrupted by a horse and rider galloping toward the house.

"Message for Colonel Campbell," the soldier called out as he rode to the door. "Are you him?"

"Yes, right here."

He jumped off the horse, marched up and saluted. "Compliments from Colonel Samuel Clyde, commandant of Fort Plain on the Mohawk, sir."

"And how is our cousin?" Sam asked, returning the salute.

"He and Mrs. Clyde plan to move back to Cherry Valley as soon as the colonel can give up his post." The soldier drew himself up very straight and took a deep breath almost to bursting. "I've come with news: On July 31st some distinguished visitors will be traveling from Fort Plain to Cherry Valley and desire to spend the night with you."

"Distinguished visitors, with us? Who?"

"Governor Clinton, General Schuyler, General Hand—and General George Washington!"

68

General George Washington

General Washington was caught in time's web that summer of 1783. He was the head of an army with no more war to fight, yet prevented from disbanding until a final peace treaty had been signed. On July 15 from his headquarters in Newburgh, New York, he wrote to General Philip Schuyler:

> I have always entertained a great desire to see the northern part of this state before I returned southward. The present irksome interval, while we are waiting for the definitive treaty, affords an opportunity of gratifying this inclination.
>
> I have therefore concerted with George Clinton to make a tour to reconnoitre those places, where the most remarkable posts were established, and the ground which became famous by being the theatre of actions in 1777.

From Newburgh, Washington and his staff set out due north; en route Governor Clinton and Generals Schuyler and Hand joined them. In time, their tour turned west following the Mohawk River toward Fort Stanwix.

By July 30 the cavalcade had reached Fort Plain, where Washington and Clinton crossed the river to spend the night with Peter Wormuth and his family.

As the men strolled with their host toward his small stone house, the governor stopped and put his hand on the old man's shoulder. "Five years might have passed since Matthew's death, but such a sorrow is always with us."

276

Peter raised his head high. "My son died for our country; that is my consolation."

"Yes, Mr. Wormuth," George Washington said, "you have your country's gratitude and our most profound sympathy."

The next day Washington and Clinton recrossed the Mohawk to meet Colonel Clyde and his guard, and with full military honors were piped into Fort Plain. After a festive midday dinner, they left with the cavalcade for Cherry Valley, proceeding in triumph as farmers and their families waved and cheered them all along the road.

Meanwhile Jane waited with Sam and Cap'n, every few minutes straightening her skirts and cap, adjusting the bowl of wild flowers the children had gathered, or generally fretting over some one of her last instant efforts to beautify the log house.

"Sit down, daughter. You're like a worm on a hot griddle."

"Oh, I give up! This place is just too primitive for such important men."

"Don't be ridiculous, my dear," Sam intervened. "Most of them are soldiers and accustomed to camp life. They'll not be bothered one whit."

At last the guests arrived, virtually escorted to the door by a celebrating throng of Cherry Valley families. As the crowd dispersed and the huzzahs died away, Sam led Washington, Clinton and their entourage to chairs and benches set out under a large apple tree. "Mrs. Campbell and I thought you might enjoy tea outside in the shade. Cool breezes always seem to blow here, even on such a hot day as this."

While Jane made sure her guests were served, Sam brought over the older children to be introduced. "And this is James, my ten-year-old. He spent nearly two years with the Mohawks, mostly in Caughnawaga."

"Caughnawaga!" General Washington beckoned. "Come over here, young man. I've heard much about that town and its Christian Indians. How did they treat you?"

"Oh very kindly, Your Excellency." James' eyes grew bigger with excitement; he had been singled out by the great Washington. "My family made me happy, and I loved them very much."

"I'm pleased to learn that. Is it true the settlement has many houses made of stone?"

"Yes, sir. I lived in one of them. It was much nicer than Papa's log house here."

The general smiled, then turned almost confidential. "But James, isn't it more important to be with one's real parents?"

277

The boy thought a moment. "Yes, I think so. Only when I first came back, I sometimes wished I'd never been found. But Mama always understood when I missed my Indian family."

"And what about now?"

James stuck out his chest proudly and announced for all to hear. "Now I want to stay right here in Cherry Valley and be an American."

Everyone cheered loudly.

That evening all Cherry Valley either crowded into the Campbell's house or leaned through the open windows. General George Washington had come to their settlement and everyone was celebrating the moment **of** a lifetime.

Until the wee hours frontiersmen proudly recounted their adventures. Some had been taken prisoner by war parties; others had narrowly escaped from Indians; and a few had stayed to defend their land.

Sam Campbell took his turn. "Not long ago a friend of mine was picked up by three Tories, who started to take him to Canada. In his struggle to escape, he slammed this very musket over the head of one of his captors. Look." Sam raised the gun high over his head for all to see: the barrel was bent almost into a semi-circle.

Close-up of the actual snuff box.

279

Cap'n refought his capture by Captain Montour. "And you should have seen Queen Catherine's face when she met me. Yep, she's a real fury."

As Jane listened, her thoughts wandered back to her own experiences. How lightheartedly they do retell our stories; I'm glad. Now that's all in the past. We're free; our country's free; and with God's help we hold in our own hands our future and that of our children and our children's children.

August 1, 1783.

The Campbell family lined up to say good-bye to their guests, Sam and Jane with Cap'n, then the children in stair steps down to Robert.

The governor warmly shook Sam's hand. "Thank you, my friend. You and Mrs. Campbell made us all feel welcome. Today we're off for Lake Otsego."

"Yes," Washington agreed, "I want to see where General Clinton dammed the lake." He paused, taking an enameled snuffbox from an aide. "Colonel, may I offer to you and Mrs. Campbell this token of my appreciation for your gracious hospitality."

"Such a lovely box," Jane exclaimed. "Oh, thank you, Your Excellency."

"You're most welcome." The general bowed, kissed her hand, then moved on to say good-bye to Cap'n as Elly and her brothers stood at attention awaiting their turn.

Governor Clinton gestured toward the children. "Mrs. Campbell, *your boys will make fine soldiers in time.*"

"I hope my country will never need their services."

George Washington stopped and turned back. *"I hope so too, madam, for I have seen enough of war."*

"Yes, General," Jane said, reaching out toward Sam, "we all have seen enough of war!"

Rocking chair used by General George Washington.

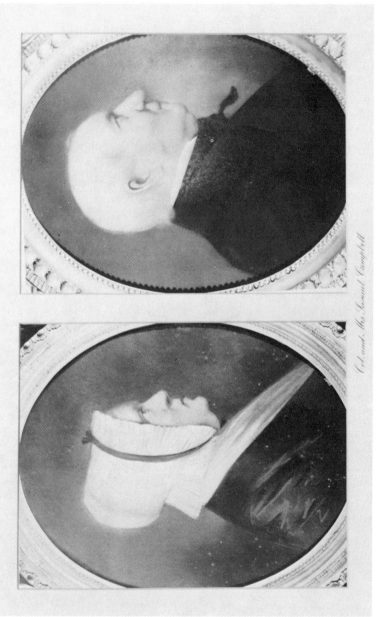

Colonel and Mrs. Samuel Campbell when they were in their eighties.
Courtesy of The New-York Historical Society, New York City.

EPILOGUE

COLONEL SAMUEL CAMPBELL

Samuel Campbell devoted most of his efforts after the war to restoring his considerable lands. He became one of the largest maple sugar producers in the Mohawk Valley, supplying places as far away as New York City.

Although Colonel Campbell was never compensated for his losses during the Revolution, in 1789 the State of New York did grant him and his family certain tax abatements because the war had forced them to leave home. By 1796 his fortunes had been sufficiently restored that he was able to build an imposing house on the site of the wartime compound; it is still owned by one of his descendants.

In 1802 the colonel was elected to the state legislature. In addition, he was active in the Presbyterian Church and in the Cherry Valley Academy.

To the end of his life Samuel Campbell enjoyed perfect health, even chopping down a tree the day before his death on September 12, 1824. He was eighty-six years old and the last member of the original families who settled Cherry Valley in 1741.

JANE CANNON CAMPBELL

Jane Cannon Campbell lived the rest of her life in Cherry Valley, surrounded by her family and friends. Her grandson, Judge William W. Campbell, described her as being of "fortitude and decision" mixed with "feminine gentleness . . . a female patriot who loved her country, its form of government and who repelled all aspersions cast upon it with great

283

ardour, clearness and force." She was "a lady of the old school, of native dignity and a firm believer in piety. Until her last brief sickness . . . the reminiscences of history of our country and of her personal acquaintance with many of the revolutionary worthies continued fresh and vivid til near the close of her life." Even in her nineties she would ride over from Cherry Valley to nearby Cooperstown to the house of her youngest son, Robert. There, she would visit with old friends who had also lived through the Revolution.

Jane Campbell died February 17, 1836, "a living chronicler of the scenes of by-gone days, and the last female representative, in the region in which she lived, of that patriotic band who achieved our independence." She was survived by all six of her children and thirty-four of her thirty-five grandchildren. The eyeglasses made for her at Fort Niagara are at the New York State Historical Association in Cooperstown, and the family Bible at the New-York Historical Society. Her mother's wedding ring is in the museum of the Cherry Valley Historical Association.

THE CAMPBELL CHILDREN

William "Willie" Campbell became a physician, practicing medicine in Cherry Valley, but soon decided his career lay elsewhere. He tried farming and merchandising before finally devoting himself to politics and science, in particular, engineering and surveying. Beginning in 1816, he served several terms in the state assembly, where he became well known for his scientific abilities. As a result, in 1825 he was chosen Surveyor General and Chief Engineer of the State of New York. Dr. William Campbell died on October 27, 1844 at the age of seventy-six, a childless widower.

Eleanor "Elly" Campbell married her cousin, Samuel Dickson, a son of Elizabeth Campbell Dickson of the flaming red hair; they had six children. She received, as part of her inheritance, the Lafayette silver coin, the remnant of her mother's wedding dress and George Washington's snuff box. She died in Cherry Valley on October 4, 1844, aged seventy-three.

Matthew and *Samuel Campbell* both became respected farmers. Matthew died in 1845 at the age of seventy, the father of nine children. His Indian pins are in the museum of the Cherry Valley Historical Association, but the tall case clock which he inherited is still owned by a descendant. Samuel, the father of six, died in 1860, aged eighty-three.

Robert Campbell became a lawyer and was considered one of the ablest and best-read members of his profession in central New York. He lived in Cooperstown and was president of the Old Otsego County Bank. He died in 1847 at the age of sixty-six.

James Campbell remained on the family lands, farming them as had his father and grandfather before him. He became a judge of the Court of Common Pleas of Otsego County and was always referred to as "Judge" Campbell. Married to Sarah Elderkin in December 1800, he fathered seven sons and one daughter, all but one of whom survived him, though he lived to be nearly ninety-eight.

In 1855, seventy-five years after his release, and when he was almost eighty-three, the judge returned to Caughnawaga with his son, William W. Campbell, also a judge. To his great disappointment, he found no one who knew him and met only one woman who could even remember her grandfather talking about the "old times." He did learn that his adoptive mother, now quite aged, was alive but away on a long visit to the St. Regis Indian Reservation. He himself recognized only one stone building, the house where he had lived.

During the Civil War, when he was in his nineties, James Campbell followed the course of *"the Rebellion"* with great interest, reading the newspapers and studying the campaign maps, all without eyeglasses. Two of his grandsons were in the Union army and captured. "He used to say, in speaking of [their] suffering[s], '*Oh, the Indians were not so cruel as are the Southerners to their captives'.*"

In 1865, when General Ulysses S. Grant was in Albany to take part in the celebrations marking the end of the Civil War, Judge Campbell happened to be visiting his son, Samuel, in nearby Castleton-on-Hudson. Invited "to sit on the platform with other distinguished guests, [he had] quite a conversation with General Grant who [showed great] interest in the old man [then ninety-three], and in the fact that he was [speaking] with one who in his youth was a prisoner in the Revolutionary War, and who remembered talking" with General Washington in his own home.

James Campbell died in Cherry Valley on March 23, 1870, one of the last prisoners of the Revolution. He was also the only man to have spoken with the two victorious wartime generals who were destined to become the first and the eighteenth President of the United States.

COLONEL AND MRS. JOHN BUTLER

Colonel and Mrs. John Butler lived out their remaining days in exile, in Butlersbury, Ontario, Canada. He became the first district Indian Superintendent and later judge of both the Nassau District Court and of the Court of Common Pleas. He also founded the first masonic lodge in Ontario, lodge number two, which is still functioning. To his great chagrin, in 1792 Butlersbury was renamed Newark. [It is now Niagara-on-the-Lake, Ontario.]

Catalina Butler died on May 29, 1793, aged fifty-eight, and the colonel, on May 14, 1796, aged sixty-eight. Not long after John Butler's death, Chief Joseph Brant conducted an Indian "condolence ceremony" in his honor, saying, *"Our grief is equal to yours, for our worthy brother, whose life has been spent with us both in War and Peace—none are remaining that understand our manner and customs as well as he did."*

* * *

June 18, 1979 marked the anniversary of Colonel John Butler's rescue of Jane Cannon Campbell from her Indian captivity. In celebration, a reunion was held on the shores of Cayuga Lake, about a day's walk from Kanadesaga [Geneva, New York], between members of the Campbell clan, James' descendants of the third, fourth and fifth generations, and Charles Lorne Butler and his wife, Mildred, he being a fifth generation descendant of Colonel John through his son Thomas. Butler's first words were: *"Well, I guess it's been 200 years since we last met."* Needless to say, that week-end the Campbells and Butlers buried the hatchet.

GLOSSARY OF INDIAN WORDS, NAMES AND PLACES

Canandaigua—also present-day Canandaigua, New York

Cattaraugus—also present-day Cattaraugus, New York

Cauche quando—Come out.

Caughnawaga—also present-day Caughnawaga, Province of Quebec, Canada

Chemung—also present-day Chemung, New York

Deyonwadonti—Mary (Molly) Brant's Indian name, meaning "Many opposed to one"

Duxea—Captain Walter Butler's Indian name, meaning "Leader"

Este quato—Go away.

Goahwuk—Daughter

Ganowauges—now Avon, New York

Hahnih—Father

Hineaweh—Thank you.

Hocnoseh—Uncle

Honeoye—also present-day Honeoye, New York

Joggo—Get going.

Kanadesaga—now Geneva, New York

Karitongeh—Cherry Valley

Kayahdah—Grandchildren

Kendaia—near present-day Kendaia, New York

Little Beard's Town (Deonundagaa)—now Cuylerville, New York

Naho!—I have finished! I have done!

Neahgah—now Youngstown, New York

Nohyeh—Mother

O Sago—Greetings.

Ona—Now

Onaquaga—near present-day Windsor, New York

Oneonta—King George III's Indian name

Oonah! Oonah!—A mournful cry signaling retreat

Ot Kayason?—What do you call this?

Oyehgwahahweh—Tobacco

Quah, Quah, Quah!—Hail, hail, hail!

Shawhiangto—now South Windsor, New York

Shechquago (Catherine's Town)—now Montour Falls, New York

Sugantah—Colonel John Butler's Indian name, meaning "The Lodging
Tree"

Tioga (Point)—now Athens, Pennsylvania

Togeske—Very True.

BIBLIOGRAPHY

PART I

Beach, Allen C., *The Centennial Celebrations of the State of New York,* Albany, Weed, Parsons & Company, 1879.

Buckman, Peter, *Lafayette: A Biography,* Paddington Press, Ltd., New York and London, 1977, pp. 67–71.

Butler Family Genealogy, compiled by C. Lorne Butler (unpublished documents).

Campbell, Cleveland J., Manuscript, 1881 (unpublished).

Campbell, Jane Cannon, Memorial (unpublished).

Campbell, Sarah Mynderse (Mrs. Samuel Robert), Diary, 1823–1829 (unpublished manuscript).

Campbell, William W., *Annals of Tryon County,* 4th edition, New York, Harper, 1929, pp. 2-115, 235-41.

Clinton, Governor George, *Public Papers . . .* published by the State of New York 1899–1909, 10 vols, New York & Albany.
—*Vol. II,* p. 203, August 9, 1777, Peter Deggert to Goosen Van Schaick; pp. 821–23, February 23, 1778, Cherry Valley to Governor George Clinton.

—*Vol. III,* pp. 104–05, March 31, 1778, James Willson, Samuel Campbell, Samuel Clyde to Lafayette; pp. 126–27, April 4, 1778, Benjamin Dickson to Albany; pp. 203–04, April 21, 1778, Abraham Yates to Clinton; June 5, 1778, Jacob Klock to Clinton; pp. 409–10, June 5, 1778, Campbell & Clyde to General John Stark.

—*Vol. IV,* pp. 222–28, October 28, 1778, William Butler's Journal; pp. 289–90, November 17, 1778, Clinton to John Jay; pp. 290–92, November 17, 1778, Abraham Ten Broeck to Clinton; pp. 338–40, November 26, 1778, John Moore, Campbell, Willson to General Edward Hand; pp. 410–15, December 2, 1778, William Harper to Clinton; pp. 457–59, January 1, 1779, James Clinton to Walter Butler; pp. 574–78, February 16, 1779, Harper to Clinton.

—*Vol. V,* pp. 414–18, June 23, 1778–December 13, 1779, Case against William Hudson Ballard, Captain, 7th Massachusetts Regiment.

The Connecticut Gazette, Friday, December 18, 1778, New London, #788.

Crèvecoeur, Guillaume St. Jean de, *Journey into Northern Pennsylvania and the State of New York . . . ,* University of Michigan Press, Ann Arbor, 1964, p. 412.

Cruikshank, Ernest, *The Story of Butler's Rangers and the Settlement of Niagara,* Tribune Printing House, Welland, Ontario, 1893. Reprinted 1975, Lundy's Lane Historical Society.

de Paor, Liam, *Divided Ulster.* Penguin Books, c. 1970.

Dickson Family, Manuscript (unpublished).

Dickson, Tracy Campbell, compiler, *Some of the Descendants of William Dickson & Elizabeth Campbell of Cherry Valley, New York,* Stephen Daye Press, Brattleboro, Vermont, c. 1937, pp. 13–25.

Draper, Lyman, Manuscripts, Series 5F 1, 3–38, 146; F 20/16; 4S:23, State Historical Society of Wisconsin.

Flexner, James Thomas, *Lord of the Mohawks, A Biography of Sir William Johnson,* Little, Brown & Company, Boston, c. 1959, 1979.

Graymont, Barbara, *The Iroquois in the American Revolution,* Syracuse University Press, 1972, pp. 48, 64–66, 93–94, 129–89.

Grider, Rufus A., *Scrapbook,* New York State Library, Albany, Vol. 4, pp. 72ff, Vol. 7 (unpublished).

Haldimand, General Frederick, *Papers,* British Museum, Public Archives of Canada (verified copies), PAC B 100 pp. 82–88, November 17, 1778, Walter Butler to Mason Bolton; B 105 p. 439, to Philip Schuyler, Prisoner list . . . ; February 1779; B 183 p. 16, "Prisoners sent back the 18th Nov. 1778 . . ."; B 114 pp. 25–27, Daniel Claus to General Haldimand.

Hand, General Edward, letter to Clinton, November 10, 1778 (Duane-Fetherstonhaugh Manuscript Collection, New-York Historical Society).

Hinman, Marjory Barnum, *Onaquaga: Hub of the Border Wars,* 1975, pp. 3–84.

Lafayette, Marquis de, *Letters of Lafayette to Washington, 1777 to 1799,* edited by Louis Gottschalk, Helen Fahnestock, Hibbad, New York, 1944, pp. 33–35.

Little, Mrs. William S., *The Story of the Massacre of Cherry Valley,* Rochester Historical Society, 1890, pp. 9–16, Appendix, pp. 1–3.

Lossing, Benson J., *The Pictorial Field Book of the Revolution,* Benchmark Publishing Corporation, New York 1970. New York, Harper Brothers, 1859–60, 2 vols. *Vol. I,* pp. 386–87, p. 387 footnote #3, *Vol. II,* p. 632 footnote #3.

McKendry, Lieutenant William, Diary, Massachusetts Historical Society Collection, 2nd Series, *Vol. II,* pp. 452 ff.

Morgan, Lewis Henry, *League of the Iroquois,* Citadel Press, Secaucus, New Jersey, 1962, pp. 190, 218, 328.

New York State, *Minutes of the Commissioners for detecting and defeating Conspiracies in the State of New York,* Albany County Session, 1778–1781, Edited by Victor Hugo Paltsits, State Historian, Albany, 1909, 3 vols.

Roberts, James A., Comptroller, *New York in the Revolution ... Records ... ,* 2nd edition, Albany, New York, Press of Brandow Printing Company, 1889, 2 vols, Supplement, p. 180.

Sawyer, John, *History of Cherry Valley from 1740–1898,* New York Gazette Printers, 1898.

Scott, John Abbott, *Fort Stanwix and Oriskany,* Rome, New York, 1927, pp. 199–217.

Scudder, William, *The Journal of William Scudder, 1779–1784,* Garland Publishing Company, Inc., New York & London, 1977, p. 33 ff.

Seaver, James E., editor, *A Narrative of the Life of Mary Jemison, the White Woman of the Genesee,* New York, New York Scenic and Historic Preservation Society, 1932, 1824.

Siebert, Wilbur H., *Loyalists & Six Nation Indians in the Niagara Peninsula,* Ottawa (Royal Society of Canada, Vol. IX), 1915.

Simms, Jeptha Root, *The Frontiersmen of New York,* 2 vols., Albany, Geo. C. Riggs, 1882–83, pp. 68–77, 192–93, 204–11, 530–33.

Stone, William Leete, *Life of Joseph Brant—Thayendanegea,* New York, Blake, 1838, 2 vols. *Vol. 1,* pp. 113, 233–48, 318–42, 370; *Appendix:* LXVIII.

Swiggett, Howard, *War Out of Niagara, Walter Butler and the Tory Rangers,* New York, Columbia University Press, 1933, p. 158, November 12, 1778, W. Butler to Philip Schuyler.

Transcripts of American Loyalists, Mss., Books and Papers of the Commission of Enquiry, etc., *Vol. XXII,* Book VI p. 155.

Warren, Benjamin, Diary ... at Cherry Valley, *Journal of American History, Vol. 3 #3,* pp. 377–84.

PART II

Campbell, Cleveland, Manuscript, pp. 13–14.

Campbell, Jane, Memorial.

Campbell, W. W., *Annals,* pp. 113–247.

Cartwright, Richard, *Life & Letters* . . . Toronto, Bedford Bros., 1876, "Continuation of a Journal of an Expedition into the Indian Country 1779".

Clinton, *Papers, —Vol. IV,* pp. 334–37, November 28, 1778, Clinton to Abraham

Yates; pp. 338-40, November 26, 1778, Campbell & Willson to Hand; pp. 345–46, December 3, 1778, G. Clinton to James Clinton, pp. 363–64, December 12, 1778, Yates, *et al* to Clinton; pp. 412–15, December 2, 1778, Harper to Clinton, December 23, 1778, Clinton to Harper; pp. 457–59, January 1, 1779, J. Clinton to W. Butler; pp. 528-29, January 31, 1779, J. Clinton to G. Clinton; p. 704 (n. date), John Campbell to J. Clinton & Philip Schuyler.

—*Vol. V,* p. 414, August 15, 1778, Stark to Colonel Ichabod Alden.

Conover, George S., *Seneca Indian Villages . . . ,* Geneva, New York, March 1889, pp. 80–109, 189–238, 506–47 (unpublished)

Draper, Lyman, Mss. 5F 146(3), 147(1); 4S:23.

Edmonds, Walter D., *In the Hands of the Senecas,* Little, Brown, & Co., Boston, 1937.

Ellet, Elizabeth F., *The Women of the Revolution,* New York, 1850, pp. 179–90.

Elwood, Muriel, *Towards the Sunset,* Manor Books, New York, 1947, pp. 87–88ff.

Enys, John, *The American Journals of Lieutenant John Enys,* Syracuse University Press, 1976.

Flick, Alexander G., "New Sources of the Sullivan—Clinton Campaign in 1779" (New York State Historical Association, *Quarterly Journal, Vol. X,* no. 3, July, 1929), pp. 203-07, 218–20, June 5, 1779, John Butler to Mason Bolton; p. 220, May 21, 1779, Butler to Bolton; p. 221, May 28, 1779, Butler to Haldimand; p. 222, May 28, 1779, Butler to Bolton.

—*Vol. X,* no. 4, October 1929, "The Indian—Tory Side of the Campaign," pp. 265–66, June 18, 1779, Butler to Bolton.

Gilbert, Benjamin, *The Captivity and Sufferings of Benjamin Gilbert and His Family,* Cleveland, 1902.

Graymont, *Iroquois,* pp. 10–20, 122–95.

Grider, Rufus, *Scrapbook, Vol. IV,* pp. 72ff.

Haldimand, *Papers,* PAC, B 100 p. 81, November 30, 1778, Bolton to Haldimand; B 100 p. 82, November 17, 1778, W. Butler to Bolton; B 43 p. 169, July 2, 1779, Lord Germain to Haldimand; B 96 pt. 1, p. 238, February 8, 1779, Bolton to Haldimand; B 96 pt. 2, p. 109, April 8, 1779, Haldimand to Bolton, p. 162, April 8, 1779, Haldimand to J. Butler; B 105 pp. 427–28, May 1779, W. Butler to J. Clinton; B 147 p. 103, September 28, 1779, Haldimand to Sir Henry Clinton.

Halsey, Francis Whiting, *The Old New York Frontier . . . 1614–1800,* New York, Scribner's Sons, 1902.

Henry, Thomas P., *Wilderness Messiah, The Story of Hiawatha and the Iroquois,* Bonanza Books, New York, 1955.

Hinman, *Onaquaga,* pp. 3–84.

Little, *Cherry Valley*, pp. 14–19, *Appendix*, p. 2.

Morgan, *League of the Iroquois*, pp. 80–86, 104–12, 154–55, 207–374, 416–34.

Priest, Josiah, *Stories of the Revolution . . .* , Albany, Hoffman & White, 1838, pp. 15–20.

Scudder, *Journal.*

Seaver, Mary Jemison, pp. 41–48, 75–76, 150, 170–86.

Slocum, Frances, *The Lost Sister of Wyoming*, compiled and written by her Grandniece Martha Bennett Phelps, Knickerbocker Press, New York, 1905, pp. 14, 55, 97.

Stone, *Brant, Vol. I*, pp. 189, 377–78, 388–90, *Appendix* VI-XXXI: *Vol. II*, pp. 61–66.

Swetland, Luke, *A Narrative of the Captivity of . . . in 1778 and 1779, among the Seneca Indians*, Written by Himself, Waterville, New York, 1875, pp. 6–23.

Swiggett, *Niagara*, p. 180.

PART III

Armour, David A. and Widder, Keith R., *Michilimackinac During the American Revolution*, Mackinac Island State Park Commission, Mackinac Island, Michigan, 1978.

Boatner, Mark M., III, *Landmarks of the American Revolution*, Stackpole Books, 1973, pp. 313–14.

Campbell, W.W., *Annals*, pp. 148–53, 178–83.

Cartwright, *Expedition.*

Claus, Daniel, *Papers*, Public Archives of Canada, MG-19 F1 Vol. 25, June 26, 1780.

Clinton, *Papers, Vol. V*, pp. 700–01, Daniel Uhlendorph's testimony (n.d.).

Crèvecoeur, *Journey.*

Cullen, Joseph P., "I Have Almost Ceased to Hope," *American History Illustrated, Vol. XIV*, no. 9, January 1980, pp. 30–35.

Dickson, T.C., *Descendants*, etc., p. 270.

Ellet, *Women*, pp. 179–90.

Fraser, Mary M., *Joseph Brant, Thayendanegea*, The Joseph Brant Museum, Burlington, Ontario, c. 1969.

Goring, Francis, *Reminiscences*, Niagara Historical Society, Family History & Reminiscences of Early Settlers, pub. #28.

Grant, Anne McVicar, *Memoirs of an American Lady . . .* , Boston, W. Wells, 1908, *Vol. II,* p. 91.

Graymont, *Iroquois,* pp. 192–233.

Hagan, William T., *Longhouse Diplomacy and Frontier Warfare,* New York State American Revolution Bicentennial Commission, n.d., pp. 47ff.

Haldimand, *Papers,* 1778. PAC B 96 pt. 1, p. 216, fall 1778, Bolton to Haldimand, p. 227, November 11, 1778, same to same.

—1779. PAC B 96 pt. 1, p. 238, February 8, 1779, Bolton to Haldimand; B 98 pp. 190–201, February 1779, same to same; B 96 pt. 1, p. 251, March 5, 1779, same to same; B 99 p. 67, May 15, 1779, Diederich Brehm to Haldimand, p. 88, July 5, 1779, same to same; Michigan Historical Collections, v. 9, pp. 425–26, July 1779, Haldimand to Bolton; PAC B 105, p. 140, August 1779, Bolton to Haldimand; MG 1, Q 15, pt. 1, pp. 360 ff, August 16, 1779, same to same; B 54 p. 155, September 13, 1779, Haldimand to Germain; B 96 pt. 2 p. 17, October 2, 1779, Bolton to Haldimand; B 119 pp. 90–95, October—November 1779, Minutes of the Indian Council; B 127 p. 101, November 7, 1779, Alexander Fraser to Haldimand; B 105 pp. 146–49, November 11, 1779, Haldimand to Bolton; B 100 p. 313, November 15, 1779, Bolton to Haldimand; B 114 pp. 88–89, November 19, 1779, Robert Picken to Claus; B 127 p. 110, December 1, 1779, Fraser to Haldimand; B 119 pp. 113–14, December 7, 1779, Guy Johnson to Schuyler.

—1780. PAC B 119 pp. 115–18, January 23, 1780, Schuyler to Johnson; B105 p. 101, February 2, 1780, W. Butler to Mathews; B 100 pp. 104–06, February 10, 1780, Haldimand to Bolton; B 105 pp. 172–76, February 12, 1780, Haldimand to J. Butler; B 175 p. 1, February 13, 1780, Henry Watson Powell to Van Schaick; B 175 p. 4, February 23, 1780, Van Schaick to Powell, p. 8, March 4, 1780, same to same; B 114 pp. 100-01, March 4, 1780, Jelles Fonda to Peter Hanson; B 100 p. 347, March 10, 1780, Arent de Peyster to Bolton; B 133 p. 159, March 11, 1780, Christopher Carleton to Haldimand; B 175 p. 1, March 15, 1780, Powell to Van Schaick; B 114 p. 102, March 16, 1780, Mathews to Claus; B 133 p. 163, March 18, 1780, Carleton to Haldimand; B 114 pp. 103-04, March 23, 1780, Claus to Mathews, p. 106, March 27, 1780, Mathews to Claus; B 104 pp. 113–15, April 16, 1780, Haldimand to Bolton; B 114 p. 115, April 17, 1780, Haldimand to Claus; B 113 p. 83, April 17, 1780, Mathews to (British Lt. Colonel) John Campbell; B 111 p. 154, April 20, 1780, (British) Campbell to Haldimand; B 105 pp. 208–09, April 29, 1780, J. Butler to Haldimand; B 105 p. 209, May 3, 1780, same to same; B 96 pt. 2 pp. 26–27, May 16, 1780, Bolton to Haldimand, p. 23, May 16, 1780, same to same; B 104 p. 124, May 18, 1780, Haldimand to Bolton, p. 163, May 18, 1780, same to same; British Museum Added Mss. #21787 p. 150, June 21, 1780, Fraser to Haldimand.

Halsey, *Frontier.*

Hounsome, Eric, *Toronto in 1810,* Coles Publishing Company, Toronto, Canada, c. 1975, pp. 38–39, 43–44, 53.

Hultzen, Claud H., Sr., *Old Fort Niagara,* Old Fort Niagara Association, c. 1939.

Indian Records, Public Archives of Canada, R.G. 10, ser. 2 XII, pp. 126–78.

Klinger, Robert Lee, *Distaff Sketch Book . . . Women's Dress in America, 1774–1783,* Pioneer Press, Union City, Tenn., 1974.

Larue, Arlene C., "Brides: 1770 to Early 1800s," *Syracuse Herald American,* p. 56, 110.

Little, *Cherry Valley,* pp. 19–21, *Appendix,* p. 1.

Loyalist Narratives from Upper Canada, edited by James J. Talman, Toronto, Champlain Society, 1946 (Journal of Adam Crysler, pp. 59–60).

McClellan, S. Grove, "Old Fort Niagara." Reprinted from *American Heritage, Vol. 4,* no. 4.

McIlwraith, Jean N., *Sir Frederick Haldimand,* Toronto, Morang & Co., Ltd., 1906 (Makers of Canada), pp. 153–71, 236–37.

Marshall, Orasamus H., "The Niagara Frontier." Buffalo Historical Society, *Publications, Vol. II,* pp. 421–22.

Porter, Peter, *A Brief History of Old Fort Niagara,* 1896, p. 54.

Priest, *Stories of the Revolution.*

Ray, Frederic, *Old Fort Niagara, An Illustrated History,* 1954.

Scudder, William, *Journal.*

Seaver, *Mary Jemison,* pp. 75–76.

Severance, Frank, "With Bolton at Fort Niagara." *Old Trails of the Niagara Frontier,* pp. 66–103, 244.

Siebert, *Loyalists.*

Slocum, *Lost Sister of Wyoming,* pp. 28–98.

Stone, *Brant, Vol. II,* pp. 55–68, 80.

Strach, Stephen G., *The British Occupation of the Niagara Frontier, 1759–1796,* Lundy's Lane Historical Society, Niagara Falls, Ontario, 1976.

Swiggett, *Niagara,* pp. 30–31, 40, 218.

Whittaker, Mrs. Jane (Strope), "Captivity," in Schoolcraft, Henry, *Indian Tribes.*

PART IV

Béchard, Henri, S. J., *J'ai cent ans!* Le Messager Canadien, Montréal, 1961, p. 14.

Campbell, Sarah M., Diary.

Campbell, W.W., *Annals,* pp. 183–85.

Clinton, *Papers,* —*Vol. VI,* pp. 238–39, September 18, 1780, Udny Hay to Clinton; pp. 288–90, October 12, 1780, Stephen Lush to Clinton; pp. 290–91(n.d.), Articles of Capitulation of Fort George; pp. 291–93, October 13–14, 1780, Robert Van Rensselaer to Clinton, Clinton to Van Rensselaer, W. Malcomb to Van Rensselaer; pp. 306–07, October 18, 1780,Clinton to George Washington; pp. 324-25, October 20, 1780, Schuyler to Clinton; pp. 325–26, October 26, 1780, Clinton to Schuyler; p. 326, October 20, 1780, Ebenezer Russell to Clinton; pp. 331-32, October 24, 1780, Alexander Webster to Clinton; pp. 343–44, October 27,1780, Schuyler to Clinton; pp. 344–45, October 28, 1780, Lewis Van Woert to Ten Broeck; pp. 345–47, October 29,1780, Clinton to James Duane; pp. 351–58, October 30, 1780, Clinton to Washington; pp. 363–64, August 31, 1780 (?), Examination of James Van Driesen; pp. 364–65, November 1, 1780, Schuyler to Clinton; pp. 368–69, November 2, 1780, Clinton to Schuyler; pp. 373–74, November 3, 1780, Clinton to William Heath; pp. 374-75, November 3, 1780, Clinton to Washington; p. 376, November 23, 1780, Ten Broeck to Clinton; pp. 376–78, November (3), 1780, Schuyler's appeal to the Militia; pp. 393–95, November 7,1780, Lush to Clinton, November 9, 1780, Clinton to Lush; pp. 405–07, November 12, 1780, J. Clinton to G. Clinton.

Enys, *Journals,* pp. 40–50, 101–171, 293–305.

Flexner, *Lord of the Mohawks,* p. 99.

Gilbert, *Captivity.*

Graymont, *Iroquois,* p. 76.

Haldimand, *Papers,* July 1780. B 105, July 13, 1780, Haldimand to Bolton, July 20,1780, same to same.

—August 1780. B 105 pp. 222-26, August 15, 1780, J. Butler to Mathews; B 131 pp. 68–69, August 31,1780, Mathews to Allan MacLean.

—September 1780. B 151 pp. 269–70, September 10,1780, Adam McAllen to William Chambers; B 141 p. 260, September 10, 1780, Chambers to Haldimand; B 143 p.98, September 14, 1780, Mathews to Chambers; B 133 p. 227, September 14, 1780, Mathews to William Monsell; B 135 pp. 131–32, September 17,1780,Haldimand to Powell; B 131 pp. 74–75, September 17, 1780, Haldimand to MacLean; B 133 p. 225, September 18, 1780, Monsell to Haldimand; B 135 p. 133, September 18,1780, Mathews to Powell; B 114 p. 139, September 18, 1780, Mathews to Claus; B 131 p. 77, September 21,1780, Mathews to MacLean; B 135 p. 135, September 21, 1780, Mathews to Powell; B 175 pp. 39–40, September 22,

1780, Powell to Van Schaick; B 133 p. 230, September 24, 1780,Powell to Haldimand, p. 233, September 25, 1780, same to same; B 135 pp. 136–37, September 25, 1780, Haldimand to Powell, pp. 138–39, September 28, 1780, same to same; B 133 pp. 234–36, September 30, 1780, Powell to Haldimand.

—October 1780. B 133 pp. 237–39, October 1, 1780, Powell to Haldimand; B 135 pp. 140–41, October 5, 1780, Haldimand to Powell, pp. 143–44, October 7, 1780, same to same; B 133 p. 246, October 8, 1780, Powell to Haldimand; B 141 pp. 275–76, October 9, 1780, Chambers to Powell; B 133 p. 249, October 10, 1780, Powell to Haldimand, p. 252, October 16, 1780, Haldimand to Monsell; B183 pp. 286–87, October 16, 1780, "Detachment returned to Crown Point;" B 133 p. 264, October 19, 1780, Monsell to Haldimand; A.L.S.1, October 19, 1780, Monsell to Van Schaick; B 135 p. 149, October 22, 1780, Haldimand to Carleton; B 133 p. 265, October 22, 1780, Monsell to Haldimand; B 175 p. 47, October 24, 1780, Carleton to Van Schaick; B 141 pp. 303–06, October 24, 1780, Chambers Diary on Lake Champlain; B175 p. 47, October 24, 1780, Carleton to Van Schaick; B 133 pp. 268 ff, October 25, 1780, Carleton to Haldimand; B 141 p. 295, October 25, 1780, Chambers to Haldimand; B 180 pp. 42–58, October 26 to November 30, 1780, Journal of Justus Sherwood; B 183 pp. 286–87, October 1780, Prisoner List; B 133 pp. 276–79, October 31, 1780, Carleton to Haldimand.

—November 1780. B 175 pp. 50–52, November 2, 1780, Peter Gansevoort to Powell; B 133 pp. 280–81, November 6, 1780, Carleton to Gansevoort.

Hannon, Leslie F., *Forts of Canada,* McClelland & Stewart.

Hough, Franklin Benjamin, *The Northern Invasion of October 1780,* New York, 1866 (Bradford Club, publications #6).

Hutchinson, Abijah, *Memoir of, A Soldier of the Revolution,* by his Grandson K. M. Hutchinson, Rochester, Wm. Alling, 1843.

McIlwraith, *Haldimand.*

Montreal, City of, *A Visit to Old Montreal,* 1977.

—, *A Walking Tour of Old Montreal,* 1977.

Montreal and environs, Gourvernement du Québec, Québec, 1976, pp. 53–54, 64.

Morgan, Lewis H., *League of the Iroquois,* p. 86, footnote 1.

New York State, *Conspiracies, Vol. II,* pp. 561–63.

Pell, John, *Ethan Allen,* Adirondack Resorts Press, Inc., 1929, pp. 198–206.

Scudder, William, *Journal.* pp. 45-46, 88, 98-99.

Sawyer, *Cherry Valley,* p. 147.

Steele, Zadock, *The Indian Captivity of . . . ,* Montpelier, Vt., E. P. Walton, 1818.

Wrong, George M., *Canada and the American Revolution,* Cooper Square Publishers, New York, 1968, p. 449.

PART V

Campbell, W.W., *Annals,* pp. 174–90.

Clinton, *Papers, Vol. VI* pp. 707–08, March 19, 1781, Clinton to the Legislature; pp. 811–12, Andrew McFarlan to Clinton; p. 876, May 16, 1781, J. Clinton to G. Clinton; pp. 877–78, May 13, 1781, Robert Cochran to J. Clinton; pp. 878–79, May 16, 1781, J. Clinton to Cochran; pp. 879–80, May 16,1781 (J. Clinton?) to Philip Van Courtlandt, pp. 880–81; May 15, 1781, Schuyler to J. Clinton; pp. 898–99, May 21, 1781, Schuyler to G. Clinton; pp. 903–04, May 22, 1781, J. Clinton to G. Clinton.
—*Vol. VII* pp. 472–75, November 2, 1781, Marinus Willett to G. Clinton.
—*Vol. VIII* pp. 93–94, March 23, 1783, William Floyd to G. Clinton.

Glen, Henry, *Journal of a Trip from Schenectady to Quebec,* 1783. (Glen Papers, N-YHS).

Grant, A. McV., *Memoirs, Vol. II* p. 131.

Graymont, *Iroquois,* pp. 245–58.

Greene, Nelson, *Fort Plain—Nelliston History, 1580–1947,* Ft. Plain, N.Y. Standard (Publication #5 of the Fort Plain Nelliston Historical Society, 1947) pp. 50–55.

Haldimand, *Papers,* B 107 pp. 301–07, from October 5, 1781 Journal of Gilbert Tice; B 124 pp. 25–33, November 11, 1781, John Ross to Haldimand; B107 pp. 309–11, November 11, 1781, David the Mohawk (translation) to Guy Johnson.

Little, *Cherry Valley,* pp. 17–22.

Lossing, *Field Book, Vol. I* p. 244.

New York Colonial Manuscripts, Plantations General S.P.O. CCLXVI #15, pp. 796–97, July 26, 1780, G. Johnson to Germain, #17, pp. 812–13, October 11, 1781, Johnson to Germain.

Roberts, James A., *Revolution,* Suppl. p. 180.

Roberts, Robert B., *New York's Forts in the Revolution,* Rutherford, etc., Fairleigh Dickinson University Press, c. 1980, pp. 45–46, 87–91.

Simms, *Frontiersmen, Vol. II* pp. 656–62.

Stone, *Brant, Vol. II* pp. 185–93, 234.

EPILOGUE

Campbell, James, Memorial.

Campbell, Jane, Memorial.

Campbell Family scrapbooks.

"The Centennial Celebration at Cherry Valley," Otsego County, New York, July 4, 1840. The Addresses of William W. Campbell . . . . New York, Taylor & Clement, 1840.

Ellet, *Women.*

Killman, Murray, U. E., "A Commemorative Portrait Exhibition: The Many Faces of Brant."

Little, *Cherry Valley.*

Niagara Falls Review, "John Butler, 200th Anniversary of Butler's Rangers," (Niagara-on-the-Lake, September 20, 1977).

OTHER WORKS CONSULTED

Adams, James Truslow, Editor-in-Chief, *Atlas of American History,* New York, Charles Scribner's Sons, c. 1943.

American Loyalists, Calendar of the Original Memorials, etc. preserved amongst the Audit Office Records in the Public Record Office of England, 1783–179? in 6 vols.

Bradley, A. G., *Sir Guy Carleton (Lord Dorchester),* University of Toronto Press (c. Canada, 1966. Makers of Canada series, 1907, reissued in 1926 . . .).

Brandon, William, *The American Heritage Book of Indians,* Dell Publishing Company, New York, 1961.

Brandow, John Henry, *The Story of Old Saratoga,* Brandow Printing, Albany, 1919.

Brick, John, *King's Rangers,* Doubleday & Company, 1954.

Caulkins, Frances Manwaring, *History of New London, Connecticut,* New London, 1852.

Chambly Canal: Richelieu River, Parks Canada . . . , Ottawa, 1976.

Claus, Daniel, *Papers,* Public Archives of Canada (Unpublished manuscript).

Clune, Henry, *The Genesee,* Holt, Rinehart & Winston, 1963.

Crown Point, A Short History of, adapted from notes by Paul Huey . . . New York State Office of Parks and Recreation.

Crown Point, Historical Archeology at . . . , New York State Parks and Recreation.

Cruikshank, Ernest A., editor, Niagara Historical Society Publication #38, "A Collection of Documents Relating to the First Settlement, 1778–1783. . . ." 1927.

Cumming, William P. and Rankin, Hugh F., *The Fate of a Nation, The American Revolution through Contemporary Eyes,* Phaidon (London).

Cummings, Uriah, *Indian Trails of Western New York,* Akron, New York Herald, 1907.

Drake, Samuel G., *Indian Captivities or Life in the Wigwam,* New York, 1857.

Dwight, Timothy, *Travels in New England and New York,* 4 vols., New Haven (1833).

Edmonds, Walter D., *Drums Along the Mohawk,* Boston, Little, Brown, 1936.

Encyclopedia of American History, Bicentennial Edition, edited by Richard B. Morris, Harper & Row, New York.

Furnas, J. C., *The Americans, A Social History of the United States, 1587–1914,* G. P. Putnam's Sons, New York, c. 1969.

Guillet, Edwin C., *Pioneer Travel in Upper Canada,* University of Toronto Press, Toronto and Buffalo (1933 reprinted . . . 1976). Series; Canadian University Paperbacks.

Howard, Robert West, *Thundergate: The Forts of Niagara,* Prentice-Hall, Englewood Cliffs, New Jersey, 1968.

Hazen, Moses, *Moses Hazen and the Canadian Refugees in the American Revoution,* Syracuse University Press, 1976.

Kenney, Alice P., *Albany, Crossroads of Liberty,* Albany, 1976.

Lancaster, Bruce and Plumb, J.H., *The American Heritage Book of the Revolution,* Dell Publishing Company, 1958.

Lodge, Henry Cabot, *Alexander Hamilton,* Houghton Mifflin, Boston and New York (Series: American Statesmen . . .).

Long, J., *Voyages and Travels of an Indian Interpreter and Trader . . . 1791* (Facsimile edition . . . , Coles Publishing Company, Toronto, 1974, Coles Canadiana Collection).

McAdams, Donald R., "The Sullivan Expedition, Success or Failure" in "Narratives of the Revolution in New York," New-York Historical Society *Quarterly,* 1975, N-YHS, no. 14, pp. 304–30.

McAlpine, J., *Genuine narratives . . . of J. McAlpine . . . from the time of his Emmigration from Scotland to America 1773–1788.*

McCarthy, Richard L. and Newman, Harrison, "The Iroquois," Buffalo and Erie County Historical Society, *Vol. IV, Adventures in Western New York History.*

Mollo, John, *Uniforms of the Americn Revolution in colour,* London, Blandford Press, 1975.

New York State, *The Mohawk Valley and the American Revolution,* Albany, New York, January 1972.

New York State, State Historian, *The American Revolution in New York,* edited by Alexander C. Flick, 1967.

Ontario Register #4, October 1968, "Transcription of original rolls of settlers of Upper Canada, November 30–December 1, 1783," From British Museum transcripts (Haldimand 105 A).

The Revolution Remembered, Eyewitness Accounts of the War for Independence, Edited by John C. Dann, University of Chicago Press, Chicago, London (Clements Library Bicentennial Studies).

Ryan, Dennis P., editor, *A Salute to Courage, The American Revolution as Seen Through Wartime Writings of Officers of the Continental Army and Navy,* Columbia University Press, New York, 1979.

Scheer, George F. and Rankin, Hugh, *Rebels and Redcoats,* New American Library, 1957.

Schoolcraft, Henry, *History of the Indian Tribes,* 6 vols, Philadelphia, 1851–57.

Severance, Frank H., *The Tale of Captives at Fort Niagara* (Publications of the Buffalo Historical Society, Vol. IX, 1906).

Simms, Jeptha R., *History of Schoharie County and the Border Wars of New York,* Albany, 1845.

Smith, Page, *A People's History of the American Revolution, A New Age Now Begins, Vol. II,* McGraw Hill Book, 1976.

Sosin, Jack M.,*The Revolutionary Frontier 1763–1783,* University of New Mexico Press, Albuquerque (Histories of the American Frontier), 1967, Holt, Rinehart & Winston.

Swiggett, Howard, *A Portrait of Colonel John Butler,* New York State Historical Association, 1936.

Swinnerton, Henry U., *The Story of Cherry Valley* (n.d.)

Syracuse Herald American, Sunday, June 27, 1976. (Bicentennial Edition).

Taft, Pauline (Dakis), *The Happy Valley,* Syracuse University Press, 1965.

Tharp, Louise Hall, *The Baroness and the General,* Little, Brown and Company, Boston, Toronto, 1962.

Ticonderoga, Guide Book to, The Meriden Gravure Company, Meriden, Connecticut.

Venables, Robert W., *The Hudson Valley in the American Revolution,* New York State American Revolution Bicentennial Commission, Albany, 1975.

Vermont 1977: A Guide to the First Republic . . . , Agency of Development and Community Affairs, Montpelier, Vermont.

Wallace, Anthony F. C., *The Death and Rebirth of the Seneca* . . . , New York, Vintage Books, 1969.

Wilson, Bruce, *As She Began, an illustrated introduction to Loyalist Ontario,* Dundurn Press, Toronto and Charlottetown, 1981.

Young, Philip, *Revolutionary Ladies,* Alfred A. Knopf, 1977.

Zaboly, Gary, "The Battle on Snowshoes, March 10–13, 1758, Rogers' Rangers," *American History Illustrated,* December 1979, *Vol. XIV* no. 8, pp. 12–24.

Biographical Information

Eugenia Campbell Lester grew up with the story of Jane Cannon Campbell, her great-great-great grandmother. As a child she was intrigued with the perilous tale; as an adult she found researching the complete history a fascinating and rewarding experience. For *Frontiers Aflame,* Eugenia found a wealth of new material from British, Canadian and American sources. Eugenia is a graduate of Radcliffe College, Harvard University with an AB *cum laude* in Romance Languages and an MA from Johns Hopkins University. She lives in New York City with her husband Dennis and son Campbell and summers in the Finger Lakes, where so much of the action of Jane's story took place.

In 1976, **Allegra Branson**, a writer and researcher, also became intrigued with the story of Jane Cannon Campbell and its documentation. Holding a BA in Music and an MA in Library Science from the University of Michigan, Allegra is an avid student of the American Revolution. A long time resident of New York City, she has been for twenty years a writer-editor with WCBS Radio and has served as chairman of the National Council of the Writers Guild of America.

Illustrator **Peggy Scott** is an alumna of the Parsons School of Design and the National Academy of Design. Elected to the American Watercolor Society in 1968, she has twice been chosen for the Society's national traveling exhibit. Peggy lives in New York City.

Typeset in 11 point Garamond with a baseline of 12½ on an Itek Digitek 3000 photocompositor.

Printed on 60 pound book white and bound in a 12 point, UV coated-one-side cover with four-color process printing.

Contact Walt Steesy for your book publishing needs.

A *quality* publication from
Heart of the Lakes Publishing
Interlaken, New York 14847